The victim of a traumatic childhood event, Angela Harwell's life is forever changed. As she grows up, she trains relentlessly and becomes a Domestic Violence Detective for the Memphis Police Department. A disturbing case of abuse puts Harwell on the trail of Tyrone "T-Bone" Reed, the ruthless head of a powerful gang called The Family. Rich, smart, and connected, the cunning gangster proves no easy target. A heartbreaking night of bloodshed, however, turns things personal for Harwell. Having lost everything she cares about, she becomes driven by revenge, vowing to crush Tyrone and The Family.

She is clearly outnumbered, but sometimes help comes from damndest places.

Driven

A novel by
Rick Jacobs, Sr.

Edited by
Rodney Rastall

Book Cover design by Hazel A. Morgan
Cover photographs by Theresa Jacobs

Cover models:
Kristin Jacobs
Greg Brunson

I HOPE YOU ENJOY!

Jacobs sr

Dedication

This book is, of course, dedicated to my little sister, Becky. She had cancer. She fought this terrible disease for nearly 2 ½ years. With barely a whimper. Always with a smile. On August 23, 2014, her fight ended. She was only 52. Wife of Lee, mother of Kevin and Monica, and grandmother of Aubrey and Bailey. She was, and still is, my inspiration.

This is for you, Becky. You were Harwell. Beautiful, strong, fearless. A heart of gold. Fighting demons you didn't deserve. Driven to succeed, no matter the odds.

I miss you, Sis.

Acknowledgements

It would be safe to assume that an author, especially a first-time novelist, works alone.

I certainly thought that's how it would be. It would be me and my computer, typing away whenever I could grab an hour or two, sandwiching in my day job and my duties as a caregiver husband, father and grandfather.

In a way, it was like that. But it became so much more.

My mother, God bless her, is nearly 80 years old and I wasn't going to ask her to try and edit. Then she told me she would never forgive me if I didn't.

My son, Ricky, who is a United States Marine and an Air Traffic Controller, supplied the authentic radio conversation between the tower and the jet.

Another son, Sean, is a Special Forces Airman in the United States Air Force. After I wrote the radio banter in the latter chapters, he read it and said, "Dad, do you want that to be realistic?" I thought that would be a lot better than unrealistic, so he helped me out.

And what would I have done without my little sister, Terri Matz? She was my biggest fan, and my most vocal critic throughout this entire process. Believe me when I tell you, you need both.

If something in a chapter I sent her sucked, she would tell me. And she would tell me why. And virtually every time, she was exactly right and I would promptly rewrite it. You need someone like that. You don't want everyone to be a cheerleader and just love every single thing you hand them.

Conversely, if I sent her a chapter and she said, "It's perfect! Don't change anything!" I knew it must be perfect because she would tell me if it wasn't.

Finally, my lifelong friend, Rodney Rastall. He wears many hats. He's the golden-voiced narrator of the audio book of *Driven*.

He wrote the Foreword.

Most importantly, Rodney was the literary editor of my manuscript. What does that mean? He took a magnifying glass and went over every word of my original manuscript. He'd take a 20-word sentence, cut it down to seven and make it sound better. He'd scratch out complete paragraphs if he felt they were unnecessary or a distraction. He caught mistakes and blunders that would have made me look foolish. And, together, we rewrote the last chapter and made it infinitely more exciting and believable than my original.

In other words, I gave him a steak and he added all the spices and marinades that took a decent piece of meat and transformed it, if I may, into a mouth watering culinary delight that, when you take the last bite, only leaves you wanting more.

It was absolutely that way for us. Ultimately, he became such an invaluable part of this project that I began to refer to *Driven* not as *my* book, but rather *our* book.

Suddenly, I realized, I had a team, all with a specific job and everyone on this team wanting the same thing: that this novel not only be written, but written well and to wind up with a product that we could all be proud of.

I would now like to share three gems of wisdom that kept me going throughout the months and months of writing and rewriting, of low points and high points, of staring for hours at a screen without writing a single word, then not being able to write fast enough and culminating one night when I woke too excited to sleep because I had actually dreamed the perfect way - at least in my ever so humble opinion - to end my book.

One: Never, never, never give up. Two: Never, never, never give up. Three: Surround yourself with people who tell you to never, never, never give up.

Thank you everyone, from the bottom of my heart.

Rick Jacobs

Foreword

Rick Jacobs and I have been best friends for decades, and I was honored when he asked me to write this foreword. Driven is a perfect name for this book, for Rick was driven in its creation. I remember when he first told me "I'm thinking about writing a novel. I have a few ideas...." That began years of creating a world that never existed before, populated by people who never lived.

And yet, his creation has become real. Throughout the process of editing the copy, and recording the audio, we changed, refined and rewrote until make believe was as believable as we could make it. In recording the audio, Rick gave me great direction, and incredible latitude in coming up with a voice for everyone who lived in the book. For me anyway, the characters came to life. I can truly say in my thirty plus years producing media of all kinds, this is one of the most creatively satisfying things I have ever done.

Look between the lines of this adventure and you'll see the essence of a good man's character, integrity, and sense of justice. I hope you enjoy it.

Rodney Rastall

Prologue

Summertime in Memphis, on most days, is downright brutal.

High temperatures, negligible wind and merciless humidity all combine to send heat indexes soaring - often into the 100's - especially in July and August. Weeks can pass with little or no rain. And, even after the sun sets, there's little relief, especially from the humidity.

Twenty-seven year old Zachary Harrington was feeling the full impact of this weather as he ran full-out along the mostly empty, late night streets in a drug-laden area known as Nutbush. Only the occasional meth addict, unable to sleep, noticed him, or those who chased him, and they quickly lost interest. Harrington's dress shirt was soaked with sweat and clung to his emaciated torso. The stains and filth were typical for clothing that had been worn for nearly three weeks without changing or washing.

There was also the stench. His trousers were much the same. They were far too large now, but they were all he had. His shoes were falling apart and he wore no socks. Despite all of this, he was actually covering decent distance, partly from anxiety-induced adrenaline, but also because his long legs worked from memory from his days in high school track where he had been the very essence of health. He'd been a rising star in the 5,000 and 10,000 meter distances, until he discovered that cocaine would help him run even faster.

But it also made passing random drug tests impossible. Overnight, his track and field glory days ended; his college scholarship offers were rescinded. His drug habit, however, remained.

Harrington was able to graduate from college, and eventually find work as a broker. He worked more hours and harder than anyone else and discovered he excelled at handling his clients' money.

He had exceptional people skills and good instincts. Within two short years he was one of his company's top producers. He met a beautiful co-worker named Andrea and they married. His son and daughter were now five and six, but he hadn't seen them since they were four and five.

For the most part, Harrington was able to keep his addiction a secret, but his boss should have figured it out. Harrington would work all night for three or four nights in a row, then sleep for 24 hours straight. Andrea was aware, of course, and she tried everything she knew to try before giving up on him. In desperation, she and the kids moved in with her parents, hoping it would, finally, be the incentive he needed to get and stay clean.

It had the opposite effect.

He went on a binge that nearly killed him. His boss, feeling he owed Harrington something, placed him in a six month rehabilitation program, paid for by the brokerage firm. Harrington lasted three weeks before he walked out. That decision cost him everything that was important. His job, his marriage and his family. And it was about to cost him his life.

He reached his car, parked where he had left it earlier in the day, and desperately pressed the "unlock" button on the remote. He silently prayed the battery hadn't died or been stolen. To his great relief, the driver's door unlocked.

He threw the door open and quickly got in. The BMW 5 Series now bore little resemblance to the showroom vehicle he'd proudly driven between his home and office every day. In fact, the car had been his home for the last few months, and it looked it. It was filthy inside and out. The bald tires barely held air and the rims were chipped and ugly. There were dents and scratches throughout the body. The windshield had a crack which ran full length from side to side. The passenger seat and the back was filled with soiled clothes and trash.

He would sit behind the wheel and lay the seat back, and that was his bed, but it was nearly impossible to sleep in the suffocating heat. It was all he had, though. He'd been evicted from the tiny studio apartment he'd been forced to move into after everything had crumbled around him. He tried once more on his own to get sober and had actually kicked it for a while. But, like everything else in his life, it hadn't lasted. He was weak, and cocaine was incredibly strong. He began dealing, knowing full well what a conviction would mean if, or really when, he was caught, but it didn't matter. He would do anything to get high, including resorting to violence.

Just days ago he'd met the kid who always brought the rocks he was supposed to sell, and in a surreal moment, when years of addiction finally made rational choices impossible, he grabbed the kid's head and slammed it repeatedly against a brick wall until he was sure the kid was out. He then rifled through the kid's pockets and found cash and more cocaine.

In the back of his mind, Harrington was vaguely aware that what he had just done was unpardonable. He'd been warned, more than once, about street justice should he go awry of their laws. So he'd hidden and binged until the drugs were gone, then found the overwhelming desire to get high again far outweighed concern for his own safety. When he emerged from the shadows, they were waiting.

Harrington tried desperately to put the key in the ignition, but his hand was trembling and it took much too long. His pursuers were almost on him, and when he was able, finally, to push the key home and turn it to the right, the engine turned, but it wouldn't start. If he'd been thinking clearly, he'd have recalled that it was parked where it was because he'd run out of gas. But he wasn't thinking clearly. He was in a full-blown panic. His cocaine addiction, which had begun innocently enough at a party when he was 17, was about to run its course. He looked in his rear-view mirror and saw five shadowy figures approaching. In an absurd move borne of desperation, he locked his door.

The largest one walked around and, with the butt of a Sig Sauer P229 DAK handgun, shattered the window beside Harrington. He unlocked the door and opened it, then pulled Harrington out and threw him brutally to the ground. It was easy enough. Harrington was six foot three inches, but he was rail thin. Conversely, his nightmare was a large, heavily muscled black man, but Harrington didn't notice his race or his size. All he could see was the barrel of the Sig.

"Please," Harrington said, "I'll pay you the money. You... you can have the car. The keys are in it. Please..." And then he began to cry.

"You stupid white mother *fucker!*" the man over him said. "Do you really think this is about *money*? I don't want this piece of shit car. I want *you!*"

Harrington looked up at the man, but, again, all he could see was the gun. He could've reached up and touched it, but he knew that would do no good. Things happen when your mind is able to grasp that you're likely about to die, especially so young. There's an overwhelming feeling of regret, and it generates an agony way down deep inside you that's almost impossible to bear. He pictured Andrea and his children, safe inside their upper middle-class Germantown home. He wanted desperately to be there with them. He wanted to tell them how sorry he was. He wanted to walk through the door as he had so many times, announce he was home, kiss his young wife and marvel at the joy of being a dad. He wanted to make love, one last time, with Andrea. He wanted...

"Look at me!" the man demanded, and Harrington was suddenly brought back to reality. "You messed up, man. You fucked with my *Family*! That was my cousin's head you busted up. Then you just left him there to die. Now you're gonna know how that feels."

The first silenced shot sent a bullet into the kneecap of his left leg. Almost before he could react, a second round pierced his right. He was turned over, and two more bullets were shot point blank into his buttocks, the calling card, so to speak, of a gangland execution. He was vaguely aware, once again, of being turned over and onto his back. He wanted to scream, not so much from pain - and there *was* pain - but rather from pure, unqualified terror. It seemed strange he couldn't. He reasoned he must be in shock. He knew drugs, also, played a part. He was having trouble breathing, and blood was pouring from his wounds. The man then put the barrel of his gun against his belly, and fired once more. Finally, apparently satisfied, he leaned over and put his face inches from the dying man.

"How does it feel? Huh? *Knowin'* you gonna die? 'Cause, see, ain't nobody around here gonna help you. Ain't no ambulance on the way. Police'll eventually come but it'll be too late. Any second now, the lights are gonna go out, and they ain't never gonna come back on. Now, let's see..." He pretended to count in his head. "You got *five* holes in you, not countin' the ones you was born with, and they all bleedin'. It looks bad to me. How's it look to you, mother *fucker*?"

Harrington couldn't answer. He was gasping for breath, and he felt himself fading. His body was shutting down from the rapid blood loss. He suddenly noticed that he was alone. He tried to call for help, but his mouth simply opened and closed, akin to a fish out of water. He heard a far off police siren. He felt his heart skipping beats here and there because there was less and less blood to pump. After a minute or two, the lack of blood to his brain, mercifully, rendered him incapable to understand what was happening. And even though he was unable to see, he instinctively fought the urge to close his eyes. He lost the fight. Blackness enveloped him. All sound ceased. Nothingness, from which no creature has ever returned, was a final breath away.

Then, on a hot summer's night, on a dirty Memphis street, Harrington's pitiful life ended. Whatever happens when a soul passes from this world, happened. He was Tyrone's first kill, and the budding gangster had found it easy. Even exhilarating.

What Harrington didn't know was, even if the kid whose head he'd battered hadn't been Tyrone's cousin, he would still be dead. Because he had stolen drugs and money from The Family. And no one stole from The Family.

And lived.

Chapter One
One Year Later

Thirteen-year-old Angela Harwell sat alone inside the dark closet, in her pajamas, desperate and terrified. She hugged her favorite stuffed animal tightly against her chest with both arms. It was Tigger, from Winnie The Pooh, a birthday present from her grandmother a long time ago. Angela had him facing away from her, towards the closed door, as if to protect her. There had been many times when she wished he was a real tiger and could actually keep her from harm, and this was one of them. But the silly grin on the animal's face never changed and since he wasn't real he was, of course, oblivious to anything that may be happening to her. This wasn't *Toy Story*.

It was well past midnight and she should have been sound asleep, safe underneath the covers on her bed. She had school in the morning. Just a few hours earlier she had finished her homework, brushed her teeth and told her mother goodnight. Her mother's boyfriend, Billy, had not yet come home and the familiar ache of dread began to build in her stomach.

Billy was 24 and had moved into their tiny trailer with them a couple of years before. Her mother, Joyce, had met him where she met most of her men, in a bar just a stone's throw from the trailer park where they lived in Bartlett, Tennessee, a suburb of Memphis. Joyce's drink of choice was bourbon. His was beer.

Billy was quite a bit younger than Joyce and was nice enough when he was sober. He was a licensed armed security guard and made decent money. The living arrangement more or less kept her mother home nights and that made Angela happy. Most of the time her mother was able to function fairly coherently with her daughter up until bedtime, but that's when her drinking began in earnest. According to family members, the first time they had ever seen Joyce drunk was the day word came that Angela's father had been killed in Iraq. Angela was only two at the time and had no memory of him whatsoever. Only the picture of him in his Marine dress blues hanging in the hallway was left. Angela would stare and try hard to remember but it did no good. Her mother refused to talk about him so Angela quit asking.

Tonight, alone in her closet, she wished he was here to protect her.

Sometimes, when Billy was late, he was working and everything was fine. Other times he would drink, and come home very drunk. Angela prayed that this night she would fall asleep, wake up at her usual time - nearly always alone - fix her own breakfast - *if* there was milk she would have a bowl of cereal, *if* there was cereal - and then catch the school bus at the trailer park's front entrance.

Angela loved school. She loved her teachers. She felt safe there. She made excellent grades, especially in math and science. She dreamed that one day she'd be a doctor. But, on this night, all alone and more afraid than any young teen should ever be, all she wanted was that the closet door remained shut until she was sure it was safe for she and Tigger to crawl into her bed and fall back asleep.

She had tried more than once to tell her mother what was going on, but she didn't know how to begin. She was too ashamed and embarrassed to come right out and describe what Billy was doing, especially in any detail. She couldn't tell her mother that while there had been no penetration - at least not yet - there had been, well, contact. Billy would rub himself against her and tell her that there was nothing wrong with what he was doing. He warned her not to tell anyone, especially her mother, because no one would believe her anyway.

And now, she was very afraid that it was about to happen again.

Angela had awoken a few minutes earlier, when she'd heard Billy's heavy footsteps coming down the hallway just before he entered her room. She'd begged God for Billy to keep going and to leave her alone, but her prayer hadn't been answered. She smelled the familiar odor of alcohol on his breath as he leaned over her. He gently shook her shoulder.

"Angie?" he whispered, "Sweetie, are you awake?"

She lay on her back with the covers up to her chin. She kept her eyes shut. Tigger covered her face and she pretended not to hear. She felt the mattress move as Billy sat down on the edge of the bed. His hands began to caress and squeeze her arms and shoulders. His fingers played with her blond hair and then, moving the stuffed animal, he kissed her forehead.

"I know it's late, but I wanted to tell you good-night." He pulled the covers down to Angela's knees. Then, breathing heavily, he began a more aggressive massage on her small body - she was barely five feet and no more than 80 pounds - touching places where her teachers taught her no one should touch. Puberty had begun a year earlier, and Billy noticed. That's when things began to happen. She started to tremble and this caused him to suddenly pull his hands away.

"I'm sorry sweetie," he said, his voice remaining a low whisper. He immediately pulled the covers back over her. "You're cold. I tell you what. You stay right here," he said as he stood up, "and I'll be back lickety-split with another blanket. And then I'll tuck you in."

She fearfully opened one eye, just enough to watch him exit her room. And that is when she went into her closet. She began shaking again when she heard him come back.

Naturally he noticed her bed was empty. She heard the bathroom door open and close. Her body began convulsing as she heard his footsteps approach the closet. Tears streamed down her face and she began whispering, over and over, two words that were more prayer than supplication.

No, Billy! No, Billy! No, Billy!

He knew where she was of course. She had hidden there before. The door opened and he was there, towering over her. Only now his uniform was off and he was dressed only in his boxers.

No, Billy! No, Billy! No, Billy!

He was over six feet and seemed a giant to her. She noticed the front of his shorts. She opened her mouth to scream.

No, Billy!

There was no sound.

His hand covered her mouth. He pulled her from the closet.

Tigger remained behind.

****

Joyce woke suddenly, her head pounding mercilessly. She sat up, confused, not knowing at first where she was. She was relieved to discover she was in her own bed. There had been times - although not since Billy moved in - where this wasn't the case.

She clutched her forehead with both hands and pressed hard against the pain. It was a pitiful, and futile, attempt to make her head feel better. She felt around the top of her nightstand hoping she'd remembered to place a glass of water and three aspirin there before she'd stumbled to bed. She often did this in anticipation of the alcohol-induced headache, along with the cotton-mouth, she so frequently suffered. Not this time. She groaned. She would have to get up, knowing further sleep was impossible until she did.

She looked over and noticed Billy wasn't beside her. Nor was his blanket disturbed. She squinted at the clock on his side of the bed. It was nearly one o'clock in the morning. She hoped he was working late and not out spending money somewhere.

She managed to swing her legs over and stand. Every movement further tormented her skull. She remained woozy, her body yet to dissipate the shots of bourbon she had consumed earlier. She debated whether another shot or two might help.

Joyce had a routine. Angela - only Billy called her Angie - would tell her goodnight and go to bed. When Joyce was certain she was asleep, she would sit at the kitchen table with her bottle and glass, and pour. From her purse she would produce an old, worn picture of Brad, in his Marine uniform, taken just before his deployment. She would talk to Angela's father until the bourbon blurred her vision and slurred her speech. Tears always followed. She cried because she missed Brad terribly and also because she was so ashamed at what she'd become. She knew she was an alcoholic. She knew she was neglecting Angela. She realized that their daughter was the only part of Brad that she had left. But it wasn't enough to make her quit the booze. Even after eleven years, it wasn't enough.

She doubted it ever would.

She hated that - seriously hated it. She hated that her life had transformed from a fairy-tale story into a living nightmare. She hated knowing she was a lousy mother. She hated that she lived in a piece of shit filthy trailer with a man who was way too young and drank almost as much as she did. Joyce knew it was more about his paycheck than anything else. The money that Social Security sent her every month didn't come close to paying the bills. The life insurance money was long gone. The pain remained, however; so strong at times that not even the bourbon could dull it.

Brad had been her whole life. It was that simple. His death had left a hole in her heart and soul so massive that nothing on earth could fill it, not even Angela. There were even occasions where she almost resented their daughter. Always around. Always a reminder of what had been and never would be again. She was fairly certain she loved Angela. It was what, and who, she hated that consumed her. She hated Iraq and everybody in it. She hated her country being involved in something that didn't even matter. Not to her, not to anybody.

Except Brad. It mattered to him. He was proud. So damn proud. Proud to be a Marine. Proud to be fighting for his country.

Even proud to die for it.

And leave his wife and daughter behind, utterly alone.

And that, other than perhaps herself, is what she hated most of all. It made her wonder just how much longer she'd be able to go on, if nothing changed.

Joyce shuffled around the bed and towards the bedroom door, holding onto whatever she could find so that she wouldn't fall. She noticed the door was closed, which confused her even further. She never, ever closed her bedroom door, a habit formed when Angela was a baby and she needed to hear if she woke during the night. Even during her most serious binges the door remained open. It was instinctive. Joyce searched the wall beside the door until she found the light switch, and flipped it on. It took a moment for her eyes to adjust to the light. When they did, what instantly caught her eye was Billy's clothes and gun belt laying in a pile on the floor by his side of the bed, as if he had undressed in a hurry.

So where the hell was Billy?

She walked quietly, slowly down the hallway. She heard noises inside Angela's room. She paused outside of the door for a moment and heard Billy shushing Angela. She opened the door.

At first, her clouded mind wouldn't accept what she was looking at. Had she been stone-cold sober, still the reality would have been beyond comprehension. And when she finally understood, when there was simply no denying the obscenity that was in front of her, it was as if a baseball bat had been slammed into her stomach.

Billy was sitting on Angela's bed, naked.

A struggling Angela was in his lap, unable to scream because Billy's hand remained over her mouth. Her tear-filled eyes were pleading for help,

Finally, most telling of all, light blue pajama bottoms and a small pair of pink panties lay on the floor, next to a pair of boxers. The panties were torn.

Billy's eyes were wide open, horrified. Joyce looked directly at him, then simply turned around without a word and walked - stumbled, really - back towards their bedroom. Her stomach ached. The hallway spun. In the back of her mind she heard her name desperately called by a voice that seemed far away. She burst through her bedroom door so violently that it ricocheted off the wall and closed behind her. She fell to the floor and wretched a vile, burning fluid that tasted like sour bourbon.

Seconds later, the door opened. Billy stood at the doorway, boxers on. He said softly, "Joyce, honey. It isn't what you think." Joyce did not speak or move.

"Really, babe, you can ask her. Go ask Angie. We were just

playing. That's all it was. Go ask her." Still, Joyce did not move.

"Stay there," he said, the increasing desperation in his voice patently obvious. "I'll... I'll go get her. She'll tell you. It's okay, really." He started to turn, but stopped when Joyce said, "Wait."

She pushed herself up to her knees, her back toward him. When she turned, his gun was in her hand. They were barely five feet apart. Billy froze.

"Joyce, no!" he managed. "I swear to God, it'll never happen aga..."

She pulled the trigger of the revolver three times. Three .38 caliber slugs found their mark, two penetrating his stomach and one his chest. Blood poured from the wounds. Billy somehow remained standing, his face at first registering confusion, then disbelief, and, when he realized he was in the final moments of life, horror. He placed a hand over his stomach, then raised it up toward his face. He stared at his blood-covered fingers for a moment, then looked at Joyce one final time. He opened his mouth as if he was trying to say something to her, but instead gagged as blood began pouring from his mouth. He blinked once, his eyes closed, and, at last, he fell. Joyce heard a gurgled breath noisily escape his lips as his body hit the floor just inches from her.

He didn't breathe, or move, again.

She got up and dropped the gun beside the body. She looked down, then began kicking him, over and over. As she kicked, she screamed, "You son-of-a-bitch! You fucking bastard! How could you?" Finally, she stepped over him and walked down the hall to Angela's room. Angela was sitting on her bed, facing the door, her face expressionless. She'd put her pajamas back on. Joyce stood there for a long minute, then came to a decision.

She continued past her daughter's room, into the living room and found her cell phone. She noticed with relief that there was enough battery to make a call. She dialed the numbers, then sat heavily on the couch, rocking back and forth as she waited for an answer. After four rings she was relieved to hear the click of someone picking up.

"Dad?" she said, "can you come over here please?" A pause. "Yes, Dad, I know what time it is." Her voice quivered, and she began to rock again. She wiped her eyes with her arm. "Dad, please, it's important. I need you to come here." Another pause. She rolled her eyes. "No, Dad, I'm not drunk. Not anymore." Another pause. "Jesus Christ, Dad!" she shouted, "Do you think I'd be calling if it wasn't goddamned important?" Then her voice softened. "Daddy, Angela needs you. You need to get here right now. It can't wait until tomorrow." She ended the call, then turned the phone off. If her father called back, it would go straight to voicemail. She dropped the phone, then went back to Angela's room. Angela had not moved.

"Oh, honey," her mom wailed, tears streaming down her face, "I'm so sorry." She walked into the room hesitantly, then slowly lowered herself onto the bed beside her daughter. She wanted to put her arms around her but was afraid to. Angela had not looked at her. Joyce tried to place her hand on her daughter's arm but Angela jerked away. Joyce began to cry harder.

"You tried to tell me, didn't you?" she sobbed. "You tried, but I wouldn't listen." Angela turned her head toward her mother. Her eyes seemed unspeakably sad. With tears of her own forming, she nodded.

They sat together for a minute or two, their bodies touching. Joyce finally rose off the bed and walked toward the door. At the threshold she stopped. Then, without turning around, spoke in a clear, strong voice.

"He'll never hurt you again, Angela." There was a pause. "And neither will I." Then, she whispered, *I love you,* so softly that Angela didn't hear.

Her mother walked away. Angela heard the bedroom door close.

Seconds later, Angela's body jerked to the sound of a fourth gunshot. She slid off the bed and walked back to her closet. She picked Tigger up, then got back into bed. Holding Tigger close, she pulled the covers over her body and laid down on her pillow.

Then, very softly, she cried, but she wasn't sure why.

She heard sirens in the distance outside her window.
And then she fell asleep.

****

Within minutes the trailer park was awash in blue and red lights. Along with several police cars were two ambulances and one fire truck. Angela's grandfather, 59-year-old Detective Rodney "Rocco" (pronounced Rock-o) Rocorro, after being unable to reach his daughter on her cell, had made the call to roll the emergency vehicles. Two additional calls had been made to 911 by neighbors reporting suspected gun shots, but Rocorro provided the actual address.

When he arrived, the lights on his black-and-white Bartlett Police cruiser added further excitement for the curious onlookers who had gathered to watch whatever events might unfold. Dozens of cameras and camcorders were either clicking or recording, capturing every moment, their owners hoping to encapsulate the biggest thing most of them had ever seen. Or thought they might see. Later these people would, no doubt, entertain scores of friends and family who find some sort of satisfaction, or perhaps fascination, in real-life drama that involved violence. Something big had happened here and rumors were flying. As many as ten to fifteen shots was now the going total, depending on who was telling the story.

His heart sank when he saw the crime-scene tape placed around his daughter's trailer. There had been no radio traffic preparing him for this, and that was because he'd turned his police radio off. If something terrible had occurred, he didn't want to find out from emotionless voices over the radio. Before now, the only hint that something serious had happened here was his daughter's use of "Daddy" at the end of their conversation. It had been years since she called him that. They had slowly grown apart since the death of his son-in-law. As the years passed, and her drinking worsened, he had tried to intervene. She'd resented his efforts, however, and pushed him away. Finally, all he could do was make sure his granddaughter, the love of his life, was provided for and taken care of. From the looks of things, this just might be the night he feared would eventually come to pass.

Rocorro parked his car beside the others, exited quickly, then ducked his lean six foot frame under the tape and sprinted to the front door. Though he was almost 60, he was in superb shape. He lifted weights almost daily and still ran half-marathons a few times a year. He'd lost his hair twenty years before but that no longer bothered him. His wife of nearly 35 years didn't mind, so what the hell? Hair was overrated and there was nothing he could do about it anyway. He could, however, do something about his body, and his heart, and he worked hard to counter the physical deterioration that inevitably came with too many birthdays.

He took the four steps that led to the trailer's front door two at a time. With each passing second, his chest increasingly tightened with dread. He walked through the open door and into the living room. Four officers were there, and the looks on their faces spoke volumes. He had been to hundreds of crime scenes but this would be the first time where family, *his* family, was involved. Bartlett was a small town, and violent crimes were extremely rare. But, judging by the sullen faces of his fellow officers, he knew that someone inside this trailer was dead.

He rushed past the men and went straight into Angela's room. Sitting on the bed with his granddaughter was one of the department's female officers. As soon as Angela saw her grandfather, she rushed from the bed towards him. Rocorro knelt and received her embrace, the desperation in it unmistakable.

He wrapped his arms around her, and held her as tightly as he dared, and all he could say was, "Thank God you're okay," again and again. He fought to contain himself. He would not cry in front of the officer, or Angela. Finally, he held her at arm's length and looked her over.

"Hi, Angel," he said. "How's my girl?"

"Oh, Grandpa," she whispered, "You came! I heard Momma call you. I'm so glad you're here. I think Mom..." Then she fell into his chest, and began sobbing.

Again, his powerful arms encircled her body and, he hoped, provided the comfort and protection she so desperately craved. "It's okay, Angel," he said, "everything's going to be just fine now." He took a handkerchief from his pocket and wiped her eyes. "Stay here with Stacy, Angel, and I'll be right back. I promise." Angela nodded, and he carried her back to her bed. He looked at Stacy. She said, "Go ahead, sir, I'll take care of her."

He got up and walked out of the room. He went down the hall towards his daughter's room. A lieutenant who had been on the force almost as long as Rocorro guarded the closed door. His name was Keith Couples and was one of Rocorro's best friends. Rocorro's years on the job kicked in. "What've we got, Cup?"

Couples pursed his lips, and shook his head. "It's bad, Rocco. Real bad."

"Joyce?"

"Yeah, Rocco," he said slowly, "it's Joyce." Then he added, "And her boyfriend."

Rocorro let that sink in. "Both... *dead*?"

Couple's silence told him everything. "Listen," he said, "you don't have to go in there."

Rocorro reached around Couples, opened the door, shoved past him and entered the room. Billy lay on the floor where he had fallen, a large pool of blood beneath him. Joyce was on her back on the bed, both arms outstretched, her legs straddled over the edge of the mattress, sightless eyes wide open. The gun she had pressed against her temple lay just out of reach of her right hand. There was blood and splatter everywhere.

Rocorro took in the horrific scene. Had it been two strangers he still could not have prepared himself for the gruesome nature of what he was seeing. And while the hopes and dreams he and his wife had had for Joyce while she was growing up had long ago faded, he felt devastation at seeing his little girl's lifeless body on the bed in front of him. Murdered. It was a parent's worst nightmare. And, at that point in time, that's what he was. He was a father, not a police detective. He suddenly felt faint, and it must have been apparent because at that moment he felt an strong hand on his right arm. Rocorro leaned into it until the dizziness passed.

He fought to regain his composure. He swallowed hard. "My God." was all he could say.

Couples hold on his friend's arm remained. "I'm really sorry," he said. "I... I can't imagine."

Rocorro began to study the scene. There was something about it that didn't make sense to him. He pointed at his daughter. "How in the hell did he shoot her, Cup? And then the gun end up...?"

Couples waited a while for Rocorro to sort it out on his own. Then he said, "I don't think it happened that way."

Rocorro realized the implication of what Couples was saying. It was impossible to fathom, yet he heard himself asking, "*She...* shot *him?*"

Couples exhaled. "It sure looks that way to me, Rocco. From what we were able to get from your granddaughter, and the gun being where it is, well... I believe that's what happened."

Rocorro shook his head. "But Joyce didn't own a gun. That had to be Billy's gun. How in the hell did she get it away from him? And what did he do to make her want to kill him?" He paused as he again looked at his daughter, and the gun beside her hand. "And then she...?"

He looked down at Billy, dressed only in his boxers. He tried to force the unimaginable out of his mind. He finally asked. "What did Angela tell you?"

"She told us that Joyce opened her door and saw Billy in her bed *before*," he emphasized, "anything had really happened. I don't believe he actually raped her, Rocco." He took a notebook out of his shirt pocket, flipped a couple of pages, read for a second, then said, "She said Joyce came back in here and he followed her. She heard two or three shots. She heard Joyce call you. Joyce went back to Angela's room, told Angela how sorry she was, then came back in here. Angela heard one more shot. After that, she said she went to sleep."

Just then there was a knock behind them. There was an officer at the door. He said, "Sir, the coroner's here and so are the crime guys. They need to come in here. What should I tell them?"

"Tell 'em to *wait!*" Rocorro yelled, then slammed the door closed, barely missing the officer who delivered the message. He turned back around. He felt a calmness settle over him as he began to accept the finality of what happened. He'd learned long ago to recognize what he could change, and what he couldn't. This was one of those times where there was nothing he could do. At that moment he began to see his daughter in another time, in a better place when she was still his little girl, and her future remained bright. He was almost able to smile as he remembered.

"You know something, Cup?" he said, "she was a good girl. A good mom. A good wife. Right up until Brad was killed. Then she changed."

"I know, Rocco," Couples answered. "I remember."

"After that, it was like something broke inside her. I imagine it was her heart. And her spirit. Just broke in little pieces. She was never the same." He looked at his friend. "*My* Joyce," he said, "died with Brad. And now," he continued, "they're together again. I have to believe that. There's no way God would put her in the same Hell as *him.*" He pointed to the floor at Billy. "I think I'm going to take Angela out of here now. Take her home with me." A single tear flowed down his cheek. He wiped it off.

Couples nodded. "That's a good idea Rocco. If we need anything it can wait until later. I'll let you know."

He took one last look at his daughter. "I know how bad this looks, but I have to believe she did what she thought was right, Cup. She was protecting Angela the only way she figured she could." He was quiet for a moment, then said, "I need to go home now. I have to tell her mother."

When he got back to Angela's room, he reached down and scooped her up into his arms, covers and all. She wrapped her arms around his neck and said, "Grandpa, I want to live with you and Grandma now. I don't want to live here anymore."

"Then that's what we're gonna do, Angel," he said. He carried her outside and placed her gently in his cruiser. He slid in behind the wheel, and started to leave, but suddenly braked and got back out. Leaving his door open, he ran back inside the trailer and emerged seconds later with Tigger. He got back in the car, handed the stuffed animal to Angela, then drove away.

Angela never went back to the trailer again.

Chapter Two
Ten years later

"Last load, Timi!"

Timecia Harrison watched as the drycleaner placed an armload of pants on the curved metal rack next to her press. She was glad to see it wasn't a full load. When the 55-lb capacity drycleaning machine was full, there could be as many as 30 pair for her to press. Instead, there were maybe half that many and it would not take long to get them done.

It was July and miserably hot out. It was worse, by far, inside the walls of the cleaners where she worked, surrounded by steam and steam-return pipes. Though the pipes were insulated, it didn't seem to help much. She didn't want to imagine what it would be like had they been bare. The one bright side was that business dropped off this time of year. People simply didn't wear as many clothes in July and August. She was normally gone before the real heat of the day hit.

She was anxious to leave; not just because she craved the air-conditioning of her apartment, but also because she had studying to do. She had a test that evening at the community college she was attending. She was on schedule to graduate next spring and she always smiled when she imagined herself a paralegal and spending the day in an office, cool and comfortable. The noise and heat of a cleaning plant, with the endless days and low pay, would soon be a distant memory.

Timecia, just a month past her 20th birthday, was the single mom of four-year-old Kristin. She was glad Kristin was with her grandmother today and would be spending the night. Timi would be free of the constant demands of a toddler and could spend four or five serious hours of uninterrupted studying. She flew through the last few pairs of pants, careful not to double-crease - they were uncompromising when it came to quality and would return every pair that didn't live up to the high standards the owner required -

then grabbed her purse and hurried to clock out.

"Hey, Timi!" a voice yelled over the noise. It was Annie, talking as she pressed dress shirts on a three-piece unit. "Where you goin' in such a hurry, girl?"

"Gotta go Annie," she said, "big test tonight."

"You smart, girl," Annie told her as she dressed the bosom-shaped form with a damp men's dress shirt. She was a big woman, in her mid-40's and had worked her entire adult life in one drycleaners or another. The damp towel around her neck helped fight the heat and was also handy to mop the sweat from her brow. "You gonna get outta here. Gonna make some real money. Won't have to spend your life workin' hard and nothin' to show for it like me. You smart, girl." she repeated.

Timecia stopped, then said, "You can do it, too, Annie."

Annie laughed. "Me? Shit! No, it's too late for me, girl. I done got too old. Tell you what, though," she said as she pushed two buttons in front of her and sent the form sliding toward two shiny, spit-dancing hot, stainless-steel buck plates, "after you get to be a big-time lawyer, I want you to represent me. I wanna sue that bastard right there." She pointed to her boss, who was inspecting finished shirts.

"Watcha gonna sue me for, Annie?" he asked, smiling.

"Don't know," Annie said as she removed the newly pressed shirt from the form, "but we'll think of somethin'."

Timecia knew she would miss Annie. Annie had been an employee there for years and they had become good friends, *close* friends. Timecia didn't have any close friends, other than Annie. Annie knew everything about her past and also the dreams she had for the future. Whenever she felt it was all a waste of time, Annie would set her straight. Timecia loved her like a sister, despite the age difference.

Driving home, Timi thought of their conversation. Annie had said "big-time lawyer." *Wouldn't that be something?* she allowed herself to imagine. *Me, a lawyer!* She glanced down at her incentive, a picture of her daughter she had taped to the center of the steering wheel of the '96 Crown Vic she owned. It wasn't much but it was all hers. Her boss had helped her buy it and she'd paid him back every penny. It was one of the proudest days of her life when he presented her with the title, free and clear. Maybe, just maybe, *one day* she'd tape that picture on a brand new car. The car she'd park in the driveway of a home that she longed, *one day*, to own. A home where she and her daughter and - *should she dare hope?* - her man would live. A good man who loved her, who she loved and didn't have to fear. A man who would protect her and her daughter, in a place where they'd be safe. Where they could be happy.

One day at a time, she reminded herself, *one day at a time.*

These were the words her rehab counselor had framed on the wall above his chair in his office. Dr. John was one reason she was sober, there was no doubt about that. He'd given her the first glimmer of hope that she could beat the drug that threatened to destroy her. She'd contemplated suicide many times, thinking it was her only way out of the hopelessness and depression a methamphetamine addiction created. The high was so powerful she often was awake for days at a time. Conversely, the crash so complete as to be utterly devastating, and the overwhelming urge to return to the illusion of a world where literally nothing mattered was all-encompassing and would shut out any other thought. It was a double edged sword that, had it not been for Dr. John, would likely have made her another statistic.

Timi's mother also deserved credit. When she filed for custody of her granddaughter - when she wanted to take her little girl *away* from her - Timecia woke up, finally understanding what was at stake. She suffered through a week of detox, then was admitted to a long-term rehabilitation center for women with no insurance or money. The center was a safe house as well, and the identities of the patients living there were well-guarded and virtually unobtainable. She'd now been sober for 18 months and six days. She cut off contact with all of her so-called friends from her darker days because she feared - no, she *knew* - even after this much time, if the drug was in front of her, she would smoke it again.

It was a terrifying admission.

Meth was that powerful.

She steered the Vic into the parking space in front of her apartment. Detective Harwell, yet another extremely important person in her life, had helped her get it. It wasn't the nicest apartment in the world, but it was home. She kept it immaculate, and had it furnished as comfortably as she could afford. It wasn't in the best area of town but she felt safe enough. There was a security gate at the entrance that required a card to open. There was also a wrought-iron fence surrounding the complex and a security guard who was on duty 24/7. The rent was reasonable and she was careful to pay it on time. A process server was regularly seen on the property, knocking on doors and diligently serving the dreaded Detainer Warrants to tenants who fell behind. Timecia had never been served one, but she had been told it was the beginning of the eviction process.

And there were plenty of evictions. You had to pay to stay, it was that simple.

Timecia slipped the key into the dead bolt, unlocked it, and placed the same key into the door knob and turned. She walked into the cool air of her apartment and it felt heavenly. She only ran her car's air when Kristin was with her. Otherwise, she rolled the windows down and hoped she didn't get caught by too many lights. She heard it burned extra gas to run the AC and gas was expensive.

She locked the door behind her, threw her keys on the coffee table and hurried to her bathroom. She hated using the unisex bathroom at her job and usually was able to hold it until she got home. When she finished, she washed her hands, then pulled the sweat stained t-shirt up over her head as she walked into her bedroom. She wanted out of her clothes and underneath a cold shower as quickly as possible. She also wanted to be able to grab a quick nap before one last review of her notes. She found she was able to score better if she managed a power nap before a test.

She walked back into the living room dressed only in her bra and shorts, planning to grab a cold bottled water from the fridge. As soon she reached the outer edge of the hall, she froze.

Tyrone Reed, Kristin's father, was sitting on her couch.

"You know, baby," he said, holding up a locksmith's pick, "the locks on these doors are just too easy. You ought to put that little chain on your door when you get home, otherwise folks can just walk right in. Ain't that right, boys?"

Timecia looked where Tyrone indicated. Two men who Timecia knew well walked toward her from the dining room. She knew exactly why they were here. She screamed and turned to run. They grabbed her from behind. One of them accidentally found a handful of breast in the scuffle. The other covered her mouth, and they returned her, kicking and trying to scream, back to Tyrone.

Tyrone placed a gloved right index finger against his lips. "Shhh. Calm down, baby," he said, "and I'll tell Rod Man to take his hand off your mouth. Can you do that, baby?" She nodded, eyes wide open with fright. "Well, alright then. But understand me, you scream again, and you won't scream no more. I promise you that. Okay Rod Man, let the girl talk now."

Rod Man did as he was told. Timecia stared at Tyrone, afraid to breathe.

"What's wrong, baby? Ain't you glad to see me?" Timecia nodded, but said nothing.

He rose off the couch. He was dressed in jeans and a plain, black t-shirt. "Then SAY it!" he shouted

Timecia nearly screamed again, but muffled herself before it came out. He glared at her, his nostrils flaring as he breathed, the anger in his eyes apparent. She finally managed to say, in a voice that was barely a whisper, "I'm.. I'm glad to see you, T."

He calmed a little, then sat back down. "Now that's better. Only thing is, I'm having a hard time believing you, 'cause you never came to see me while I was trying to clear my good name. Not one time. Now, don't that seem strange to you? All those months and not one visit?" She nodded. "Yeah. It did to me, too. It got...

lonely." He got back up from the couch, walked up to her, and put his face inches from hers. "I tried to get my boys to find you, but they say they can't. I called Rico, and even he had a hard time. He finally found out you was in some kind of hospital. Why'd you go to a hospital, baby? You sick?"

She nodded again. "I was," she whispered.

"But not anymore, right? You all better now?" She nodded again.

He backed away, seemed to ponder that, then said, "I'm glad to hear that. I really am. But now I'm wondering," he moved closer again, "why'd you move? I mean, without telling me where you went?" She didn't answer.

"Maybe you didn't hear me. I'll speak a little louder." He put his mouth against her ear. Then, screamed, "WHY DID YOU FUCKING MOVE?!!"

This time she couldn't help herself. She screamed. Rod Man instantly clamped his hand over her mouth again. She struggled against the restraint the two thugs had on her but they were far too strong. She was utterly terrified now. She knew what Tyrone was capable of. He watched as she fought, a small smile finding its way to his lips. Eventually she stopped struggling. Tyrone nodded at her, as if in approval of something.

"You got some fight in you now, don't you baby?" he said. "Never seen that before." He cocked his head to one side. "You off the junk now?"

She nodded again, this time with a little more force. "Good for you," he said. "I mean that. Good for you." He walked back over to the couch, and sat back down. He looked at her, then said nonchalantly, "Where's Kristin?" She became wide-eyed again. "C'mon," he said, "that's the easiest question so far. Rod Man, take your hand off. Good. Now, baby, I'll ask you one more time. I'll even slow it down a little." He stood up.

"Where. Is. Kristen?"

"She's... she's spending the night with a friend."

"That's nice," Tyrone said. "What friend?"

"She's, uh... her name's Monica."

Tyrone smiled. "Monica. And now tell me where Monica lives."

She shook her head. "I don't know. I'm not sure. My mother came and got her for me. I have a test tonight." She indicated with her eyes the thick schoolbook on her kitchen table.

He thought about that for a minute. "So what you're telling me is, my daughter, *our* daughter, is having a sleep-over with Monica, and you don't know where she lives?" Timecia was frozen. She just stared at him. "Well, can you call her?"

She shook her head.

"Hmm," Tyrone said, "you can't call her." It wasn't a question. "That seems strange to me. Does that seem strange to you, Rod Man?"

"It does, boss," he said.

Tyrone was walking around, finger on his chin, pondering. He stopped suddenly and looked at Timecia. "Tell me something. Is she white?"

"Is she what?"

"Is her little friend white, or is she black?"

"I... she... she's black."

He shook his head. "A black child named *Monica*? Really? Now I know you're lyin' to me. Ain't no sister I know gonna ever name her kid Monica."

He walked over to the three of them. "Y'all let go of her now." Each man released her arms, but stayed where they were. Tyrone looked at them. "Go on now. Wait for me over by the door. She'll be fine." They both started to move away, but Tyrone unexpectedly grabbed one of them by his arm. It wasn't Rod Man. He slammed him against the wall, pulled a pistol from the back of his jeans, and jammed it against the bewildered man's crotch.

"Danny Boy," he said, "are you still using this?"

"What?" Danny managed.

"Are you still using *this*?" He pressed harder. "I mean, you got a pretty wife, you want to hang on to it for a while longer, right?"

Danny nodded. "Yeah." was all he said.

"You EVER touch my woman in an inappropriate manner again, I'll give you a sex change. I will blow that little mother fucker clean off. You understand me?"

"Tyrone," he said, "you don't think I did that on purpose, do you?"

"If I thought that you'd already be castrated. But I didn't ask you that. I asked you if you understood me?" He pressed still harder into Danny. The pain was becoming unbearable.

He desperately nodded. "Yeah. I understand. I'm sorry. It was an accident. I swear it won't happen again." Tyrone let him go. Danny nervously made his way past him.

Tyrone turned his attention back to Timecia. He put the barrel of his weapon on the exposed flesh of her breasts. He traced a figure-eight on each one. He said, "You know somethin' baby? You bein' clean and all done you some good. You got some meat on your bones now. You're lookin' real nice. How long has it been since you been high? Long time?" She nodded, her eyes focused on the gun in his hand, afraid to move, terrified that it might go off. He continued his eights, back and forth. The cold steel on her bare skin made her shiver. "Been a long time for me, too. You did hear about the terrible things they was saying about me, right?" Timecia nodded. "Anyway, what I meant was, I was looking for you for some..." He waved the gun around as he searched for the word. "Companionship. Maybe some sympathy." He suddenly placed the barrel of the weapon against her throat. She recoiled at the touch. He reached around her with his free hand until he had a handful of hair, and pulled. She yelped in pain.

"I need to ask you about something. I need you to help me understand. A man, some lawyer, came to see me a few months ago, even had a Deputy Sheriff with him, and he brought me this legal looking piece of paper. He said you were trying to keep me from seeing my daughter. He said I was dangerous, that I was a gangster, that I was violent - all kinds of shit like that. I mean, paragraph after paragraph of this bullshit. What bothered me most, though, according to this paper, is I'm not supposed to get within like 500 feet of you and Kristin. You know anything about that?"

Timecia didn't answer him. There was nothing she could say. She, of course, knew about the order of protection. He pulled even harder on her hair.

"One last time," he said through clenched teeth, "I'm asking you. Where's Kristin?" He abruptly let go of her hair, then gently smoothed it out. "I'm not going to hurt her, baby. I just want to see her. I have a *right* to see her. And ain't no goddamn piece of paper gonna *keep* me from seeing my daughter. Now where the fuck *is* she?"

Timecia, at that moment, wanted, like she had never wanted before, to get high again. To return to that familiar place where absolutely nothing mattered. To escape the terror she was feeling. She knew she would never tell him where Kristin was. And she knew Tyrone might kill her because of it. No one ever told Tyrone "no." She had to do the unthinkable. She would defy him because she'd rather die than put her daughter in harm's way again, and she knew her mother would feel the same way. And with this realization came resolve. And with this resolve came strength. She could not save herself, but she could save Kristin and her mother.

She looked Tyrone dead in the eyes, and without blinking said, "I told you, Tyrone. She's at a friend's house."

"That," he said, "is the wrong answer."

She took the first blow without flinching. He struck her face with an open backhand, and the pain took her breath away. She started to fall, but he caught her. Again he asked her, "Where's Kristin?"

She felt blood pooling inside of her mouth. She spit it directly into his face. "Fuck you."

The last things she remembered clearly that day was the look of shock on Tyrone's face, her own blood and saliva sliding down his cheeks, and finally the wild, animal-like guttural roar that erupted from his throat.

The pain of her nose being broken was unmistakable. The lights dimmed. She again was vaguely aware of the sensation of falling, this time hitting the floor. She felt someone begin to kick her. And then the lights went out completely.

****

The three men looked down at Timecia. If she was breathing it was hard to tell. Tyrone found a handkerchief. With shaking hands, he wiped his face. He looked at the red spittle that he had removed from his skin, and, enraged, kicked her again. He finished cleaning his face, then nudged her with a polished, brown Italian loafer. Nothing.

"Oh, man," Danny Boy said, shaking his head. "I think you killed her, Tyrone."

Tyrone looked down at Timecia, and for a moment felt something. Then he remembered what she did, and the rage built up again. "She *spit* on me, Danny Boy. Spit in my *face!*" Then he looked at the two men and said, "No one spits on me. If my own momma spit on me, I swear before God I'd do the same thing to her."

He stuffed the handkerchief back into his pocket, made a mental note to destroy it later, then looked around the apartment. He closed his eyes for a few seconds. He became visibly calmer. The anger was gone. "Okay, boys," he said, "let's clean it up. We were never here."

Rod-Man and Danny Boy put on latex gloves and set about meticulously wiping down the entire apartment. After a few minutes they were satisfied no evidence remained that might place them inside. Tyrone took one last look at Timecia's motionless body. He sighed deeply, then took a cell phone out of one of his pockets. He quickly dialed a number and waited. "Hey, baby," he said, "I need you to do something for me. Call 911. Do it right now. Tell them to come to 1800 Garden Gate Cove, apartment number one. Tell 'em the door'll be unlocked. Tell 'em to hurry. And use the safe phone. Thanks, baby." Tyrone put his phone away, then carefully looked through the blinds "I don't see anyone," he said. " Let's go."

As soon as they left the apartment, Timecia opened her eyes. Somehow, she found the strength to reach into her back pocket and retrieve her cell phone. The pain was incredible. Then, despite being barely able to see, she managed to find her contacts, and then her mother. The phone rang twice. To her great relief, she heard her mother say, "Hello?"

"Mom," she said, "you need to leave."

"Timecia?" her mother said, "Are you alright, dear? I can barely hear you."

"Momma," she said again, then coughed several times. Finally she was able to speak again. "Momma, you and Kristin need to leave right now. Tyrone might be coming over there."

"Tyrone's coming here? Why?"

"Momma!" Timecia said, still louder, and this caused her to cough again. The coughing made her wince in pain. There was something wrong with her chest. Tears were seeping from her swollen eyes, streaming down her bruised face. When she finally stopped coughing, she tried again. "Momma, please. You need to leave. Leave right now."

And then she dropped the phone, and lost consciousness. If she'd stayed awake, she'd have heard her mother's desperate voice over the phone, screaming, "Timecia! *Timecia!*"

Chapter Three

"Some days are better than others."

This was Detective Angela Harwell's stock answer when asked how she was doing.

Today wasn't a good day. That's why she was seeking solace here, at the shooting range.

Yet, as she slapped the magazine to her Glock 17 handgun back into place, she had to admit it hadn't helped nearly as much as she'd hoped.

She'd gotten the phone call a couple of hours earlier. She didn't know how, but Tyrone had found Timecia.

Timecia Harrison had been one of Angela's priorities for over a year now. Tyrone Reed was her baby's daddy. His street name, T-Bone, was whispered on the streets with both reverence and fear. He was 28 and had been involved with Timecia since before Kristin's birth. He'd been in and out of jail throughout his teens, but had since proven nearly untouchable. Tyrone was now a powerful gangster, the head of a local gang called The Family, and was a capable and ambitious leader. Under his control, The Family prospered and, naturally, so did Tyrone. He was listed as the owner of a successful logistics company, ideal for laundering The Family's lucrative drug sales profits. To the IRS he was a young, dynamic, tax-paying business owner with a 50,000 square foot warehouse full of goods being loaded and unloaded daily.

To the Memphis Vice Squad, he was so much more. They just couldn't prove it.

They'd almost been able to put Tyrone away recently. A "lucky" traffic stop, and subsequent search of his vehicle, produced enough cocaine to charge him with felony possession with intent to sell. But he and his high-profile lawyers were able to ask for, and receive, postponement after postponement. During the months all of this was happening, Tyrone became the very pillar of society. He was filmed going to church and feeding the homeless. He donated piles of money to various charities around Memphis. And he distanced himself from Family business, especially when the cameras were rolling.

The charges were eventually dropped after allegations of an illegal search and evidence planting surfaced. Harwell halfway believed it was true. One of the arresting officers had just buried a young daughter who'd died from a heroin overdose. There were other irregularities as well. She was never convinced that, as smart as Tyrone was, he would actually have drugs in his car, especially since he was a non-user. Still, it was frustrating. Harwell knew, *knew,* that he and his gang were involved in everything from large-scale drug trafficking to murder, but Tyrone was always one step ahead. A lifetime of crime had taught him many lessons. None of his victims would ever testify against him. Tyrone never made any serious mistakes. He covered his tracks. He had nearly unlimited resources and could afford the best lawyers. He paid his cronies well and never touched any of the drugs that he sold to others.

Tyrone was sinister and cunning. He was highly intelligent, despite not finishing high school, and had a remarkable memory. He could be charming when he needed to be. He was loyal to his friends and aware of his enemies. He was generous when he needed to be. His temper was legendary and explosive. He ran The Family with an iron fist. He ordered executions with the same demeanor as he would order lunch.

And, regardless of the crime, Tyrone always had an air-tight alibi. Always.

Tyrone had impregnated Timecia when he was 24 and she was barely 16. No charges had been filed because she wouldn't tell anyone who the father was. She had been in love with Tyrone. He had money and he seemed to care for her. At the time, he was second in line in The Family hierarchy, and was promoted to the top job when the former head was killed in an ambush by a rival gang. Tyrone was big - well over six feet - and powerfully built. His eyes were hypnotic and penetrating. His skin was almost completely covered with tattoos, the most prominent being the gang's logo, the initials "T" and "F" inside a circle, with "Once Family" over the top of the circle, and "Always Family" underneath. It was dead center in the middle of his chest, almost like a target. The top half of the logo was red for blood, the lower half black for pride. There were no white members. Nor Hispanic. That was by design.

The first time Harwell met Timecia was in the emergency room of Methodist Hospital in midtown Memphis. The nurses had been suspicious of her injuries and called the police. When asked how her jaw was fractured, Timecia told Harwell simply, "I fell." Tyrone was there also, and with then 2-year-old Kristin on his knee, he also told Harwell, "She fell." When she asked him angrily if there were any witnesses to this "accident" he had calmly replied, "How many witnesses do you want, Detective? I'll get them for you."

Timecia also had a drug problem but had been working hard to get clean. Lately there was reason for great hope. A few months ago, she'd passed the one year anniversary of being clean and sober, widely recognized as the yardstick of a successful rehab from meth. If you could make it a year, your chances greatly increased to beat it forever. But even after a year, it remained dicey. Kristin was, and remained, Timecia's motivation. She was determined that her daughter would have a good life, free of gangs and drugs. To do that, though, Timecia finally understood she would also have to be free of Tyrone.

Possibly even more daunting than beating meth.

This was where Harwell came in. She was determined to help and she was in a position to do so. Timecia knew that all she had to do was call and she'd come running. Harwell had helped Timecia get her job at the cleaners and found an apartment she could afford. Harwell derived great satisfaction from this. This was one of the reasons why she became a cop. She cared. She cared very deeply. She wanted to make a difference in Timecia's life.

And she was furious with herself for not anticipating - and preventing - this latest assault.

Harwell wasn't the least bit afraid of Tyrone. Besides the fact that his drugs had ruined countless young lives and continued to do so, his physical abuse of women enraged her and she dreamed of the day she would take him down. She suspected that if one fought back - her for example - he might make a mistake. He would assume she was as helpless as the others. That would be all she'd need. Tyrone was one reason why she trained so relentlessly.

Almost since the day of her mother's death, Harwell had been in some form of training. Her grandfather had seen to it.

"You can't help being female," he'd told her, "but you sure as hell don't have to be helpless."

He enrolled Angela in self-defense classes and she excelled in them. She especially loved Krav Maga, an Israeli form of martial arts. Students of Krav Maga are taught to avoid confrontations first, but, should that prove impractical, they are trained to end the fight as quickly as possible. She learned that carefully placed blows to the eyes, throat, groin, knees, etc, would quickly put a loud-mouthed aggressor into a fetal position.

Harwell had the same personal trainer who'd kept her grandfather in such good shape. She enjoyed lifting weights and could bench-press 180 lbs. She was now 5'8" - she'd had a dramatic growth spurt between her junior and senior year in high school - and weighed 133 lbs. Her body/fat percentage hovered between 6 and 8 percent. She was lean and fit - damn near a perfect physical specimen. She'd long outgrown the vulnerable little girl that Billy had preyed upon.

She was fiercely devoted to staying in shape and, of course, didn't smoke and only sporadically enjoyed a beer. One occasion was when she and her grandpa would attend Memphis Redbird's baseball games together at the downtown stadium. They would split a barbecue nachos and would each enjoy a cold one. It was tradition and she relished their time together. Grandma had died suddenly just days after her high school graduation and pretty much all they had now was each other. He hadn't remarried and she seldom dated. She was too busy for a relationship and rarely went out with the same guy more than once. Harwell liked living alone and her memories of Billy remained strong. She had yet to find, other than her grandfather, a man she completely trusted. There were other reasons as well.

While it was true that her grandfather inspired her to join law-enforcement, it was her bitter hatred of Billy, and anyone like him, that led her down a specific path. She became driven to help those who were too weak to help themselves. She would graduate from high school, get her degree in Criminal Justice from the University of Memphis in just three years and then join the MPD. She was made a detective. She asked for, and was assigned to, Domestic Violence, and also worked closely with the Sex Crimes/Juvenile Abuse Unit. This was how she met Timecia and her daughter, and the reason she stayed involved. She was determined that Timecia and Kristin would have every opportunity for a better life.

But Timecia, at this moment, was lying in the critical care unit at The Med, short for The Regional Medical Center at Memphis. Paramedics had been alerted by an anonymous call to 911 from a cell phone. The caller's voice had been female. The phone was untraceable. A neighbor perhaps. Harwell was relieved to discover that Kristin was with her grandmother at the time of the attack.

Tyrone - and Harwell would never be convinced that it had not been Tyrone - had left her for dead, she knew that. Harwell also knew that Tyrone would lay low for a while and would be difficult to find. She also knew he would be busy manufacturing an alibi and finding witnesses who would account for his whereabouts at the time of the assault. And it wouldn't be long before it would all be air tight.

She knew all of this but could do little to prevent it. At least not yet. What Harwell needed was Timecia to point her finger at Tyrone, but she doubted that would ever happen. Understandably, Timecia was too afraid of him. No, Tyrone would have to be gotten some other way. Until then, though, more people would get hurt. More kids would buy his drugs. More women would fall victim to his charm, his money and ultimately his fists. And this filled her with a fury that consumed her nearly to her breaking point. And that was dangerous. It could affect her judgment, could cloud her thinking and cause *her* to make mistakes. And when a police officer made mistakes, the wrong people could get hurt.

There was only one person who Harwell wanted to hurt. She wanted it more than anything in the world.

She raised her pistol, flipped her blond hair away from her eyes and took aim at the head-and-torso cardboard target downrange. In what seemed to her to be no more than a second or two, she had expelled all fifteen 9mm rounds she had loaded into the clip. And though the target was fifty yards away, every round which screamed from the gun's barrel at more than 1200 feet per second penetrated the torso, dead center, in a tight grouping no larger than a fist.

Her grandfather had also taught her to shoot. It was second nature to her now.

It was suddenly eerily quiet after the deafening noise her weapon had made, especially after rapid-firing the last load. She removed her noise-protection headphones - she was the only one there - and dropped them into a duffle bag beside her on the floor. She'd been there about an hour, and had gone through three hundred rounds. She decided to call it a day. She released the now-empty clip from the grip and insured the chamber was free of a wayward round. She knew it was, but it was a habit she formed when she first began shooting was now automatic. She then reloaded the clip, snapped it back into her weapon, chambered a round, then placed the gun into the holster on her hip. She reached up to her left and pushed a button. The target she'd been aiming at began moving towards her. When it stopped just in front of her, she snatched it off the clips and stared at it for a moment. Instead of the blank, faceless shape, though, she now saw *him*. She angrily ripped off the head, crumpled it and threw it aside. Then, with a sudden sweep of her arm, she cleared the table in front of her of all the empty shell casings which had earlier been ejected from the Glock, but had not fallen to the floor. Neither act accomplished anything.

But it did make her feel better.

Just then she got a text message from a nurse she knew at the hospital. It read, simply, *She's awake. Hurry.*

Harwell grabbed her duffle bag and ran out to the parking lot.

She needed to see Timecia. She needed to talk to her. She needed to find out what really happened. She didn't know how much time she would have to get this information. She didn't know yet how badly Timecia was hurt. She knew it was possible Timecia's injuries might be fatal.

With the assistance of her lights and siren, the trip to the hospital was swift.

****

Danny Boy eased his late-model silver Malibu into the drive of his middle class home, pushing the garage door remote at the same time. He parked beside his wife's Lexus SUV and was pleased she was home. He needed to talk to her.

Danny Boy was born Daniel William Sullivan on the 4th of July and had recently celebrated his 22nd birthday, quietly, with his wife, Jasmine, and their two-year-old twin boys, Donnie and Ronnie. His 21st birthday had been an extravaganza he would never forget, though he wanted to. Paid for by Tyrone, he had found himself at a downtown strip club, rented for the night and closed to the public, with more food, booze, girls and drugs than he had ever seen in one place. Danny had nearly died that night from a lethal mixture of alcohol and cocaine. He woke up in a hospital the next day with a distraught Jasmine standing by the bed. She'd been both relieved and hysterical, crying uncontrollably, furious with him for nearly making her a widow and a single mom at age 22. He had no recollection whatsoever of the night before. He'd had an epiphany of sorts at that moment, realizing that she loved him and he loved her and it was a for real, lifetime, forever love. He understood he'd nearly lost this and what that would do to his wife and kids. He'd promised her he would never do drugs, or drink, again.

And he hadn't.

But he kept working for Tyrone because he simply didn't know what else he could do. And also because Tyrone paid him well. Jasmine also made good money as an OR nurse at the Med, and between them, they were very comfortable. They paid their bills and even managed to save a bit. They'd made many friends in their Whitehaven neighborhood. None of them had any idea who Danny worked for. He told them he did consulting work when they asked. They didn't press. He did not wear The Family tattoo, nor any other tattoo. He told Tyrone he had an allergy to ink that made tattoos dangerous for him.

It was still daylight when Danny put the car in park and got out of the Chevy. After they'd left Timecia's apartment they'd driven Tyrone to one of the many homes that were available to him. Tyrone told them he'd be in touch, that he was going to chill for a while until this thing settled down. He knew he'd be a prime suspect, although he also knew there was a good chance Timecia wouldn't say anything.

If she was still alive.

Tyrone told him and Rod Man to take some time off, with pay. He'd warned them not to call him, and that he would call them when he needed them. And that, in a nutshell, was Danny's job. While Rod Man was nearly always at Tyrone's side, Danny, like a dog, came when he was called. He provided extra muscle for Tyrone. Danny was an impressive human specimen. He was just over six feet, around 220 lbs, and had trained as a boxer since his early teens. Danny had been convinced, at one time, that he had a future in boxing. He had the build. He had most of the skills. He had the desire. He had the intelligence and the endurance. And he was absolutely fearless in the ring. But what he lacked was the lightning fast reflexes that a successful prize fighter required, that maybe one in a million had. That was what had made Ali so unbeatable. He was blindingly fast, and Danny wasn't. And this is also how he'd met Tyrone. Tyrone had approached him after a losing bout three years earlier. He'd fought valiantly, but hit the floor after a vicious right hook in the 9th round. Although he tried desperately, he was unable to get back up before the count reached ten. Tyrone had bet a bundle on Danny's opponent and therefore had won. But Tyrone liked what he saw in Danny. Big, imposing, tough, utterly unafraid and trained to fight. He told him that night, "You'll never make it as a pro. You want a job, come see me. I'll take care of you." Danny and Jasmine had just discovered she was pregnant, she was still in nursing school, so he went to see him. The money Danny was offered was too good to be true. He'd been with Tyrone ever since.

He'd learned, over time, to do what he was told, show no outward emotion and to keep his mouth shut about whatever he saw. He was given a gun and always had it with him, but had never used it. Normally Danny had little to do but provide visual evidence that Tyrone was never to be touched.

Today had been immeasurably different.

Man-handling Timecia had sickened him. He and his wife both knew her, and her daughter. Watching Tyrone beat her senseless disgusted him. A fight was supposed to be fair. Having Tyrone push a loaded weapon into his manhood and berate him like a schoolyard bully had incensed him, and, right after it happened, it was all he could do not to pull his own weapon and empty it into Tyrone.

And that possibility was downright terrifying to him.

Had he gotten to the point where he was actually capable of murder? Had enough of Tyrone, and this job, rubbed off on him that he had become the kind of thug that Tyrone was? He'd always been able to justify what he did because he'd kept his hands relatively clean. And now Danny knew, even though he was one of the few privileged enough to get close to Tyrone, that he was expendable. And possibly even more than most since he was privy to parts of Tyrone's world that almost no one else was.

In other words, what he knew could get him killed.

He'd even flown with Tyrone recently to El Paso, Texas, in a plane that Tyrone would hire from time to time. They'd then driven into Mexico, where there'd been a meeting with Tyrone and a Mexican businessman. It took place in a massive mansion 30 or so miles south of the border. The entrance to the mansion was gated and patrolled by two Hispanic guards armed with AK-47s and side-arms. They'd leveled their guns and eyed Tyrone and Danny suspiciously as the two men slowly drove towards them. Tyrone told Danny to relax, lowered his window of the rented Mercedes and said something in Spanish to the guards. While one kept his gun aimed squarely at the Mercedes, the other walked over to the gate and made a call from inside the guard shack. Soon the gates were swinging open, and they were waved through.

They traveled a tree-lined, black asphalt curved drive for at least a half-mile. Suddenly the trees ended, and they were treated to a panorama of 20 acres or more of an incredibly green, manicured lawn, and in the distance a mansion that appeared worthy of royalty. It was the biggest dwelling Danny had ever seen. Another well-armed guard was waiting just outside the main entrance of the mansion as they drove up. Without taking his eyes off the car, the guard reached around and knocked. Almost immediately, the door opened and a casually dressed, and very fit, Hispanic gentleman made his way down the steps, followed closely by the guard. He was smiling; his teeth were dazzling white and he seemed genuinely pleased to see them. As he got closer, the man's affluence was obvious. He had several diamond rings on his hands and a gold Rolex on his wrist. A gold medallion the size of a silver dollar hung on a thick gold chain around his neck. His jeans nestled over the tops of handmade snakeskin boots. When Tyrone opened the door to get out, Danny followed.

"Tyrone!" the Hispanic man said, his voice genuine and warm, "it is so good to see you again, my friend."

Tyrone smiled and extended his hand. "Ah, Ricardo! *Como esta, amigo!*" The two men shook hands and embraced. "Thank you for inviting me."

"I assure you, it is my pleasure. I am pleased to welcome you to my humble home. And now," he said, "please introduce me to your friend."

Tyrone looked at Danny. "Come on over here, Danny." He did so. "Ricardo, this is Danny Boy." He then said, "Danny's just a... well, a little insurance policy that I like to have with me when I'm out and about. You understand." It was a statement, not a question.

As the two men shook hands, Ricardo said, "Of course I understand, but there's no need for that here, I assure you. Tell me Danny," he said, "do you have a weapon?"

Danny looked at Tyrone, and Tyrone nodded. "I do," he said.

"Of course, that was a silly question. I apologize." He turned to his guard, spoke quickly, and the guard instantly stood in front of Danny. "Now," Ricardo said to Danny, "if you would, please, very, very carefully give this man your weapon. I promise, when our business is done here, and before you leave, you will get it back."

Again, Danny looked at Tyrone, and, again, Tyrone nodded. "It's fine, Danny Boy," he said. "Give him your gun."

Danny, without thinking, reached inside his sport coat, forgetting that he was instructed to do so very, very carefully. When he did the guard immediately chambered his weapon and aimed it directly at Danny's temple.

"No, Carlos, no!" Ricardo said, and moved the barrel of the gun away from Danny. "It's okay," he said, "*esta bien, amigo, esta bien.*" He looked at Danny apologetically. "Please excuse him," he said. "But, you see, he is very protective and cannot help himself. If you'll allow me, please, just open your jacket and I will remove the gun." Danny did as he was told. Ricardo removed his gun and handed it to Carlos. "There!" he said, "and now we can relax! Please, Danny, while Tyrone and I sit and discuss business with members of my family inside, you are welcome to enjoy my pool. I am sure you will be pleased with the, shall we say, scenery? It is a hot afternoon. Should you wish to swim, you will find a bathing suit that will fit you in the guest house beside the pool. And whatever you desire in the way of beverages or food, I will see to it that it is done. I assure you, we won't be long."

And with that, Tyrone and Ricardo climbed the steps to the front door and disappeared inside. Carlos led Danny to the pool, where, for the better part of three hours, he watched several beautiful young Hispanic ladies splash and sun in very nice, and very tiny, swimsuits. He had no idea what was discussed at that meeting. Whatever it was had to have been important.

Danny was certain then, and remained certain, that Tyrone had, somehow, incredibly, made his way inside one of the Mexican Cartel families, and was now dealing with them directly. As impossible as that sounded, the evidence seemed indisputable. At the time, Danny actually felt a sense of pride that Tyrone allowed him to accompany him to this meeting. He felt both valuable and secure. His job was important. He was the #2 guy.

All that changed when he felt the gun in his crotch. He'd been kidding himself.

And what did Danny know really, about Tyrone and The Family? He knew Tyrone kept up with the money, made sure the major deals were made and the distribution was organized. But the actual dirty work was carried out by scores of underlings, most of which Tyrone, and Danny, didn't know. And, didn't want to know. Only a very select few in the organization, maybe a dozen souls, give or take, knew Tyrone personally. To most of those on his payroll, he was a name and a face. Similar to the President, they knew he existed but, even if they wanted to, could not get anywhere near him, much less provide anyone with information about him. And wouldn't even if they could. They were too afraid of him.

And that's what kept Tyrone in business and out of prison. He'd explained it to Danny once. How he stayed out of trouble. How he was protected. And how feared and respected he was. Tyrone was able to do things that no one else could. He had money and power. When you have those things, he explained, good things happened. He found cops and politicians he could bribe. He steered clear of the ones he couldn't. He was, outwardly, a model citizen. All of this, Danny now knew, simply meant his boss was above the law. And while he could pay those who were in a position to help, Danny knew Tyrone would, if he had to, eliminate those who would hurt him.

Except cops. Any cops. It was his golden rule.

And now, in his time of soul-searching, Danny finally admitted to himself that he was protecting a gangster who sold drugs. To addicts. To children. To perhaps his own children one day. He'd been so mesmerized by the money, he'd failed to stop and understand where it had come from and just how dirty it was. He knew also he was just as guilty as if he had sold the drugs himself. He recalled a documentary he'd watched once. It was on the Nuremberg trials after World War II. While Hitler had committed suicide, all those under him went on trial for war crimes and were either executed or sent to prison for many years. They'd merely followed orders, they claimed, from a superior officer. But, they would later find, that was not a defense. Blind obedience was Danny's excuse as well. Sure, times were good now, but how long would it last? Would things ultimately come to a crashing halt in a courtroom for him as well?

Tyrone might be protected, but Danny doubted he was. And going to prison scared the living shit out of him.

Danny didn't go into his house right away. Instead, he walked outside of the garage and into his drive and yard. He looked around his neighborhood. Kids were playing here and there, some on bicycles, yelling and laughing and enjoying their last days of summer vacation before school started again. There was a group of six playing basketball in the street, a three-on-three game, shooting toward a portable goal. There were folks working in their yards, cutting grass or tending to flowers growing in beds bordered by bricks or lumber. Most of the yards were at least decently maintained. Some were neglected but that was to be expected. His own was perfect and he took great pride in that. Jasmine had the flower beds bursting with color and devoid of weeds. Danny cut and edged at least once a week. He loved yard work. He could think of few things that delivered the instant gratification of a newly cut lawn.

But, suddenly, he felt all of these things slipping away from him. He wondered what Jasmine would do if he *were* to go to jail, possibly for life? He'd just been an accomplice in a violent crime, perhaps a murder. Then Tyrone, a man with a violent temper, pulled a gun on *him*. What if he had, accidentally or otherwise, pulled the trigger? He would have been left to die along with Timecia. And, because of that, Danny had been tempted to kill a man. Would he, if it happened again, be able to stop himself as he had today?

He didn't know. God help him, he just didn't know. And that meant it was possible that he would, given the circumstances, take a life, just as if he was God Almighty Himself. He'd then certainly go to jail for life, or worse. Danny didn't have the protection or connections that Tyrone enjoyed. He would lose, forever, Jasmine and his boys. He felt a dull pain in his gut as he realized that if Timecia died, this was already a possibility.

He had to make a change. If he wanted any chance to grow old with Jasmine. If he wanted to see his boys graduate, get married and have kids of their own. If he wanted a normal life, the kind of life that surrounded him at this very moment, he had to be free of Tyrone.

But, in this business, in this gang, change was nearly impossible. He couldn't simply quit; give his two weeks notice and walk away, and he knew it. Tyrone would never allow it. He'd heard him say it many times: "Once Family, Always Family."

He closed his eyes and tried to think. There *had* to be a way. His thoughts were interrupted when he heard his name called.

"Danny?" It was Jasmine, calling to him from the kitchen door. "Danny, you coming in?" She walked through the garage and out to him. "What are you doing out here? Supper's nearly ready." She immediately sensed his distress. "Sweetie, you okay? What's wrong?"

He put his arm around her and brought her in close. "You remember Timecia? Timecia Harrison?"

She thought for a moment. "Yeah. She used to be with Tyrone, didn't she?"

"That's right. She's in the hospital. She had an accident. She's hurt bad, Jasmine."

"Oh my God, Danny, that's terrible. What happened? She's got a little girl, doesn't she?"

Danny nodded. He hugged Jasmine tight. She was tiny next to him, just five feet and change. She still had a stomach, left over from her last pregnancy and her addiction to chocolate. She was self-conscious about it but Danny was oblivious. He looked down and said, "Baby doll, after the boys go to bed, we need to talk."

Jasmine felt alarmed. It was the way he said it. "About what, Danny? Is this about Timecia? Is everything okay?"

"It'll wait," he insisted, "until after the boys go to bed."

"Well, alright then," she said, but it wasn't alright. She felt it. Something *was* wrong, really wrong, but she did as her husband asked.

They walked back into the house. Danny pushed a button next to the kitchen door and the garage door motor started humming. Just before the door closed, two boys gleefully yelled, "Daddy!"

The garage door settled against the concrete floor. The humming stopped. Around their neighborhood, life went on. A weed was picked. A goal was scored. The same was true in countless neighborhoods around the globe. Danny wanted this to continue for himself and his family. He was determined to hang onto it. He understood that, what it all boiled down to was this:

Your job should make you a worthwhile living, but your family is what makes living worthwhile.

He hoped he had realized this before it was too late. Before it was all taken from him.

Chapter Four

Timecia opened her eyes, and the first thing she noticed was glorious sunshine pouring through a window bordered by open curtains. She stretched luxuriously beneath her blanket, smiling widely. Her eyes fluttered between slumber and awake. Either was fine with her. She didn't have a care in the world.

She felt strangely drawn to the window's light, but had no inkling why. The light seemed soothing yet ominous, so she resisted leaving her bed for the time being.

She suddenly realized she was in her old room. The room she shared with three sisters, in her childhood home. But how could that be?

She let her head fall sleepily to her left, then was suddenly wide awake. A single word formed on her lips.

"Daddy?"

He was seated in the rocker, and the familiar creaking sounds as he rocked back and forth were music to Timecia's ears. His hair was a mixture of black and gray, and his teeth were noticeably white when he smiled at her, a stark contrast to the deep blackness of his skin. He was a true black man, and, at that moment, the most beautiful thing Timecia had ever seen.

"*Daddy!*" she yelled as she leapt from her bed and rushed to him. He took her in his lap and wrapped his arms around her. She felt pure contentment, safe and in a place where nothing could ever hurt her. It was how she always felt when her daddy held her. He rocked her and patted her back tenderly. Somehow, she was eight years old again, the same age she was when he died.

"Oh, Daddy!" she said as she snuggled against him, "I've missed you so much."

"I know, baby, I know," he said softly. "I've missed you, too."

They remained that way for several minutes. Finally, Timecia said, "Daddy? How are you here? Am I in Heaven?"

Her father laughed. " Well, now, baby, that's up to you. Do you want to be?"

She contemplated that for a while, then said, "I *want* to go to heaven. Someday." She sat up and looked at him. "I've got a little girl, Daddy. Her name's Kristin."

He nodded at her. "I know," he said, "and she is so beautiful. Just like her momma."

That made her smile. "I wish you could meet her, Daddy. She doesn't have a grandpa." He didn't respond, and for a time the only sound was that of the rocker. Then Timecia said softly, "When you died, Daddy, I was so very sad. My stomach hurt for a long time. I don't want Kristin to be sad like that."

He nodded at her. "I know, baby," he said. He stood up and carried his little girl back to her bed. He covered her with the blanket, then bent down and kissed her cheek. She found that she was, once again, grown. He smiled at her, then said, "I have to go now." His hand lovingly brushed her cheek. "I want you to know that I am very proud of you."

Her eyes filled with tears. "Oh, Daddy," she cried. And then she rose up toward him, and they embraced for a long time. Finally, he tenderly laid her back down, then said, "You know what, sugar? There's an angel watching over you, all the time. You're going to be just fine." She nodded up at him, and said, "I love you, Daddy."

"I love you, too, baby." He used his thumb and finger to gently coax her eyelids down. "Time for you to sleep now, baby," he whispered. He kissed her forehead.

He then walked over to the window and drew the curtains.

The room was suddenly very dark.

And Timecia slept.

****

The Regional Medical Center at Memphis is the oldest hospital in the state of Tennessee. Chartered in 1829 as Memphis Hospital, it was officially renamed in 1983, but most refer to it as simply: The Med.

It is home to the Elvis Presley Trauma Center, the hospital's most renowned wing. Critically injured patients within 150 miles of the hospital would likely receive their treatment here. The Trauma Center is internationally known for superior care and excellence.

In a nutshell, if you're facing life-threatening injuries, you *want* to be at The Med. Harwell was glad Timecia was here, but she remained anxious.

Harwell avoided hospitals of any kind, but especially Inten-sive Care and Critical Care Units. She received her first taste of these when her grandmother suffered a massive coronary barely a week after Harwell's high school graduation. Grandma was only 61 and in good health. While she was on medication for blood pressure and cholesterol, more precautionary than treatment, like her husband, she was robust and energetic.

It's what made her heart attack, and subsequent death, so devastating.

There *had* been chest pains, almost a year earlier, and she was taken to the emergency room. She passed a thallium stress test and the pains went away. The diagnosis was simple acid reflux. The doctor explained that the symptoms of acid reflux can be remarkably similar to those of a heart attack. She was given a prescription and was released.

Ten months to the day of her hospital visit, the pain returned in earnest. At first her grandparents assumed it was just another bad case of reflux. But this time her chest pains grew progressively worse. Within minutes, Grandma collapsed. Grandpa desperately performed CPR but Grandma never responded. When paramedics arrived, they immediately used a defibrillator and, on the fourth shock, was able to detect a slight pulse. She was rushed to the emergency room, and was admitted into the Cardiovascular

Intensive Care Unit at Methodist Hospital.

But too much time had passed where blood hadn't circulated through Grandma's wonderful brain, and tests revealed only minimal activity. She was kept alive by machines that breathed for her, circulated her blood and monitored her vitals. Harwell and her grandfather were told there was little hope for recovery.

For three days and nights, they literally lived at the hospital, getting little sleep, hoping against hope that a miracle would occur. Grandpa would talk to his beloved wife, sing to her, hold her hand and pray. There was no response. Finally, with his granddaughter by his side, he took his wife's limp hands in his, knelt down beside her, and whispered in her ear.

"Honey," he said, "I want you to do something for me. I know how scared you must be. It's dark, and lonely and you don't know where you are. If you can hear me, follow the sound of my voice and come back to us. But," he continued, and fought the urge to cry, "if there's another way out, and you feel like that's where you're supposed to go, don't fight it. You go ahead, honey. Angel and I will be fine." He then kissed her unresponsive lips, and they both left the room.

Per his instructions, life support was removed the next morning. Grandma's warm, caring heart stopped forever a few minutes later.

It was then that Harwell began to question the existence of God, at least the God who was preached about at the church that she and her grandparents attended. She'd experienced and seen far too many things that directly contradicted, in her opinion, this naïve way of thinking. How many times had she prayed to God to stop Billy from coming into her room? Yet God allowed it to happen. Billy had robbed her of her innocence and now, as an adult, her ability to get close to men. God had taken her father away, then her mother, and now her grandmother.

She became convinced that life was a game of chance, a roll of the dice. The world wasn't perfect. Sometimes you got the breaks, sometimes you didn't. She acknowledged the marvel of life, the miracle of birth, the way the human body worked. The way our world sustained itself and the balance of nature. She understood as well that, without great evil, we would not appreciate goodness. Without ugliness, we would not grasp beauty. She knew that humans were capable of hatred, but also love. She got that.

But life after death? Heaven and Hell? She wondered if that were simply conjured up long ago by human minds who were desperate to believe that death wasn't the finality that it appeared to be. Our survival instinct so strong, and our wonder of everything so overwhelming, that God simply had to exist because no other explanation made sense.

But, she had to admit, the fear that Hell just *might* actually exist scared, well, the hell out of her. If it did, she hoped that it was reserved for people like Tyrone and Billy and not someone who may have lied about a golf score, and then was suddenly struck by lightning before he had a chance to ask for forgiveness.

She did have her grandfather, though, and he was there on the night she needed him most. And she had never been happier than when she was living with him and her grandma. Did God send him on that horrible night? And did God push her from wanting to be a doctor to instead help those who may be as desperate as she once was?

There seemed no doubt.

This was the God in which she chose to believe. One who never planned terrible things, but one who would be there to make terrible things better. Whether it was a frightened 13-year-old girl hiding in a closet, or a young single mom fighting for her life in a hospital room, God was watching and listening.

Harwell actually found herself saying a little prayer as she parked her cruiser in front of the main entrance to the Med.

"Please God," she whispered, "let her live."

Harwell entered the hospital and ran past the elevators, opting to take the stairs to the fourth floor. She took them three at a time, and very quickly found herself in front of the Critical Care waiting room. She walked in and immediately saw Timecia's mother and Annie. Her mother, a rather large woman in her late 50's, sat stone-faced, hands on a cane, her expression unchanging even as Harwell walked towards her. Annie was dabbing her eyes with a tissue and immediately got up when she saw Harwell, and the two ladies embraced. Harwell looked down at Timecia's mother. "Hello, Mrs. Harrison," she said.

Slowly, she looked up at Harwell. "De-*tec*-tive," she said, pronouncing each syllable as if it were three words instead of one, "I thought you was going to protect my daughter and granddaughter from that man."

Harwell didn't know what to say. She had been adamant about the order of protection, and that it be served on Tyrone right away. She had underestimated his reaction so soon after his highly publicized criminal case. Harwell squatted down and looked Mrs. Harrison in the eye. "I'm sorry. I never thought..."

"Never thought *what*, Detective?" she interrupted angrily. "What *did* you think? That my granddaughter's father would get some piece of paper and then do what it said? That he, for the first time in his life, would actually *obey* the law? Did you really believe that would happen?"

Her words crushed Harwell. She felt responsible for the terrible thing that happened to Timecia, and also for what it was doing to her mother. She finished her thought. "I never thought he'd find her. Not this quickly."

"Detective," she said incredulously, "no one hides from Tyrone Reed. Not forever. You don't know that? Aren't you *supposed* to know that? Isn't that your job?"

Harwell took a deep breath, then exhaled a long, loud frustrated sigh. "It is my job, Mrs. Harrison. And I am so sorry."

Mrs. Harrison softened. She placed a hand on Harwell's arm, and said, "I know you're doing your best, Detective. I know you're trying to help my baby. If not for you, Timecia probably been dead a long time ago. And I'm grateful for that. But you being sorry? That ain't going to fix my baby's face. That won't protect her or my granddaughter. What you have to do is quit being sorry, find that man and make sure he doesn't hurt anyone else, *ever* again. Do you know what that *means*, Detective?" Angela nodded. She knew exactly what she meant.

Annie, however, said it out loud.

"She means kill that bastard dead, Miss Angela. *Dead*!" Nearly everyone in the waiting room stared at them. Annie softened her tone. "You should see what he did to that pretty face of hers, Miss Angela. He messed her up. He beat her damn near to death is what he did. Big ol' man beatin' up a little girl! Why would he do that, Miss Angela?"

Harwell stood, and looked into the red eyes of the sweet woman who so loved Timecia. "I don't know, Annie. He's never hurt her that bad before. I think maybe Timecia might have stood up to him. But I don't care *why*. The *why* just doesn't matter." She looked at Timecia's mother and asked, "Where's Kristin?"

Mrs. Harrison answered. "She's just fine detective. She's with some of my boys who think Kristin hung the moon. Got 'em *all* wrapped around her little fingers. And while they may not be big shot gangsters like Tyrone, 'cause they know I'd whup 'em if they were, there's no way in hell or heaven that *anyone* would stand a chance of taking that baby. Not from *my* boys."

Harwell allowed a smile. "That's good, Mrs. Harrison. You keep her right there. Do not bring her here, under any circumstances. He'll know if you do."

Annie spoke up. "When you do find him, Miss Angela, can you do me a favor?"

Harwell looked at Annie. "What's that, Annie?"

"Just put that coward in a room, with me, and nobody else, and then close the door. Just give me five minutes. I promise you, that bastard won't never hurt Timecia again. Just five minutes. I ain't no little girl. I swear I'll make sure that man meets his maker before I'm through. I've been married four times, Miss Angela. I ain't afraid of no man, especially not no rat bastard coward."

Harwell understood why Timecia loved this woman. "I'm not afraid of him, either, Annie. But he's not a man, and that's what makes him dangerous. He's not human. To be human he'd have to care about people. He's an animal. You'd better leave him to me." Then she asked, "What room is Timecia in?"

Annie answered her. "She's in 419. Last one on the left. Prepare yourself, Miss Angela. If her name wasn't on the door, you'd never know it was her."

She found the room, and Annie was right. Even outside the door looking in, Timecia was completely unrecognizable. Her face was swollen. Bandages covered most of it, and what wasn't covered was purple with bruises. Several teeth were missing. Her right arm was in a cast and two fingers of her left hand were splinted. There was an IV dripping into a line attached to the top of her left wrist. There were monitoring machines everywhere and it immediately rekindled memories of her grandmother and the all too familiar ache in her gut returned.

She forced herself to go into the room. There was a male nurse inside, busily typing information into a laptop computer. He looked up when he became aware of Harwell. "I'm sorry," he said, "but you'll have to wait outside until I'm finished."

"I'm a Detective," she said, showing him her badge. "MPD. If it's possible, I need to talk to her."

He looked at her for a moment, then said, "Okay. Just let me save this. Don't want to lose it." He punched a few more keys, then closed the computer. "Okay Detective, she's all yours, but only for a few minutes. Don't know if you'll get anything out of her, though. She's heavily sedated."

"How's she doing?" Harwell asked apprehensively, afraid of the answer.

"I think she's out of the woods, actually," he said, "despite the way she looks. Her vitals have improved since she's been here. That's promising. The X-rays actually look pretty good - some broken ribs but no other internal damage that we can tell. We're keeping a close eye on her urine output, but so far there's been no blood. Pretty amazing really. Other than those ribs, a broken arm and nose, two fractured fingers and of course the rest of her face looking like she went through a windshield, she's relatively intact.

She'll likely remain in ICU for at least two more days, though, just to be sure. When they first brought her in, she was just barely alive. She was in shock and had lost a lot of blood. Then, all of a sudden, she began to get better, like her will to live had just miraculously returned. We see it from time to time. Someone upstairs apparently was watching over her." He picked up the laptop and said, "I'll leave you alone with her. I'll be right outside in case, well, just in case. Again, Detective, just a couple of minutes."

"Is she awake?" Harwell asked. "Will she be able to hear me?"

"I'm not sure. Hard to tell with all the bandages. She'll not be able to do much more than nod, or speak much above a whisper, *if* she responds at all. Good luck."

Alone with her, Harwell leaned over and spoke directly into her ear. "Timecia. It's Detective Harwell. It's Angela. Can you hear me?" There didn't seem to be any reaction, so she repeated the same words into her other ear. There was a definite reaction this time. Timecia rolled her head towards Harwell. She licked her lips, then very faintly, whispered, "*Thirsty.*"

Harwell looked around, and found a swab inside a cup filled with water and ice. She took the wet swab and placed it inside Timecia's mouth. She moved it around, and Timecia swallowed the small amount of liquid. Harwell replaced the swab back inside the cup. She leaned back over to the good ear. "Timi, I need your help. Who did this to you? Was it Tyrone?"

She licked her lips again, then, almost imperceptibly, shook her head.

Harwell pressed. "Timi, you have to help me here. I *know* it was Tyrone, but you need to tell me. Did Tyrone do this to you?"

Once more, Timecia shook her head, then whispered, "*Fell.*"

Harwell's heart sank. "No, Timecia, *no!* You did *not* fall. Someone beat you up. Was it Tyrone?"

Again, she whispered, "*Fell.*" She rolled her head away from Harwell, and Angela knew this would be the only answer she'd get. Through the tiny slits of bandages left open for her eyes, Harwell noticed a tear forming. Then, with great effort, Timecia managed to lift her left arm, and point. Harwell looked where she was pointing and saw a picture of Kristin, taped to a bedrail. She immediately understood. As long as Tyrone was out there, her baby was in danger.

Something stirred deep inside Harwell at that moment. Timecia was being held hostage, just as surely as if Tyrone had her tied up in a basement somewhere. And right now she was screaming for help, and hoping someone would hear. Her eyes pleaded with Harwell, and in those eyes she saw herself, 13 again, a hostage inside a trailer, and the memory of how she felt returned, as vividly as ever. The only way it ended for Harwell was with Billy gone. And the only way it would end for Timecia was if Tyrone was gone.

"Okay, Timi," she said, "I understand. Look, honey, you just get better. Kristin's safe, I promise. You get back on your feet, and you leave Tyrone to me. This is the last time he will ever lay a hand on you. Please tell me you hear what I'm saying to you. As God is my witness, this is the last time, okay?"

Timecia closed her eyes, nodded, and began sobbing. Harwell stayed with her until the nurse returned. Before she left the hospital, she told Mrs. Harrison and Annie what the nurse had said about Timi's promising improvement.

Harwell had to get out of the hospital. She needed to get outside and do *something*. Somewhere in this city there was a monster, hiding from her, feeling smug, feeling safe. He was smart, but so was she. He was powerful, but she was strong and well-trained. He had almost unlimited resources and he had protection. But he was pure evil, and preyed on the weak and helpless. If history showed us anything it was that evil, regardless of how mighty it seemed, always, *always* lost in the end. Hitler, Mussolini, Hussein - they all had their run, but eventually their ruin. It only ended when someone finally stood up to them and said enough is enough. It would be the same for Tyrone.

Harwell was down the stairs and outside in an instant. She

remembered little of her return to the cruiser. She was too preoccupied with what she needed to do. She needed to get to her desk and make a report. She needed to call the crime scene guys and see if they found anything. There had to be *something* that put Tyrone in Timecia's apartment.

Above all else, she needed to get to the ballpark before seven. She had a date.

The Redbirds played tonight. She'd pick her grandfather's brain. It always helped.

Just before she got into her car, however, she hesitated, and looked around. Downtown Memphis was bustling with people and vehicles.

He was out there. She *felt* him. He was close.

Her eyes scanned up and down both sides of the street, in every direction. "Where are you, you son of a bitch?" she whispered. "Where the hell are you?"

She shrugged it off, got in and quickly drove away.

****

Two men inside a gleaming black Cadillac SUV watched Harwell's cruiser leave the hospital. They were parked some two hundred yards west, engine running and air-conditioning on high. They were invisible behind heavily tinted windows, and Tyrone peered through a pair of binoculars from the back seat. At one point, he and Harwell had actually locked onto each other, but she was unaware. When she turned a corner and was no longer in their line of sight, he dropped the glasses.

"That's the cop who's been involved with Timecia, Rod Man. I believe her name's Harwell," said Tyrone.

"Yes, sir," said the driver.

"Pretty girl. I met her once. I don't think she liked me. Can you believe that?"

"No, sir."

"I'd *love* to get to know her better. In fact," Tyrone continued, "I think that's a good idea. I'd better put in a call to Rico. I want to know everything about her. I want to know where she lives, where she hangs out. If she's got a boyfriend, girlfriend, mom, dad, husband, kids, brothers, sisters or aunties, any sort of family, I want to know," he said. He paused for a moment. "Yeah, she'll suspect me, make no mistake. If it comes to it, I need to know what'll hurt her."

"Yes, sir."

"You think Timi told her anything?"

"I don't know, sir."

Tyrone looked through the glasses again. "No," he decided, "she's too smart for that." He placed the binoculars beside him on the seat. He took out his phone and made a call.

"Johnson, this is Tyrone. Are you on the right floor? Good. I want at least two updates every day on her condition. I want to know who visits. I especially want to know when she changes rooms, when she's discharged, or," he added, "taken to the morgue. Which would," he said softly, as if to himself, "be a shame, but it would also solve a lot of problems. Can you do that for me? Excellent. You're a good man. I'll call you."

He threw the phone down on the seat beside him. "You know something, Rod Man?" he said.

"What's that, sir?"

"It is hard being a father sometimes."

"Yes, sir."

"If she makes it, first place she'll go," he mused, "is straight to Kristin." He glanced at the rear-view mirror and made eye contact with the driver. "Okay," he said, "let's go."

Rod Man placed the Caddy in gear, made sure the lane was clear, then eased into the busy downtown traffic.

Chapter Five

Danny looked in on his boys as they lay in their beds. They were watching a *SpongeBob Squarepants* DVD, a nightly ritual, and one which would normally have them asleep within a few minutes. It was early though, and both boys remained wide awake. Danny knew it would take a little longer tonight.

He and Jasmine had both felt a sense of unspoken urgency during supper, and it hung around them like a thick fog. Her look of worry and concern as she nibbled at her food was obvious. She waited for him in the living room as he watched his sons and tried to gather his thoughts. He wasn't stalling; he was anxious to talk to her. But the subject was so very complicated, that it had to be approached, well...

Hell, he didn't know how he would approach it.

He listened as his boys giggled and laughed at the silly talking ocean sponge, and he found even he smiled as he watched, despite the load he carried. He often marveled how such an improbable idea ever made it to the drawing board. But it did, and now the show's namesake was literally a worldwide sensation and probably more recognizable than any cartoon character he'd watched as a kid.

And at that moment, try as he might, he couldn't come up with any cartoon that he used to watch. Not one.

His childhood, and innocence, seemed hopelessly, unbearably distant. It was as if he'd become an adult at age six, right around the time his father left.

Stop it! He thought to himself. *This isn't about me.*

He'd made his choices. So be it. It was now about his boys and his wife. Feeling sorry for himself would accomplish nothing. He remembered, vividly, what Tyrone had done to Timecia. If driven to it, would he do the same to Jasmine? Would he hurt Donnie or Ronnie? He felt it was certainly possible, even probable. Tyrone was like a wild animal. If cornered, he'd do whatever it took to remove the threat, real or perceived. Tyrone took no chances and had no conscience. It's why he was where he was. Danny came to the sobering conclusion that Tyrone *would,* without question, hurt, or perhaps kill, his family.

This realization made him shudder. But Tyrone would have to get past him to get to them. And the only way that would happen is if he were dead.

But he didn't want to die. He wanted to live. And he wanted to walk away from Tyrone. But doing *both* of these would be next to impossible. He vividly recalled the exact words Tyrone said to him even as they shook hands the day he was hired.

"Welcome to The Family, Danny Boy," Tyrone's smile was warm and friendly. But then his grip hardened and he drew Danny closer. "But understand one thing. Once Family, *always* Family."

As he watched his sons, he allowed his mind to drift back to the day they were born. He was there with Jasmine during the long labor and delivery. They were born barely five minutes apart - Donnie was first - and both seemed impossibly tiny, especially when Danny held them and they were set against his massive frame. He recalled being terrified that he would hurt them. He had fought some of the biggest heavyweights in the business and had been completely unafraid, but his five-pound newborns had him shaking from his hair to his shoes.

That was just over thirty months ago, and since then there had many firsts. First steps, first words, first birthdays. He'd been there for most of them. Now, he had to, somehow, insure that he would be there for the rest of their firsts. Their first day of kindergarten, first Teeball game, first day of high school, first date, first day of college. He was determined they would have what he never had. Two parents, a mother *and* a father, and, perhaps, another brother or sister along the way.

Wouldn't that be something? Danny thought, as he managed another smile. *A daughter! A little girl!*

And with that, the smile left his face and was replaced by the look and mindset that he always had during his days between the ropes, when he felt nearly invincible. He'd always said, "I never worry about who I'm fighting. I let them worry about me." He fully expected to win every single fight he was in and was always stunned on the few occasions when he lost. Probably his best asset was his ability to completely shake off the losses and, within hours, regain his confidence that no one could beat him. He would need that same self-assurance when he took on Tyrone. His years of fighting could pay off for him, big time, in the situation he now found himself. Everything he learned then he could use now. That could be the edge he so desperately needed. He would carefully evaluate his opponent and develop a strategy. He would look for weaknesses and strengths, in himself and in Tyrone. He'd have to be evasive and stay just out of Tyrone's reach. He'd have to think on his feet, make instant decisions. Danny understood that this fight would not be over in one round. Success would require patience and stealth. Above all, he had to be careful. It would all be for nothing if his family was hurt. He would never forgive himself if anything happened to Jasmine or his boys.

Lastly, he knew he couldn't do it alone. He'd need people in his corner who he could trust. People who wanted Tyrone brought down as badly as he did.

And he thought he just might know where to start.

He quietly closed the bedroom door made his way into the living room where Jasmine anxiously waited. She looked up fearfully when Danny entered the room. She had a tissue in her hand and her eyes were moist. Danny quickly sat down beside her, and she fell into his chest and began sobbing. He wrapped his muscled arms around her and held her tenderly.

"Baby doll," he said, "what's wrong?"

"Danny," she cried, "are you leaving me?"

"Am I leaving..." he began, then said, "Oh, no, no, no, sweetie! Why would you ever think that? How could you ever even imagine that?"

"Oh... Danny!" she managed, "I was so scared. When you said we needed to talk, but not until the boys went to bed, I just thought... I mean, you were so serious. I didn't know..."

That was all she said, then began crying again. After a few minutes, she was able to recover. She pulled away, found a fresh tissue and wiped her eyes. She managed a relieved smile, then said, "I didn't know what I was going to do. Don't you ever do that to me again."

Danny shook his head, then said, "Listen to me Jasmine. Of all the things you need to worry about, that's dead last, okay? Bottom of the list. Everything I need is right here in this house. The woman I love, and my boys. I couldn't walk away if I tried. No way in hell. You hear me?"

She smiled again, then said, "You like being a daddy, don't you?"

He nodded at her. "Next to being your husband, best job in the whole world."

"That's good," she said, "because next spring?" Jasmine took his hand and placed it on her belly, "you goin' to be one again."

All Danny could do was stare at her, wide-eyed.

"Now," she said, "what did you want to talk about?"

****

Auto Zone Park, home of the Triple-A Memphis Redbirds, is one of the hallmarks of downtown Memphis.

Harwell had enjoyed games there almost from the day she went to live with her grandparents. Although it hadn't been quite the same since her grandmother's death, the tradition continued with just her and her grandfather. It was her favorite place to be with him and they caught every game they could. It was no surprise that *Field of Dreams* was her favorite movie. Just as in the movie, in her own crazy, sometimes surreal world, there was baseball. There would always be baseball. The one constant that made things normal again.

They usually sat along the third base line, in the $16 seats. There they enjoyed a wonderful view of the entire field and stood a reasonable chance at snaring foul balls. Her grandfather still got a huge thrill whenever he was able to grab one, and he would laugh and hold the ball up like a trophy every time. He always found a youngster to give it to, however, just as he did for her when she was little. He never kept one for himself.

Harwell, however, had every ball he'd given her.

She was running late when she was, finally, able to make her way downtown. She lived in Lakeland, less than ten miles from her grandfather, and it was about a 30 minute drive to the stadium if there was no traffic. She saw his familiar Crown Vic parked in front of the 3rd street office where he picked up part time work as a Shelby County Process Server. This was where he always parked and she was able to park behind him. She drove her personal car when she was on personal time, a tiny 10-year-old red Toyota Echo. She called it her little red roller skate. Rocorro referred to it as a death trap. It got almost motorcycle-like gas mileage, and was unfailingly dependable, despite more than 150,000 miles on the odometer.

She was late partly because she had showered and changed before she left her apartment. She was now in a pair of white shorts and a red-and-white Cardinal tank, a much cooler option than the slacks and blouse she wore on the job. She had also worn tennis shoes and was able to jog the half-mile to the park's entrance in under four minutes. Along the way she passed an array of downtown architecture, a mix of old and new commercial structures that gave this part of Memphis a feel of a partnership of sorts. The past standing side-by-side with the present, almost as if allowing that there was room for both. The older buildings were made of faded brick, having stubbornly withstood the test of time and the elements, with their antiquated metal-stair fire escapes still attached to the outside, ready to serve if needed. The more modern steel, glass and concrete structures stretched much higher towards the sky, and bore the muscle and vigor of youth despite being inanimate objects. It was like Harwell and Rocorro. Harwell's youth and vitality, and Rocorro's solidity and wisdom, side-by-side, for as long as it would last.

He was sitting on one of the benches outside the main gate, waiting for her. The area was crowded with people; some were in line to buy tickets and others, with tickets already in hand, waiting to go through the turnstiles. There was a live band playing 70's rock and roll just inside the gates, and she could already hear the beer hawkers tempting folks with promises of "Ice cold!"

He brightened and stood when he saw her. He was nearly 70 now, and though his face had wrinkled and tended to give away his age, his body remained strong and capable. Their personal trainer still worked with him three days a week and, thankfully, his body still responded. He continued to run, but slower now and much shorter distances. He'd had back surgery a few years earlier, and his surgeon warned him against the long races, in particular the half-marathons. He could still run them, he was told, as long as he enjoyed returning for more surgeries. More than four decades of long-distance running had taken its toll. He reluctantly acquiesced, and settled for power walking and an occasional 5k run. It wasn't nearly as satisfying but a lot better than nothing.

He smiled widely as she approached and open his arms for his hug, the way they began and ended every time they met. "You're late," he said, but there wasn't a hint of irritation in his voice. It was just an observation, and understandable because she was never late. "I was getting worried."

"Now, Grandpa," she said, "why would you ever worry about me? You know I can take care of myself. And what in the world is this?" She stroked the beginnings of a goatee on his chin, the hairs silvery-white, reasonably thick and probably unshaven for a week or so.

"You like it?" he asked, smiling. "It was Sue's idea. I actually think it works. Makes me look younger, like I'm 65 again. What do you think?"

She pretended to seriously study the new look. "I don't know, Grandpa. Sixty-five's pushing it. Maybe 66, 67. But," she said, "I do like it. A lot. Makes you look... I don't know. Smarter maybe."

He laughed. "That wouldn't take much. The old brain cells are dropping like flies. I feel like lately I've got full blown CRS disease."

Harwell looked puzzled. "CRS?" she said. "What is that?"

"Can't remember shit." he said.

This time *she* laughed. "I like that!" she said. "I'm going to use it. Now, come on," she said, and tilted her head toward the ticket window, "let's get in line."

Rocorro reached into the side pocket of his cargo shorts and pulled two tickets out. "Already got 'em," he said, and handed her one.

"Grandpa!" she said, admonishing him, "it was my turn to buy them!"

"Uh-huh," he said, smiling, "and now I *know* why you were late." He put his arm lovingly around her shoulder as they walked toward the entrance. "C'mon," he said, "I'll let you buy the nachos and beers."

They settled into their seats just in time to hear the lineups and umpire introductions. It was a glorious evening to be there. There was a cool breeze coming straight at them and the sun had settled far enough into the west that they were just inside the shade line. The unfortunate souls on the opposite side of the stands got neither the breeze nor the shade. The Birds were having a good year and stood just a half a game out of first place in their division. The visiting team was the Nashville Sounds, the Milwaukee Brewers affiliate, who also happened to be the team ahead of them in the standings. It was a big game for both teams.

They shared their barbecue nachos and sipped their Samuel Adams beer through a first inning that, to their dismay, found the Redbirds down 3-0. The Sounds went single - single - home-run before the Redbirds pitcher settled down and got the next three out, the last two with strike-outs. The Birds, however, went three up, three down in the bottom half and failed to cut into the lead. When the last hitter struck out looking at a 97 miles per hour fastball right on the outside corner, Rocorro shook his head. "He keeps that up," he said, "and it could be a long night for Memphis."

Harwell nodded. "That was strong," she said. "I don't think anyone could've hit that pitch."

Rocorro took a swig of his beer, then placed his arm around Harwell, his hand resting on her right shoulder. "I want to ask you something, Angel, and I want you to be honest with me."

Harwell looked at her grandfather, curious. "Okay," she said, "ask me."

"See, here's how it is," he began, "Sue and me, well, we're getting close. I like her a lot and she likes me for some God knows reason." He paused then, as if trying to decide what to say next.

"Grandpa!" Harwell said, "Of course she likes you. What's not to like?"

He scoffed. "There's plenty," he said. "I'm old, and ornery, and..."

"You are *not*!" Harwell interrupted. "You're sweet, and kind and *very* handsome. Sue's a lucky woman."

"Damn, Angel," he said, "you're as brainwashed as she is. Anyway," he continued, "she's been asking me something, and I told her I'd run it by you, see what you thought about it."

Harwell looked straight at him, barely believing what she thought she was getting ready to hear. "Grandpa," she said slyly, "are y'all thinking about getting married?"

A Nashville hitter swung at the first pitch, a liner straight back to the pitcher. One out.

"What? Married?" he said. "No! No, Angel, that's not it at all." He seemed uncertain for a moment. Harwell waited on him to continue. Finally, he said, "She was wanting to know if maybe she could come to a game with us sometimes. She likes baseball, but she knows that your grandma used to go with us, and she didn't want you to think she was trying to... hell, I don't know. Take her place or something, I guess."

The second out was a pop fly to the shortstop. While the players tossed the ball around the infield, Harwell took time to choose her words. "Grandpa," she said, "Grandma's been gone five years now. And no one could ever take her place. But, you know what?"

"What?" he said.

"I believe, if you were able to ask *her* that same question right now, she would say what I'm going to say. Of course Sue can come to the games with us. And anywhere else she wants to go, or you want to take her. Grandma would want the same thing I want. For you to be happy."

An easy fly to center ended the top of the 2nd inning. Three pitches, three outs. The starter for the Birds had found his groove.

"I'd be happy," he said, "if we could put a run or two up on the board. But I'll tell her what you said. You're a good girl, you know that?" He smiled that smile of his, then squeezed her shoulder. She knew that this conversation was over. He was not much of a sentimentalist; normally he tended to avoid any sort of touchy-feely situation. The tears he shed at his wife's funeral was the only time she had ever seen him cry. But even though he never said it, Harwell knew how much he loved her. That was unmistakable. Some men would say it, but the words would prove meaningless. She'd seen it far too many times. Other men, simply by the way they treated those they loved, never had to say it. It was obvious. That was her grandpa. And that was good enough for her.

It was her turn. "Grandpa," she said, "I need to ask *you* something now."

"Whoa," he said, "don't tell me you want to bring someone to the games as well?"

She shook her head. "No, Grandpa, that's not it."

"Damn!" he said. "I'm disappointed. You should be going to these things with someone your own age and preferably male. I'm never going to be a great-grandfather at this rate." He turned toward her, then said, "Tell you what. Why don't you ask that guy you like at work? What's his name? Terry?"

"You mean Tony?"

"Yeah, Tony! You bring him, I'll bring Sue and we'll call it a double-date!"

Harwell laughed. She did like Tony, but strictly as a friend. He was a few years older, divorced but no kids. He was also a detective and a damn good one. "Grandpa," she said, "you know the department's rules on dating co-workers."

"Screw 'em," he said. "It's a baseball game, not the prom. Just a couple of buddies going to the game. Nothing wrong with that."

"You playing matchmaker, Grandpa?"

That made him chuckle. "Would it do any good?"

Just then the home crowd came alive, and both looked up just in time to see the ball sailing out over the left field wall. When they looked on the field to see who hit it, they saw there was another Redbird already on base and rounding third. It was a 3-2 game and the Birds were back in it.

"How did we get a man on base?" Rocorro said, to no one in particular. A man directly behind him answered that he'd been hit by a pitch. They had both missed it completely. Harwell waited for things to calm down, then began again.

"Grandpa, this is important. Do you ever talk to Bo Sanders anymore?"

That got his attention. Rocorro had become acquainted with Sanders many years earlier when he'd pulled him over in Bartlett on a routine traffic stop. Rocco smelled marijuana, detained Sanders and called for backup. A search of the vehicle netted several ounces of Mississippi skunk weed hidden in the trunk, more than enough for a felony conviction and jail time. But Bo had a girlfriend and two kids and was frantic to avoid jail. He intended to sell the weed because he desperately needed money to buy expensive medicine for his very sick son. Bo poured his heart out to Rocorro, told him absolutely everything. Rocorro checked his story and found he was telling the truth. He was able to reduce the charge to misdemeanor possession. Rocco also arranged for the medicine to find its way to the ailing child. An extremely grateful Bo never forgot the kindness shown to him by Rocco. Bo was well connected, and through the years provided valuable information to both Bartlett and Memphis PD.

"Bo? No, not for a couple of years anyway. Angel, you're

strictly Domestic. Why would you want to know about Bo?"

"I've got to find a guy who beat a girl almost to death, Grandpa. His 4-year-old child's mother actually. You ever heard of a gangster named Tyrone Reed? Street name T-Bone?"

"Of course. Who hasn't? He's that gangster who just beat that possession charge. Supposed to be the leader of a Memphis gang, isn't he?"

"Not supposed to be. He *is* the leader of The Family. I want to find him in the worst way, Grandpa. He's hiding now. I know it's a long shot but I wonder if I might talk to Bo, see if he knows anything at all?"

"*You* want to talk to him?"

"It's my case, Grandpa. I'll know what questions to ask. This T-Bone is very bad news. You don't need to get involved. And besides, you're retired."

"Not completely retired, young lady. I'm still in law enforcement. Civil law enforcement, anyway. Easy work and damn good money. If I'd have known about process serving 30 years ago I just might have done that instead. I sure would've been home a lot more." He noticed that Harwell was still waiting on his answer. "I've got a number. It's probably still good. If that doesn't work I'll call a guy I know downtown. He should have a way to contact Bo. I'll see what I can do."

"Be careful who you talk to, Grandpa. Tyrone's got people everywhere. He finds out you're asking about him, he won't care who you are or why you're asking. He'll come after you."

Rocorro smiled. "Who do you think you're talking to, Angel? I haven't lasted this long without being careful." But his heart was racing. The cop in him was suddenly reawakened, and it had been a long time. He was just handed a chance to do some important police work again, and at his age these chances were rare. As he had her whole life, he would do everything he could for his granddaughter.

"Now," he said, "enough shop talk for one night. Let's watch some baseball." He finished his beer, then said, "You know, for some reason, I'm still thirsty. How about another Sam Adams?"

****

Tyrone was cutting into a piece of meat when his cell phone rang. He stopped, laid his knife and fork onto the plate, then wiped his hands and mouth on a cloth napkin before he answered.

"Talk to me."

He listened for a minute or two as the voice on the other end spoke. Then, he said, "Okay, Luther. Good job. Stay on them." He ended the call and placed the phone on the table. He looked across the table at the young lady who had joined him for dinner. He put the napkin back on his lap and picked up his knife and fork. As he cut into the meat again, he said to her, "So, she likes baseball and older men." The girl said nothing as he put the bite into his mouth. As he chewed, he appeared thoughtful. "Nah," he said, more to himself than to her, "can't be a boyfriend. Gotta be a father, or maybe a grandfather. I need to find out."

"Tyrone," said the girl, timidly, "how... how long are you going to stay here?"

He stopped chewing and looked at her, almost in disbelief. "I don't know, Kita. A while longer. Why? Is there a problem?"

"No, Tyrone," she said quickly, "no problem. It's just that... I miss my kids. And my mother, well, she doesn't have any money. My kids need things."

Tyrone put the utensils on his plate again. He nodded at her. "Okay, Kita, I'll take care of it. I'll arrange for you to visit with your kids. And I'll make sure your momma has all the money she needs. Okay?"

Kita smiled, nodded. "Thanks, Tyrone. That'd be great."

Tyrone put another bite in his mouth. "Kita?"

"Yes, Tyrone?"

"Don't ask me anymore how long I'll be here. You understand?"

Kita nodded. She understood.

Chapter Six

Danny woke the next morning much earlier than he usually began his days, but was instantly wide awake. He felt beside him, only to find her side of the bed empty. He clicked on the bedside lamp and, judging from the undisturbed blanket, knew she hadn't made it to bed at all. He quickly threw his own covers off and went to look for her.

He'd told her everything the night before. Everything. She'd listened without a word, taking it all in, her face going through a gamut of emotions. At the end of it, it was clear she was afraid. He'd tried to touch her, to hold her, but she'd pushed him away as if he was a complete stranger. She'd said, simply, "Go to bed, Danny. I'll be along in a little while." He'd laid awake, staring at the ceiling and trying to collect his thoughts, but he'd fallen asleep somehow. That was seven hours ago and he was amazed he'd been able to sleep that long.

He found her where he'd left her, in the same clothes she was wearing the night before. There was an empty coffee cup on the table beside her. The TV was on but the sound was muted. The room was dark except for the TV and a nightlight. She didn't react when he entered the room and he thought she might be sleeping. He flipped a light switch and saw she was awake. Her eyes were swollen and red, and she immediately squinted at the uninvited flood of light.

"Please, Danny," she said, "turn it off."

He turned it off, but didn't move. He said, "Jas, are you alright?"

She looked at him, then smiled condescendingly. "Sure, Danny," she said flatly, "I'm fine."

"No, you're not," he said. "You're hurt. And you're scared. And it's my fault."

She patted the space next to her on the couch. "Come here, Danny. Sit beside me." Relieved, he did as she asked. She laid her head against his shoulder. "Remember what I said to you last night when you first came in here?"

Danny thought. "You asked me if I was leaving you."

She nodded. "Yeah," she said, laughing, "that's what I said. And I actually thought *that* would be the worst thing that you could ever say."

Danny felt his heart sink, and a dread began to build in his stomach. "Jasmine..."

She put a hand over his mouth. "Shhh," she whispered, "let me finish." She placed her hand on top of his. "I've had all night to think about this, and I've come to one very definitive decision." She sat forward and faced him. She began to say something, then sighed. "My God. I've rehearsed this over and over and now I can't remember any of the lines."

She leaned against him again, and said, "Did I ever tell you I worked for the campus newspaper?"

"I... I think so. Yeah, you told me," he said.

"I actually thought about being a reporter, or a writer, at one time. I loved it. Even now, the things I write in my journal I hope will be a book one day. And this," she said, "once we get past all of it, will *definitely* be included."

Danny wasn't certain he'd heard right. He turned to look at her. "Jasmine..."

This time she only put a finger on his lips. "Not yet, Danny. Let me finish." She pushed him gently back against the couch, then resumed her position against him. She continued, "I did a story once, the second year I was there, where I interviewed a woman whose husband was convicted of murder. He was a fireman and he killed a fellow fireman, a friend of his that he owed a lot of money. He denied it at first, buried the body, but eventually caved and showed the police where the body was. He'll never get out of jail. At the time, they had two kids who were about the same ages as ours are now."

"Jasmine," Danny said, "I haven't killed anyone, I swear..."

"Danny," she interrupted, "I *know* that. Just listen for a minute."

She was quiet for a bit, then said, "His wife said something to me I'll never forget. When I asked her what she was going to do, she said to me, 'I'm waiting on him. He's my husband.' It was as if the answer was just so obvious she was wondering how I could even ask. Then she said to me, 'When you love someone, *really* love someone, it doesn't matter what they do. You never stop loving them.' I thought it was the most profound expression of love I had ever heard. And I remember that I felt so very sorry for her, but at the same time I actually... I guess I kind of envied her. I wanted very badly to know what that kind of love felt like."

Danny closed his eyes, afraid to believe what he was hearing, afraid he was misinterpreting what she was saying.

"And then, a couple of hours ago, it hit me. I love you, Danny," she said, "the same way she loved him, no matter what you've done. I've loved you since the moment I first saw you, and nothing can change that. So," she said, and sighed very deeply, "we're just going to have to figure it all out."

With her head remaining on his chest, she then looked up at him. He did exactly what she expected. He kissed her tenderly and for a very long time. He felt his heart might burst through his ribcage at any moment. Her arms wrapped around his neck, and the kiss became deliberately passionate. Eventually, they broke off.

"You know," she said breathlessly, "you are so very lucky that you are a very pretty man."

"Pretty?" he said, incredulously, "Oh, no. Hey - you're lucky you're a girl. If a dude said that to me I'd have to put him down. I'd prefer, you know, like movie star, ruggedly handsome, something like that. I am most certainly *not* pretty."

"You're right," she said, blinking seductively, "my eyes are playing tricks on me. I need sleep." She yawned and stretched. "You'd better take me to bed, Danny, before I drift off right here and now."

Danny stood, then reached down and picked her up. He carried her silently past the boys' room, not wanting to do anything that may wake them. He entered their bedroom, and gently laid her on the bed. He kissed her softly. Jasmine said, "Check on the boys, Danny, then hurry back. I have to work in a few hours."

He did as she asked. They were both sleeping soundly. He carefully closed their door, then went back to Jasmine.

He found her curled up underneath the blanket, head on her pillow, sound asleep. He groaned, but wasn't about to wake her. He leaned over her and gently kissed her cheek. She smiled happily in her dreams. He whispered, "I love you, Jasmine."

Then the smiled disappeared, and a lone tear fell from a closed eye.

He left their bedroom, more determined than ever to free himself, and his family, from the jeopardy he'd put them in. For his wife, for his children, for his unborn child, he would, somehow, find a way.

There was no option.

****

At 7 AM that same morning, Harwell sat at her desk in her office at 201 Poplar Avenue in downtown Memphis, just blocks from where she and Rocorro saw the Redbirds win in extra innings the evening before. She'd gotten little sleep, partly from the excitement of the game, but mainly because she was worried about Timecia. A quick visit to the Med on her way in had eased her mind, however. Timecia was officially out of danger and on the mend. She would be moved soon, possibly even later today, out of the Critical Care Unit and into a step-down room. It was fantastic news on two counts: One - Timecia would make a full recovery. Two - she could now focus on her primary goal.

Put Tyrone Reed away, once and for all.

Concentrating totally on Tyrone, however, put her in a precarious position. The fact remained that Tyrone was not her only case. There were others who needed her as well. In fact, in just over an hour, she had an appointment with the director of Happy Children Day School concerning a child whom they suspected was a victim of abuse by his father. She would keep that appointment. Daycares and schools did not report these on a whim and Harwell took every case very seriously.

A report on her desk confirmed what she already knew: they found nothing at Timecia's apartment that would tie *anyone* to the scene, much less Tyrone. No one saw anything, heard anything or knew anything. Copies of this report had been sent to Violent Crimes and Homicide. Hers wasn't the only department who wanted Tyrone, but it seemed they were no closer to him than she was.

How the hell could Tyrone be that damn thorough? Harwell thought to herself. She had never known anyone so meticulous, so calculating. Criminals always made mistakes. There had to be *something* that Tyrone hadn't considered. An organization the size of his always had a disgruntled employee here and there, willing to talk. But no one had stepped forward.

Yet.

As of right now, all she had was Timecia.

There had to be a way to protect Timecia and her family, and convince her that she *would* be protected, so she'd be willing to testify against him. Tyrone's power was fear. And he wielded this power like a Samurai Sword, almost daring anyone to challenge him.

She was reading the report a third time when her phone rang. It startled her in the quiet of her office.

"Domestic. Detective Harwell."

It was Marilyn Thorne, the director of the daycare. "Detective, this is Miss Thorne at Happy Children. I'm so glad you answered. He's early. He just pulled into the parking lot. Do you think you can leave right away?"

Harwell glanced at her watch. "Stall him if you can. I'll be there in five minutes." She threw the handset at the base and hurried out to her cruiser.

Chapter Seven

When Harwell pulled into the parking lot of Happy Children Day School, she hoped she'd been able to get there before he left.

"He" was Walter Miller, a 32-year-old CPA and the father of five-year-old Shawn. Miller specialized in corporate tax preparation and his company thrived. He dropped off Shawn every morning around 8:00 in his late model Lexus SUV, and usually picked him up as well. Thorne had told Harwell that she could only remember meeting Shawn's mother once, and the meeting had been unremarkable.

Based on Thorne's description, Miller seemed atypical of the profile one would associate with a child abuser, either physically or psychologically. He was just 5'6" and weighed around 145 lbs. He wore round wire-rimmed glasses. He dressed well, was soft-spoken and well educated. He carried his son inside every morning, and carried him back to his car every afternoon. Shawn didn't appear to be afraid of his father, but other things aroused Thorne's suspicions.

To begin with, while Shawn never ran from Miller whenever he saw him, he wouldn't run *to* him either. The youngster seldom smiled and never laughed. He was quiet and withdrawn throughout the day and would answer questions by either nodding or shaking his head. He cried easily and, especially recently, recoiled at even the gentlest of touches.

What prompted the call to Child Protective Services occurred two days earlier. During nap time, Thorne heard one of the children tell Shawn to stop looking at her. As she walked over to calm them down, she saw the child slap Shawn on his back. Shawn shrieked in pain, and it was clear, *this* time, the pain was real. Thorne took Shawn back to her office, and after calming him, gently lifted his shirt.

The bruises and sores were alarming. After taking pictures,

Thorne called the boy's father.

Within minutes, Miller returned to the Day School and assured the concerned director that Shawn had merely taken a bad fall from his bicycle and had received proper medical care. Thorne's suspicions were not so easily dissuaded, however. After Miller left, she asked Shawn about the accident. He meekly replied, "I fell off my bike."

"Tell me about your bicycle, Shawn," she'd said. "What color is it?"

He'd only stared at her, then finally just shrugged his shoulders. She called Child Protective Services, who called Harwell. CPS wasn't due to arrive for another hour so Harwell was on her own.

She was fine with it.

She was relieved to see Miller's Lexus - Thorne had described the vehicle to her - still running, parked by the front door. Before Harwell had even reached the door, she heard it unlock. Apparently Thorne was keeping a close eye on the video surveillance. She entered the daycare and immediately heard Miller and Thorne talking.

"Miss Thorne," Miller was saying, "I assure you I did *not* miss a payment. It isn't possible. I bring you a check *every* Monday morning. Your records are wrong."

"I know you do, Mr. Miller, and I told corporate that very thing. But they insisted..."

At that moment Harwell entered the director's office. Miller turned when the door opened, and his eyes were immediately drawn to the badge and weapon on her waist. His face registered what appeared to Harwell to be fear, or perhaps trepidation. He became visibly nervous and suddenly seemed in a great rush to leave.

"I tell you what, Miss Thorne, I'll go back home right now and, uh... get my records... go, uh... go through my... my cancelled checks... and I'll... I'll be right back."

He attempted to go around Harwell, but she blocked his path and closed, the door. "Mr. Miller, I'm Detective Harwell. I'm with

Juvenile Abuse. I'm here to investigate a report made by Miss Thorne about a possible situation involving one of the children here. Have a seat, sir."

Miller stared at Harwell with a look of deep, imbedded dread. Harwell had seen it many times. That instant when a person knows he's been caught, or inevitably will be. When life is suddenly about to forever change, when time stops and fear sets in. Harwell prepared herself for two likely scenarios: Miller would either recover and try to pretend the moment never happened, or he would attempt to fight his way past. Based on his size, Harwell figured he would use words rather than fists.

She was right. He was actually able to smile at her, but his nerves remained on edge.

"Well then, Detective," he stammered, "I'll just get out of your way. I, uh... hope that you find... uh, find him. I mean, that is, if it's... if it's true."

He attempted to casually go around Harwell. She reached out and gripped his arm and he winced in pain. "Maybe I wasn't clear the first time, Mr. Miller. I need to ask you some questions. Please, have a seat."

"You're hurting my arm, Detective," Miller whined. Then, abruptly, said, "I... I don't wish to cause a scene. Not with my son here. I'll cooperate. I'll answer your questions." Harwell loosened her grip, then led him to a chair. He sat down heavily. He looked at Thorne. "The so-called discrepancy in my account? That was a ruse, wasn't it?"

"I'm sorry, Mr. Miller," she said. "I hope I'm wrong."

He nodded. "I understand. You have a job to do. I respect that." He looked at Harwell. "My car's running and blocking the drive. I don't suppose you'd let me move it?" He smiled when Harwell shook her head. "No, I imagine not. Miss Thorne? Would you mind?"

Thorne picked up her phone and paged one of the employees to her office. Soon there was a knock at the office door. "Come in, Bailey," Thorne said. A young girl who looked to be no older than

20 stepped inside. Thorne said, "Would you please move Mr. Miller's car from the front and, *carefully,* park it in one of the spaces on either side of the lot? Thanks, dear. Please lock it when that's done, then put the keys in the safe for now." The girl smiled, then left the office, closing the door behind her.

"I trust," Miller said, "that she's a good driver?"

"Bailey's my daughter, Mr. Miller, and she's an excellent driver."

Miller was seated with his back to the office door, facing Thorne's desk. Harwell dragged a wooden chair over and placed it directly in front of him. She sat down, folded her arms and studied his face, trying to get a grasp of his mental state. He appeared calmer now, and that was puzzling. Miller spoke first.

"Detective," he said, "is this about Shawn? About the injuries on his back?"

Harwell nodded. "It is, Mr. Miller," she said. "They don't appear to be wounds from a fall from a bicycle, as you told Miss Thorne they were."

"They're not." he said immediately. "No, that was a lie, but it was the best I could come up with at the time. I've, uh... I've never been much good at lying."

Harwell glanced at Thorne. She was watching from behind her desk, her face expressionless. The detective looked back at Miller. "What happened to your son, Mr. Miller?"

"He was beaten with a belt, the buckle part," he said, matter-of-factly. "It was..." He looked up, his eyes searching for something, then looked directly at her once again. "It was three days ago."

Harwell was taken by surprise with how easy it was to learn the truth, even though she suspected something like that had happened. She said, "Mr. Miller, I haven't placed you under arrest yet, but I'm wondering if it might be better if we were to go downtown. You could make your statement there."

Miller stared at the floor for a long time, then finally looked at Harwell and said, "I think, Detective, that I'd like Miss Thorne to also hear what I have to say. Please, it's important to me."

Harwell looked at Thorne, and she nodded. Harwell stood up, took a small digital recorder from her pocket, pressed the "record" button and placed it on Thorne's desk. She said to Miller, "I'm going to record your statement, Mr. Miller, but before I do I'm going to read you your rights. You have the right to remain silent. Anything you say can and will be used against you in a court of law. You have the right to an attorney. If you cannot afford an attorney, one will be appointed for you at no charge. Do you understand these rights?"

"I do, Detective."

"And you also understand that you're being recorded?"

"Yes, Detective," he said, "I understand."

"And you are willingly giving this statement? No one is forcing you?"

"I am, and no one is forcing me."

"Please state your name."

"Walter Miller."

"Thank you, Mr. Miller. Now, what is your son's name and age?"

"His name is Shawn. He's five and turns six in October."

"How did the bruises get on his back?"

"He... he was beaten. With a belt."

Harwell then kneeled down in front of Miller in order to look directly into his eyes. "And what did a five-year-old little boy do, Mr. Miller, to deserve that?"

Miller abruptly became crestfallen. His eyes moistened. "That's the very question I asked her, Detective."

Harwell let that sink in. "Can you explain that for me, sir?"

Miller closed his eyes, and took a deep breath. Once composed, he said, "The night it happened, my wife had sent me for some Chinese food. I wanted Shawn to go with me, but she wouldn't let him. You see, Detective, my wife was rather strong-willed. There was no arguing with her."

He seemed to wait for something at this point, as if needing Harwell to acknowledge that she believed him. The room they were in was quiet, but muffled laughter and the occasional playful scream from one of dozens of children filtered in and provided stark contrast to the horror story coming from Miller. "Okay, Mr. Miller," she said, and her even tone let him know that she did, in fact, at least thus far, believe him, or at least was willing to hear him out. "What happened after you got home?"

"I heard him screaming from the garage. I ran in," he said, "and... and she had this belt. There was a large metal buckle on the end of it, and that's what she was striking him with. All he had on was his underpants, and he had... well, soiled himself. He has trouble with that, you see, and it infuriated her. He was lying on the floor, trying to crawl away, but she was standing on his foot and he couldn't get away. She was... she was *crazy*, just hitting him, viciously, over and over, and screaming at him. There was so much noise she didn't hear me come in. I ran over and just threw myself on top of Shawn, trying to shield him from her. She actually hit me a couple of times... and then she stopped. And that's when I asked her, why? Why was she doing this? What did he do? She... she threw the belt down, and then she said to me, 'He's your son, clean him up. Then explain to him what toilets are for.'"

One of Harwell's strengths was she knew whether or not someone was telling the truth. She believed Miller's story. "Mr. Miller," Harwell began, "Is your wife...?"

"Please, Detective," Miller said, "Let me finish. You'll... *want* me to finish. I carried Shawn to the bathroom and ran a bath. While the tub filled, I doctored him as well as I could. He... he couldn't stop crying. I had to carry him to the bathroom mirror and look over his shoulders to tend to him because he clung to me as if his life depended on it. I finally coaxed him into the tub. After I bathed him, I put medicine on his wounds, and bandages. I got him into clean underwear and pajamas. I put him into his bed and stayed with him until he fell asleep." As if greatly relieved, Miller dropped his head, closed his eyes and took a deep breath. He said, "The bruises are actually much better now. I've been taking very good care of him. I'm... I'm hoping that, with time, he'll forget what his mother did. I can assure you, Detective, she won't do it again."

Harwell sensed something ominous at that moment. There was a finality, an assurance that was unmistakable when he uttered those last words. "How can you be sure of that, Mr. Miller?" she asked. "Abuse like that almost never stops. Even if that was the first time, she'll likely... "

"Oh, no, Detective," he interrupted, "it was *not* the first time. There were many others. But this one was the worst by far. I think she might have actually beaten him to death had I not come home when I did. But do you know what was even harder for me to understand about that entire night?"

Neither Harwell nor Thorne said anything. They didn't need to. He answered his own question.

"When I came out of Shawn's room, after he'd fallen asleep, I found Sheila - that's my wife - eating the food I'd brought home, and just... watching TV as if nothing had happened. She didn't even ask about him. And I swear to you Detective, as long as I live, I will never, ever forget how I felt at that moment."

He sat up straight then, his eyes wide with anger. Now there was a cold edge to his voice. "I waited until she went to bed. We've separate rooms, you see, have had since Shawn was born. After an hour or so, I stood outside her door and listened. When I heard her snoring, I went and found the belt right where she had thrown it. It was important to me that I used the very belt she used on Shawn. I looped the small end of it through the opening of the buckle and formed a noose of sorts. I still wasn't positive I'd actually go through with it. But then I saw Shawn's blood on the buckle. I seldom get angry, Detective, but when I saw that blood it was as if all of the anger I had ever suppressed in my lifetime just... boiled to the surface all at once. I went back to my wife's room and went inside. She was asleep on her stomach. I stood beside the bed, and I called her name. The light from the hall was all I needed. She lifted her head up a little and looked at me. I didn't give her time to react. I put the loop of that belt over her head and around her neck.

At the same time I leapt up onto her back, planted my knees into her shoulders and pulled. I found strength I never knew I had. She fought for a while, but she would have had to cut my hands off before I let go of that belt. It only made me pull harder. Even after she was still, *I pulled!*"

Remembering, he stiffened dramatically. His teeth were clenched and his shoulders and chest heaved with every breath as he relived that critical moment, the moment that forever changed his, and Shawn's life. He swallowed hard. "I managed to wrap her body in the sheets and blanket that were on her bed, then drag her downstairs and into my wine cellar. It stays fairly cool there. I intended to turn myself in eventually. I knew it was just a matter of time before I'd be caught. I told Shawn she was on a long trip." Then, with unmistakable conviction, he said, "As I told you, Detective, she'll never hurt Shawn again."

No one moved at first. His confession hung in the air, and both Harwell and Thorne were too mesmerized to respond. Finally, Harwell stopped the recorder and put it back into her pocket. She said, "Miss Thorne, could you pull his file? We need his address and his emergency contact information. We need to make sure Shawn has family who can take care of him."

Thorne walked over to a file cabinet and opened the bottom drawer. While she was looking, Miller said, "There's a number for my sister, his Aunt Terri. It's the first one. Call her, she'll come get him. Give her the keys to my Lexus, also, if you would, Miss Thorne. Tell her it's hers to use." Thorne, finding the file, took it to her desk and opened it. She wrote down the phone number, then handed the folder to Harwell.

"We'll take care of Shawn, Detective, until she gets here," Thorne said. "But if I'm unable to reach his aunt, if it's okay, I'll take him home with me tonight. I'll take full responsibility for him."

Harwell looked at Miller, and he nodded his consent. "That should be fine, Miss Thorne," Harwell said. She looked at her watch. "CPS should be here in about a half-hour. Get with them about protocol for things like this. If you do hear from the aunt, tell her to contact me. I'll try to arrange it where she can get access to Shawn's clothes and other items she might need of his." She then spoke directly to Miller. "We need to go."

"I suppose," Miller said, "you're taking me to jail?"

Harwell nodded. "I am, sir."

"Do you have the put the cuffs on? I don't want Shawn to see me like that."

"I'm afraid so. I have no choice."

Miller nodded. "Can I tell Shawn goodbye first?"

Harwell glanced at Thorne. She was already on the phone. A few seconds later Bailey walked in with Shawn. He was hesitant when he saw Harwell, obviously shy around people he didn't know. Miller held out his arms, and Shawn went to his father. Miller hugged his son, careful to avoid his back. "Guess what?" his father asked.

"What?" Shawn said, barely above a whisper.

Miller drew back, and took Shawn's hands in his. "Aunt Terri will pick you up today, and take you home with her. Won't that be fun?"

Shawn looked at his father, uncertainty on his face. "Will you be there?"

Miller forced a smile. "I... may have to work... really late. So if it's past your bedtime, you just go to sleep, and then I'll see you tomorrow. How's that?"

"Will... Mom be there?"

With his fingers, he brushed back a tuft of hair that had fallen across Shawn's eyes. He said, "No, son. Mom won't be there. Remember? Mom's gone away. Maybe for a long time."

Shawn smiled. "So only Aunt Terri? And Uncle Steve?" Miller nodded, and smiled back. "Okay, Daddy." They hugged once more, then Bailey took him back with the other children.

Miller stood up, then turned to Harwell. He held out his arms. "Thank-you Detective. You may arrest me now."

She fished the cuffs off her belt. She hesitated, then said, "Tell you what. Why don't you take your sport coat off first." Miller started to ask why, but then quickly understood.

With his hands cuffed in front of him and with the sport coat draped across his hands, he asked her, "Is it as bad as I've seen... on TV? Jail, I mean?"

Harwell softened. She genuinely felt sorry for the man. "I'll make sure you have your own cell for now. If your story checks out, I'll see what I can do for you. You should have called us, Mr. Miller. We would have helped you and your son."

He nodded. "I know. Tell me, Detective, do you have children?"

"No."

"I'm surprised. You're a lovely girl. I'm sure you would be a wonderful mother. But since you have no children, you couldn't possibly know... could never understand how I felt when I saw my son's blood on that buckle. I acted... intuitively, I think. I had to protect him. Can you see that, Detective Harwell?"

Harwell's mind drifted back ten years, to the nightmare inside the trailer, to that little girl hiding inside her closet, and what her mother did for her. The events were strikingly similar. "I do see it, Mr. Miller. I see it very clearly."

He smiled. "I'm glad. That means a great deal to me. And you know what?"

"What, Mr. Miller?"

"It was worth it," he said. "Yes, I'm sure I'd do it again." She took his arm. Just before she opened the door, he said, "You know, I never told you the funny part, like funny-ironic." Harwell stopped, and waited. He continued, "When it was over, when I finally let go of the belt, there was an unmistakable odor that filled the room." He smiled at Harwell. "She'd done the very thing she'd beaten Shawn for. And do you know what I did, Detective?"

Harwell shook her head.

"I laughed. So help me, I laughed."

****

Jasmine Sullivan arrived at the Med that morning, thirty minutes early for her shift. She needed to talk with Timecia.

She and Danny had come up with the roughest outline of a plan. There remained much to do, but, at the very least, this was a start. She had to get to Timecia, despite her injuries, as soon as possible. Danny had explained to her just how powerful Tyrone was. His tentacles reached virtually everywhere. There was no question he had connections imbedded in the police department. The Med was probably no different. Danny had warned her not to trust anyone, even co-workers who she'd worked with for years. Keep everything she and Danny talked about to herself. Business as usual.

She parked in the employee parking lot and hurried inside. She carried a black leather purse. She took the elevator to the fourth floor. Not wanting to attract attention, she tried to walk as casually as she could as she made her way down to room 419. She avoided eye contact, but when it was unavoidable, she smiled sweetly and nodded hello.

When she arrived at Timecia's door, she knocked lightly. She heard a very cheerful, "Come in!" She pushed the door open slowly, and saw a female nurse inside. She was a little past middle-aged and slightly portly. "Come on in!" she repeated. "I'm just about done. Oh! You're a nurse," she said when she saw Jasmine. "I just took her temp and her vitals and I'm entering them into the computer. But I guess you can see that for yourself, can't you?" She had a wide smile and a bright personality. Jasmine loved nurses like that. You can do your job and be personable.

Jasmine smiled back, then said, "How is she?"

"Oh, she's just getting better and better," she answered, then, looking at Timecia, said, "aren't you dear?" She had a name-tag on her uniform that said "Pam." Jasmine remained at the doorway, not wanting to come in until the nurse was done. She was able to see into the room and notice, with great relief, that Pam was alone with Jasmine. Pam looked over at her, and said, "Aren't you going to come in?"

"No, I'll wait until you're finished. I don't want to get in the way."

"Okay, suit yourself." A minute or two later, she closed the laptop, then looked at Jasmine. "All-righty then," she said, "she's all yours!" She turned to Timecia, and said, "I'll see you later, honey. But you just press that button if you need anything at all. I got my running shoes on. I'm old but I'm scrappy!"

She made her way to the door, then stopped when she was beside Jasmine. She lowered her voice to a whisper. "Are you here officially, or to visit?"

"I'm a friend of hers," said Jasmine.

"Have you seen her before today? I mean, here at the hospital?"

Jasmine shook her head. "No."

"Try not to react when you see her. Her face is a mess. I've been doing everything in my power to get her spirits up, but it hasn't been easy." She sighed deeply. "I don't know what happened to her, but I have my suspicions. I'd bet my degree that it was a fist or a foot, or both, that caused that kind of damage."

Jasmine nodded. "I work in the OR. I've seen plenty of trauma. I'll be okay."

Pam left, pushing the cart which held the laptop, and disappeared inside the next room. Jasmine entered Timecia's room, closing the door gently behind her. When she first saw Timecia, despite her experience, it took all of her willpower not to gasp. Her once beautiful, young face remained swollen and bruised. She saw the cast on her right arm, and the pain pump being held firmly with her left, ready to press the button the instant the digital countdown wound down to zero. When Timecia saw her, there was no visible recognition. She walked around to the side of the bed and leaned over her. "Timecia," she said, very softly, and as tears began forming in her eyes, she said, "Oh my God, honey. How do you feel?"

Timecia looked at her through barely open eyelids. She was sure she had seen this nurse before. She searched her memory, but it was too cloudy. Jasmine wasn't wearing her name-tag. Finally, she whispered a very raspy, "Who are you?"

Jasmine opened her purse and retrieved several index cards. She selected one, and held it up to her. Out loud, Jasmine said, "I'm a nurse. I'm just checking on you." But the card read, in large letters:

I'm Jasmine Sullivan. Danny's wife.

Timecia's eyes opened wide, or at least as wide as her injuries allowed. Jasmine could see the fear in them. She very quickly placed a finger against her lips, and a just barely audible "Shhh" was enough to calm her. She found another card. Out loud, Jasmine said, "Your chart looks wonderful. You're making excellent progress." She held the card up.

Danny told me everything. We want to help you.

Timecia closed her eyes, then shook her head back and forth. She said, "No one... can help...me."

"Oh, of course we can," Jasmine said. "I mean, look how much better you are already." She quickly found another card and showed it to Timecia.

We need a name. Someone you trust completely.

Again, Timecia shook her head. Out loud, Jasmine said, "Do you need anything?" This time, the card she chose read:

I know you're scared. Please don't be. We are your friends.

And then again:

We need a name. Someone you trust completely.

This time Timecia didn't shake her head. She stared at Jasmine for a long time. Jasmine mouthed the word *Please!* and then folded her hands in front of her as if she were praying. Timecia put her pain pump down, then indicated with her fingers for Jasmine to come closer. Jasmine leaned over her, and put her ear next to Timecia's lips. Very softly, almost too softly for Jasmine to hear, she whispered, "Harwell."

Jasmine hurriedly opened her purse and took out a pen. She wrote the name *Harwell?* on the back of one of the cards and held it out for Timecia. She said, "Here you go. Is this what you wanted?" Timecia nodded. She then wrote *Who is she?* Jasmine, once again, put her ear next to Timecia's mouth. She whispered, "Angela. Detective." Immediately, Jasmine wrote *Detective Angela Harwell?*

Timecia smiled, then picked up the pain pump and pressed the button. She closed her eyes as the medication entered her bloodstream, and was almost immediately asleep. "Okay, sweetie," Jasmine said, "I'll leave you alone now. You let us know if you need anything." She gathered the cards and put them back in her purse. She looked at her watch and saw she barely had enough time to get to her station. She quietly opened the door, then quickly made her way back down the hall.

Jasmine didn't know it, but she had been overly cautious. There was no listening device in Timecia's room. There was, however, an orderly who was watching the room very closely. He made notes of who came in and out. He didn't pay a lot of attention to Jasmine. Lots of nurses came and went. He watched Jasmine all the way to the elevator, however.

But only because Jasmine was fun to watch.

****

Tyrone's cell phone rang, bringing him out of the TV stupor that he had fallen into. He was glad for the interruption. When he saw who it was he was even more glad. He muted the TV, then connected the call.

"Rico," he said, "talk to me."

"The old man who was with her at the ballgame is a former cop named Rodney Rocorro. He's been retired from Bartlett PD for quite a while. Still lives in Bartlett, but if you're tailing him you probably already know that. He serves court papers now, part-time, for a company called Alias Subpoena. Between that and his Social Security, *and* his pension, he's managed a pretty nifty nest egg. He goes to the gym four or five times a week. He bowls in a senior league on Tuesday afternoons. Carries a respectable 177 average. His wife died a few years ago. He's got a girlfriend now, named

Sue Donald. She bowls with him on Tuesdays as well."

Tyrone mulled over this. He said, "What's his connection to Harwell?"

"He's her grandfather, T. Simple as that. They go to ballgames together. He and his wife raised her after her mother - his daughter - capped herself when Angela was a kid, so they're close."

"Harwell's mother killed herself?"

"Yeah. Apparently her boyfriend liked little girls even more than big girls. Mom caught him one night playing doctor with 13-year-old Angela. She put three slugs in him and then one in herself."

"No shit!"

"Yeah. That had to have left a mark. Probably still has nightmares about it."

"Okay, so what do you think?"

"He's no threat to you, T. He's like 70. He's an old man. He probably takes Viagra so he can wooden up for his girlfriend. If you ask me, you're wasting your time following this guy around. I think you should leave him alone and let him collect his pension."

"I don't know, Rico," Tyrone said, "She's a cop and he used to be. Once a cop, always a cop. They talk. He may try to help, lift up an old rock or two. He lifts up enough rocks, he may find something." Tyrone got up and began pacing. "No, I'm going to stay on him. At least for a few more days."

Rico sighed. "Okay, T. I'm just telling you what I found."

"Tell me about the alibi, Rico. I'm going crazy here."

"I'm having some trouble getting the tickets, T. Everything's done online now. Tickets are printed on the home computer, so old tickets are hard to find. But I got a guy working on it. He's also a computer genius, or at least he says he is. And for what he's charging he'd better be. He's supposed to let me know by the end of the week. Everything else is already taken care of."

"I don't care about the money, Rico! I've got to get out of this house. I've got something big coming up that won't wait. You offer him double and see if it won't hurry him up."

There was silence on the other end for a while. Finally, Tyrone said, "Rico? Did you hear me?"

"I heard you, T. You wanna know what I think?"

Tyrone chuckled. "You're going to tell me anyway, so go ahead."

"You stayed clean for a whole year on those trumped-up charges, then not a month later you're in trouble again. Didn't you learn *anything*? They want you bad enough to plant evidence in your car, then you go and hand them a serious charge on a silver fucking platter. One of these days your temper's gonna put you someplace where me and all the money in the world ain't gonna help you. And you're either gonna be dead, or in a place where you wish you were."

Tyrone wasn't used to being talked to like that. "You watch your mouth, Rico. Don't forget for one second who you're talking to and what I'm capable of."

There was laughter over the phone, and then a suddenly serious Rico said. "Don't threaten me, Tyrone. You ain't nothing to me but business. What I am to you is a voice on a telephone. Nothing more. But I know where you live. I can find you anywhere on the planet at any time and you won't have any idea how I did it. Hell, I could turn your cable off right now. How the hell do you imagine I'm able to get you all this shit? All you gave me was a plate, and now you know everything about the guy. You may run Memphis, dickhead, but I'm global. You ever fucking threaten me again? SWAT will be so far up your ass you'll feel like you've had a nuclear colonoscopy."

Tyrone was on the verge of a meltdown, but he understood that, for now, Rico had the edge. He forced himself to speak calmly. "Just tell me," he managed, "when I'll have my alibi."

"I'll be in touch." Then the line went dead. Tyrone stared at the screen. He put the phone in his pocket.

He then picked up a lamp, and threw it against the wall.

Chapter Eight

Rocorro walked into the B.B. Kings Blues Club just as twilight was settling over downtown Memphis and historic Beale Street. Though the King himself rarely makes a live appearance, names like Blind Mississippi Morris, King Beez and The BB King Allstars regularly perform for blues fans from all over the world.

It was early on a weeknight and a live band was playing an upbeat blues set to a nearly full house. The diversity of young and old, black and white, affluent and not so affluent was a testimony to the universal appeal of great blues music. Especially when it was at the home of the blues, at B.B. Kings on Beale Street. Add cold beer, great food, good company and perhaps a slight buzz? It was as close to music heaven as it gets.

Rocorro wasn't a big fan of blues, but he could tolerate it. After a while it all began to sound the same to him. He preferred early rock and roll, but he also enjoyed pretty much anything live, so he was okay with the meeting place Bo Sanders had suggested. Also, like a surprising number of locals, even though he'd lived around Memphis most of his life, this was the first time he'd been on Beale Street and this club.

The volume, however, might pose a problem. Rocorro was hard of hearing and competing with electric guitars and amplifiers wouldn't be easy.

He paused just inside the door and scanned for Bo. While it had been more than two years since he'd seen him Rocorro felt certain he would recognize him. But his eyesight had declined as well - getting old could be a real pain sometimes - and even with contacts he was having trouble seeing faces in any detail. The low lighting didn't help, and he was beginning to wonder if this was such an ideal place after all. He was so focused on finding Bo that he didn't even notice the young hostess when she approached him. "Welcome to B.B. Kings, sir," she said, smiling. "Can I help you find someone?" When it was obvious that he didn't hear her, she tapped him on the shoulder. Then he saw her, and her smile, and he smiled back.

"Hello!" he said, loudly.

She was in her early 20's, had short black hair, perfect teeth and a small gold stud on one nostril. She had a slight gut that spilled over the waist of her too-tight black jeans that seemed out of place in proportion to the rest of her. She placed a hand on his shoulder, then stood on her toes in order to speak directly into his ear. "You look like you're trying to find someone. Maybe I can help?" He enjoyed her touch, her perfume, the closeness and her genuine smile. And, as he looked down towards her, her low-cut blouse.

He said. "I'm supposed to meet someone. He should be here already."

Her hand remained on his shoulder. "What's his name? Maybe I know him."

"Bo Sanders."

She brightened. "Oh! You mean Bobo?"

"I don't know about *Bobo*," he answered. "Black guy, around 45, about this tall?"

"Yeah," she said, "that's Bobo. He's here. C'mon."

He followed her to the back of the club, and they stopped at a closed door. She knocked twice, opened the door and stuck her head in. "Bobo?" she said, "you still in here?"

"Yeah, Jen," Rocorro heard a voice say.

She opened the door completely and stepped aside. "You got company!" she said.

Sanders was seated on a couch, polishing a silver trombone. When he saw Rocorro he immediately put the horn on a stand, then stood to greet his friend. He, like Rocorro, had aged in the twenty years they'd known each other. His waistline had thickened considerably and his hair was now a thinning mixture of black and gray. A half-smoked cigarette hung loosely in his mouth, and he removed it and stabbed it out. "Rocco, my friend, come on in." They shook hands and embraced, then Sanders stood back and said, "Dammit, man! How do you manage to stay so skinny?"

"I work hard and play hard, Bo," Rocorro said, "or is it Bobo now?"

Sanders laughed. "She can call me that, but you sure as hell can't."

Rocorro looked around. It was a decent-sized room which, when the door was closed, muffled the noise from the club well enough to carry on a normal conversation. Besides the couch, there were several chairs scattered around along with a coffee table adjacent to the couch. There were two overflowing ash trays on the table and the room reeked of stale tobacco. Two electric guitars rested on stands in one corner, and the walls were adorned with framed posters advertising various blues festivals from years gone by. They were in the musician's lounge where band members gathered before and after gigs and during breaks.

"You still prefer Sam Adams, Rocco?" Sanders asked.

"If you're buying, I guess I'll drink most anything," he answered.

"Jen," Sanders said, "would you mind askin' Darla or Joanie to bring two bottles, and to put it on my tab?"

"How about I bring them myself," Jen said.

"Even better," Bo said.

After she'd left, the men sat on the couch. Rocorro said, "How are things going, Bo?"

"I can't complain," he said. "I'm still sellin' used cars for Earl. Still at the same lot, even though he opened up a couple more locations. Doin' good, too. Been doin' it so long now that customers who bought cars from me years ago are sendin' their kids to me now. It's almost too easy. I just sit around the shop and holler 'next!' and someone else comes in. Won't be doin' it much longer, though. I'm fixin' to be rich."

"What now?" Rocorro asked.

"Thought of a laxative slogan. Just sent it to Ex-Lax. You know how they advertise that it works overnight?"

"I think so."

"This can't miss. They gonna have to pay me big bucks to use it. My idea is, instead of sayin' it works overnight, say 'Ex-Lax. It'll wake yo' ass up!'"

Rocorro laughed. "Bo, that one might just work. But don't quit your job until you hear from them." He nodded toward his trombone. "I see you're still playing the horn as well?"

"Yeah, now and then, but not as much as I'd like. Playin' tonight, actually. Giggin' with a band called The Blues Gang. Good horn section. Great charts. Gonna be on stage in a couple of hours. You still gonna be here?"

Rocorro shook his head. "Can't, Bo. It's almost past my bedtime now. My workday starts at four."

"Four in the *mornin'*? Seriously? Damn, Rock, that's just silly! If you knocked on my door that early, you'd just be wastin' your time. When're you gonna retire anyway?"

"I *am* retired," Rocorro said, "I just serve papers for the fun of it. Gives me something to do. *And* I get to wear my gun to work. Just like old times."

Just then there was a knock at the door and Jen walked in with the beers. The bottles were sweating and had just a touch of foam spilling out from the open tops. As she placed them on the table, Bo said, "Jen, you are truly an angel from heaven. My friend and I thank you."

Jen held out her hand to Rocco. "I'm Jenny," she said, "and you are?"

Rocco took her delicate hand in his and said, "I'm Rodney Rocorro, but everyone calls me Rocco."

She smiled, and said, "You're welcome here anytime, Rocco. Any friend of Bobo's is a friend of mine." She winked at Rocco. "You boys holler if you need anything else, hear?" And then she was gone.

"You know something?" Sanders said after the door had closed. "Anybody else calls me 'boy' and I might take offense. But she makes it sound sexy." They picked up the bottles, and Bo held his out to Rocorro. "To younger times," he said, then winked, "when 'joint pain' just meant you was out of weed."

Rocorro laughed again, then touched his bottle to Bo's. They each took a drink, then Rocorro asked, "How's Connie and the kids, Bo?"

Bo smiled. "Connie keeps me fat and happy, Rocco. I swear I don't know how I got that lucky. That woman looks at me and still thinks I'm smokin' hot. And Lucy's in medical school as you know, at Vanderbilt. Third year. You wouldn't believe how she's on me about my weight and cigarettes. So her and Connie are *both* gangin' up on me now, least ways about smokin'. And, believe it or not, DJ is a god-damned Navy *SEAL*! DJ!" He shook his head in disbelief. "I don't know, Rocco. Somethin' just happened to him in his senior year in high school. He read a book about 'em, then started runnin' and trainin' and liftin' weights. Grades went way up. All his fat turned into muscle. Just turned his whole life around. As soon as he graduated, he joined the navy. Three years later, he's a SEAL."

The pride in his voice was unmistakable. "Congratulations, Bo," said Rocorro. "I'm happy for you."

"Tell me about that pretty granddaughter, Rocco," said Bo.

"She's doing really well, Bo, putting lots of bad guys away. I'm mighty proud of her. And that's actually why I'm here," Rocorro said. He placed his beer back on the table. "She's looking for a guy. Thought maybe you might know something."

"I don't hear as much as I used to, Rocco. Who's she looking for?"

"Gangster named Tyrone Reed," said Rocorro. "His street name is..."

"T-Bone," Bo interjected. He was suddenly serious. He looked at Rocorro, took another, much longer, swig of his ale, then said, "Tell me you're kiddin' Rocco."

"No," said Rocorro. "Angela wants this guy in the worst way. She's certain he beat up a girl she's been trying to help. Apparently almost killed her. The vic and Tyrone have a child together. He's hiding somewhere, and Angela thought maybe..."

"Rocco, you go back to Angela and you tell her to forget about Tyrone Reed. Let SWAT and the Vice Squad take him down. If they can, that is. Then you serve your papers and forget about this bein' a cop again crap."

"Oh, c'mon, Bo," Rocorro said, "aren't you being just a little overly dramatic? He's just a thug, just like any other thug."

"No he's not, Rocco. Not by a long shot. Thing is, you never saw anyone like him in Bartlett. How can I put this?" He paused for a moment, thoughtful. Then he said, "There's a reason he was able to beat that possession rap a while back. In the same way B.B.'s King of the blues, Tyrone is King of the streets. He runs a gang called The Family, but you probably already knew that. He's like the Lord God Himself, Rocco. If he don't wanna be found, you ain't gonna find him. If he finds out you're lookin' for him? He'll find you first. And then you won't be lookin' for him no more. You get what I'm sayin' Rocco?"

"Bo, nobody's that..."

"Tyrone is, Rocco! Hold on a minute." Sanders got up and went to the door. He opened it just enough to be able to look around the club. He then closed it and sat back down. He finished his beer. "Listen, Rocco," he said, his voice low, "I'm telling you as a friend not to mess with this dude. He ain't the model citizen cat who was all over the news. That was all show, somethin' his lawyers told him to do. I don't have the first clue where he might be, but I do know this: there's a whole army of folks between you and him. He's got money, and power, and protection. What I hear, he's got people in the police, in the jail, in city hall - everywhere. Hell, he may even have someone outside that door wantin' to know why you're talking to me."

Rocorro looked at his friend, nodded then drained the rest of his beer. Both men stood, understanding there was nothing more to be said. "Okay, Bo," he said, then held out his hand. "I appreciate the beer, and the conversation. I'll let Angela know what you said." Sanders took his hand, then pulled him into an embrace.

Just before Rocco left, Bo said, "Look, Rocco, we've been

friends for a long time. Hell, you and Angela are like family to me and Connie. I'll never forget what you did for me. Saved my son's life. Now I'm tryin' to do the same for you. You heed what I'm tellin' you. Leave this thing alone."

Rocorro nodded, then said, "You take care. Next beer's on me."

He opened the door, then Sanders said, "One more thing, Rocco." Rocorro stopped and looked back. "*Love* the goatee!"

Rocorro chuckled. "Thanks." He walked out of the room, and into the club. Soon he was outside and walking back to his car. As Sanders watched him go, he had a strong feeling Rocorro *wouldn't* heed his warning.

He hoped tonight wasn't the last time he would see his friend.

****

Jenny, from the other side of the club, also watched him leave. As soon as he was gone she was on her cell. Almost immediately, she said, "Hey, it's me. That man you wanted me to watch for you? He just left." A pause. "Yep, just right this second." Another pause. "Why, not at all, honey. Thank *you!* Easiest hundred dollars I ever made." Another pause. "No, just Bobo. Huh? Yeah, Bo Sanders." She listened for a minute. "How would I know? I wasn't in the room when they were talk... what? I'm sorry, it's loud in here. Oh, no, he didn't talk to anyone else. No one else went in there. Hey, y'all *sure* y'all not gonna hurt him? Hello?"

But the connection was lost. For the briefest moment, she felt a stab of regret, but it quickly passed. She slipped her phone into her back pocket and went back to work.

A singer's mournful voice poured from the speakers, *"The damage is done, baby..."*

Apropos.

****

That same evening, Harwell was relaxing on the balcony of her

2nd floor apartment. The breeze from an oscillating fan a few feet away felt cool against her perspiring body, and her heart rate and breathing had returned to nearly normal.

She'd just finished a particularly vicious workout on her treadmill. She much preferred running outdoors, but the treadmill did provide a considerably cooler alternative this time of year. It didn't hurt that there was a 40-inch TV mounted on the wall just a few feet away, along with a Blue Ray DVD player and surround sound. A good movie made the miles melt away while she ran, another advantage to outdoor running with just an iPod and headphones.

Both the treadmill and the TV were gifts from her grandfather. In fact, nearly everything in her apartment had been provided by him. He struggled, initially, with her wanting to move out immediately after graduating from college, but he accepted that it was time. But he also didn't want her saddled with a furniture note on top of a new lease and so he wrote the checks. Harwell told him that she wanted to pay him back, and he agreed. He made her sign a note that required her to pay him exactly one dollar a year. They met for lunch every January 1st. She'd hand him a dollar and he'd put it in his wallet.

And that was just one of a thousand reasons why she absolutely adored her grandfather.

Harwell picked up a bottled water and took a long, cool drink. She then took the towel she'd placed around her neck and pressed it against her face. She was fully aware her body building and level of fitness bordered on obsession. As vital to life as was the water inside that bottle, her body needed to be driven to its very limit to live, to feel *alive*. Physically and mentally. She wasn't vain; rather, she was supremely disciplined. Like a warrior, she continually prepared for the battle to come.

She would be ready.

Thinking about that, she let Tyrone enter her mind once again. He was almost always there. She wondered how anyone could rise through the ranks of an organization and enjoy the sort of almost god-like power he'd attained. Like a dictator, no decision was questioned, no order ignored. Where he was looked upon with both awe and fear. This power had enabled him to dodge the law of any serious crimes or charges. No small feat considering the size of his organization and the seriousness of the crimes he was suspected of committing.

To Harwell, he was nothing more than an evil coward. He cared nothing about the families or lives he destroyed. He was obsessed with money and power. Harwell knew he was only interested in Timi and Kristin because he'd been told to stay away. There was no love for either of them. Harwell doubted Tyrone was capable of love. He simply wasn't used to being told what to do. He gave the orders. He needed to be in charge.

He needed to be stopped.

Just then, in the parking lot below, a gray SUV pulled into a space and a young family got out. Harwell knew them, at least by sight. The parents were probably in their late 20's or early 30's, and their son around eight or nine. He was dressed in a baseball uniform, wrinkled and dirty, and he carried a duffle bag with the name *Scotty* and the number *22* embroidered on it. They were animated as they talked about the game just played and Harwell saw the father put his arm around his son just before they disappeared from sight.

The image of them walking together stayed with Harwell long after they were gone. It stirred deep within her something unfamiliar. A yearning perhaps.

Or was it...wonder?

What was it like to have a child? What was it like to be married to a man? To be in love? Could it happen to her? *Would* it happen to her? She recalled the exchange between her and Walter Miller just before she arrested him:

"Tell me, Detective, do you have children?"

"No."

"I'm surprised. You're a lovely girl. I'm sure you would be a wonderful mother."

She wasn't so sure. Her own mother had allowed the death of her father to push her to alcoholism and neglect. Her grandmother had been loving and kind, but she was gone now. Harwell had no one to teach her how to be any kind of mother. She knew how to take care of herself, but a child? Did she have inside her a maternal instinct that would mysteriously surface the instant she gave birth? She didn't know. She also wasn't sure she needed it. Just because she was a woman didn't mean she possessed a biological urge to reproduce.

She looked through the patio door and into her apartment. She convinced herself she had everything she wanted or needed. She loved her job. She loved working out. There simply wasn't room in her life for anything else. And there was always the risk that she might lose her edge and hesitate at a critical moment because a picture of a husband, or son, or daughter would flash through her subconscious. She simply couldn't risk that. Not yet.

Perhaps not ever.

Besides, she was... *happy*. She really was. It wasn't like she was alone. She had her grandfather. She had her career. Every day she protected children like Shawn Miller and Kristin Harrison from harm's way, the way a mother protects her children. And with that, she decided that her grandfather would just have to wait, at least a while longer, to be a great-grandfather.

She finished her water, then wiped her face again. She went back inside her apartment, then paused in front of her kitchen table. There was an unopened bottle of water on it. In the time it took to make the decision to do it, she had leapt, turned a 360 and nailed the bottle with her right foot. She landed perfectly as the bottle sailed across the room and smashed against the far wall. She was glad the cap held. She then made her way into her spare bedroom where, instead of a bed and dresser, a bench press and free weights filled the room. She picked up a curl bar and began pumping. When she simply could not manage another rep, she replaced it on the rack. It felt as if her biceps were trying to burst through her skin.

They burned.

She loved the burn.

After a minute of rest, she began again.

****

Tyrone paced up and down in the front room of the house where he was staying. This was taking too long. He felt as if he stayed even one more day he would explode. Rico, for whatever bullshit reason, seemed to be taking his time to provide him with the alibi he desperately needed. He swore to himself. Rico *had* been right about one thing: his temper might one day betray him. He'd have to do better. It was, after all, the reason he was in this house.

He was also aware that his rage over being spit on could've landed him in jail. And he knew that what he did to Timecia was far worse than a few months for a simple drug bust. He'd get their best shot. They'd lock him up for a long time and in a maximum security facility with other hardened criminals. He wouldn't have it so easy there. There were rival gangs in these prisons that would like nothing better than to boast that they killed T-Bone. No, he couldn't have that. He'd have to be patient. This wasn't even about Timecia and Kristin now. They could wait. He had bigger fish to fry - much, much bigger - and everything had to be in place or it could all go away.

And that was unacceptable. He'd planned too long. He'd considered every possible detail.

Except being spit on.

His phone vibrated and he quickly checked the caller ID. He was disappointed when he saw it wasn't Rico. But he knew it must be important or they wouldn't be calling.

"You'd better have good news for me, Luther. I'm not in the mood for anything else."

"Sorry T," the voice on the other end said, "but there ain't much to tell you."

Tyrone sighed. "What do you have?"

"He spent about 10 or 15 minutes with a dude named Bo Sanders. Dude plays a horn now and then at B.B.'s. Girl we paid to watch him got no idea what they talked about. They were in the musician's lounge and the door was closed. Coulda just been a social visit."

Tyrone thought about that. "Yeah, maybe," he said, "but that's a real short visit. Do we know anything about Sanders?"

"I made some calls while we waited. Turns out he used to be a snitch for the old man and MPD a long time ago. Small-time shit. But he retired when the old man did."

Tyrone mulled over that for a moment. "Any chance, I mean *any* chance Sanders could know anything that could hurt me?"

"Don't see how. He's been quiet for a long time now. Seems to be minding his own business."

"Maybe," Tyrone said, "maybe not. Find out where he lives. Better yet, you, Joe and Rod Man follow him home. Talk to him. Convince him to tell you what the old man wanted. And Luther?"

"Yeah, T?"

"Do whatever it takes to make sure you *know* he's told you everything they talked about. I want there to be no doubt. No doubt whatsoever."

"Okay, T."

"Luther, one more thing."

"Yeah, boss."

"You call me as soon as you know. Either way it goes, you let me know."

"Sure, boss. Don't I always?"

The line went dead and Tyrone put the phone back in his pocket. He began pacing again.

Chapter Nine

After the final note of the night came out of his horn, Bo Sanders and the rest of the band enjoyed yet another standing ovation. Their last encore was a raucous version of "Superstitious", and though it was nearly two in the morning, the audience still wanted more. Bo loved every minute of it. He wished he could do this full time; it was way more satisfying than selling cars. However, the $100 he made tonight simply wouldn't pay the bills. He'd clear more selling just one vehicle than he could make here in a week.

Bo wasn't dumb. He'd keep his day job.

Though the rest of the band seemed to catch a second wind after the gig was over, Bo was tired. He put his horn away, collected his pay, then made his way through the crowd and towards the door. He smiled and graciously received all of the compliments thrown at him as he walked. He loved this part of the night. After every gig he'd take the long way around, and would stop and talk to fans, new and old. He kept his business cards handy just in case someone might be looking for a good used car.

Or a good used trombone player.

He'd parked in a garage just a couple of blocks away. It had rained earlier and the still damp streets glistened under the street lights. Bo never had any problems walking to his car; the garage was close and well lit. He popped the trunk of his silver Corolla and placed his horn inside. He drove through a largely deserted downtown and was soon headed over the steep viaduct which led into the riverbank community known as Harbor Town.

Bo and his wife lived in the upscale *Arbors at Riverwalk* Apartments, a gated complex located within easy walking distance from the banks of the Mississippi River. They often enjoyed leisurely sunset strolls along an asphalt path which, depending on the water level, was at times only a few feet from the muddy water. Tugboats often traveled by, pushing its load of barges either north against the current or south with it. And if the water level was high enough, it almost seemed as if you could reach out and shake the hand of the tugboat captain as he chugged by.

Bo turned off the main road and into the complex. He pushed a button on the console above his head and the gates began to open. As he waited, he noticed another car pull in directly behind him. He didn't give it a lot of thought. After all, *he* was just getting home as well.

When the opening was wide enough, he navigated through it and the headlights behind him followed. Bo was soon in front of his apartment, and saw with disgust that someone was in his reserved spot. He made a mental note to, again, complain to the property manager. As he pulled into the next available parking space, the car behind him kept going.

He got out of his air-conditioned environment and felt the humidity envelope him. He marveled at how, despite the sun being on the other side of the planet, it was still eighty degrees. He suddenly realized just how tired he was, and he looked forward to his cool apartment, warm wife and comfortable bed. He popped the trunk once more, and as he was reaching for his horn, he heard the footsteps. He straightened up and saw two men approaching from opposite sides of the parking lot.

One was bald, tall and both arms were completely covered with tattoos. The other was shorter and had long dreadlocks that split both sides of his shoulders, along with a goatee. Both men wore black pants and black muscle shirts.

Bo had no way of knowing it was Family members Luther and Joe.

Bo instinctively felt that this had something to do with Rocco's visit, and he swore softly. He was mad at himself for not paying more attention to the car that must have followed him from Beale Street. As casually as he could, he started to reach for his gun, a Smith & Wesson .38 caliber snubnosed revolver, laying on the floor of the trunk, inside a holster, behind his trombone. Had it not been in a holster, he might have been able to get it in time and deter whatever the men had in mind. Instead, the taller one, Luther, ran towards him and slammed the trunk down. Bo was barely able to get his arm out of the way. He quickly stepped back from the car and raised both his hands in the air.

"Relax, boys," he said, "nobody needs to get hurt. What do you punks want? Money?" His eyes flicked back and forth as he debated what to do should they be simple thugs who were out to roll him.

Luther smiled. "Nah, man, we don' want money, but I do respect yo' spunk. For now, jus' throw me them keys."

"My keys? You want to steal my car? Listen, you don't want this piece of shit. Tell you what, you come see me at Earl's Pearls Used Cars. You know where that is? It's on Covington Pike. I'll give you one of my cards..."

As soon as Bo attempted to reach for a card, Luther reached behind his back and drew a revolver. Bo froze.

"The only thing you gonna give me is yo' keys," he said. Bo removed his keys from his front pocket, and threw them to him. Luther unlocked the trunk, then reached inside and removed the gun and holster.

"Well, well," he said, "look what we have here." He removed the weapon, threw the holster back inside, then closed the trunk. He popped the cylinder open and saw all six chambers had bullets. He snapped it back with a flick of his wrist. He smiled at Bo. "Very nice. I think I'll keep this for myself." He put the gun inside the waistband of his pants, then turned and signaled with his hand. At that moment, two headlights came to life and a Dodge Charger sped up and stopped beside them. Luther opened the back door, then looked at Bo. "Get in." He saw, for the first time, fear in Bo's eyes. "Relax, old man," he said, "we jus' need to talk. Ask you 'bout some things. We ain't even gonna leave this here fancy complex. You tell the truth, you be back in no time, climbing in bed with yo' wife. But right now, you need to get yo' ass inside this car. Now, please, I'm asking nicely. Get the fuck in."

Before he could move, Joe shoved Bo toward the open door. Bo climbed inside the car and Joe followed. Luther ran to the other side and got in. Bo felt a stab of panic with the two thugs beside him. When the car started moving, he watched helplessly as the distance between him and his wife grew greater and greater, and his heart began to beat wildly in response. Sweat formed on his forehead and he began to feel dizzy.

"Boys, I don't... don't feel so good," Bo managed. "Why the hell y'all doin' this?"

"What'd the old man want?" Luther asked.

"What... what old man?" His breathing became labored.

"Now, now, Bo, don't be like that. You getting all worked up for nothin'. You know what old man we talkin' about. The white dude who came to see you at B.B.'s. What'd y'all talk about?"

Bo shook his head. "You mean...?" He quickly stopped himself. "Nothin' man, nothin' at all. He's a friend of mine is all."

"No, Bo, that ain't all. Now he may be a friend of yours, but he's also an ex-cop, and you a ex-snitch. And his granddaughter's M-P-D. Now, answer my question. What did y'all discuss?"

"Who *are* you guys? How do you know all that?" Bo asked. "Listen, I sell cars now. I don't know nothin' anymore about nothin'. He's... he's lookin' for a car is all." Bo's chest pain increased. He couldn't take much more.

Luther removed Bo's revolver from his waistband. He put the gun against Bo's head. With his other hand he grabbed Bo by the throat. "Now I don' want to shoot you. 'Specially with yo' own gun. But I'm real tired of askin'. I'll ask you one mo' time. I tell you what - how 'bout I make it easy? Did the name "Tyrone" come up, even one time, while he was with you?" He pulled the hammer back, then screamed, "Answer me, fool!"

Bo felt the cold steel of the revolver against the side of his head. He knew his gun had a hair trigger. He also knew that the three thugs in the car with him were members of The Family, and he knew what that meant. His life was meaningless to them. He would never tell them what they wanted to know. The hand around his throat tightened. The pain in his chest increased, and then, suddenly, he was having the heart attack his daughter had warned him about. His brain function was suddenly reduced to a chaotic blur of panic-induced electrical waves. Common sense was overwhelmed with an overpowering desire to be safely inside his apartment, in bed and next to his wife, his kids only a phone call away. A primitive instinct took control: Flight or fight.

And since he had nowhere to run, he fought.

His right hand rose up and grabbed Luther's wrist. Startled at the speed in which Bo moved, Luther stiffened and gripped the gun he held a little too tightly. His forefinger reflexively pulled back against the trigger. The hammer struck the firing pin. The firing pin ignited the gunpowder and sent the bullet through the barrel. Traveling faster than the speed of sound, the slug penetrated Bo's skull, passed through his brain and out the other side, shattering the opposite window. The explosive report inside the enclosed space of the car was both deafening and unexpected.

Bo's eyes opened wide, then closed. His head drooped down, and his arms fell limp.

The men went away, and he was no longer afraid.

****

Moments later, the Charger eased to a stop. The passenger-side rear door opened, and a body was pushed out onto the parking lot. The Charger then casually pulled away and left the complex.

There were no eye-witnesses. The surveillance footage was limited to the front gates and proved to be inadequate for facial identification through the tinted windows. The shattered window was facing away from the camera. The license plate was hidden behind a tinted cover as well.

Later, authorities would study an all but useless, grainy recording of a black Charger entering the complex at 2:23 AM, then exiting at 2:41 AM. At 3:01 a call to 911 from a morning paper carrier alerted authorities to the crime scene. Police and ambulance sirens alerted nearly everyone else to the activity outside their windows. This included Connie Sanders.

At that very moment two things happened: She discovered that Bo was not in the apartment. There was a knock at her door.

She felt panic building up inside of her as she slowly made her way to the door. The two policemen with solemn faces ignited the beginnings of a scream which began in the depths of her soul, only to erupt from her lips when one of them said, "I'm very sorry to have to tell you this..."

****

Rocorro drained the last swallow of coffee, placed the cup in the sink and filled it with water. It was a few minutes before 5:00 and time for him to go. He was alone this morning as Sue was visiting her grandchildren in Nashville. He was used to it and thought for a time he actually preferred it. But then Sue came into his life and he found himself enjoying her company more and more. Though she would never take the place of his wife - they were too different in almost every way - he discovered she rekindled feelings he thought were long gone.

Physical love, for instance. For a long time he'd been content with merely her companionship and conversation. They enjoyed movies, dinners and, occasionally, an off-Broadway show, something which Sue especially enjoyed. It was a far cry from an evening at a Redbird's game, but Rocorro had to admit he found it intriguing as well as entertaining. They had attended *Wicked* recently, far and away the best show he'd ever seen.

Hell, maybe he was getting soft in his old age.

But he'd been unsure if he would ever be able to make love to Sue. He'd been faithful to his wife to her dying day and felt, until recently, that he should maintain that fidelity until *his* dying day. Sue had been patient. She'd let him know, clearly, that *she* was ready. But she understood his reluctance. She'd been widowed three years before Rocorro and had this same disinclination until she met him. There'd been men who'd tried - she was a few years younger than Rocorro and had aged well - but only Rocorro gave her that *tingle* - that's how she'd described it - again.

Then, one night, it happened, and they were both good with it. It was sweet, comfortable and satisfying. She'd slept in his arms the rest of the night, and they'd shared his bed most nights since then. Neither brought up the subject of marriage. They liked what they had.

He turned the kitchen light off, then paused at the alarm keypad next to the door which led into the carport. He armed the system, then stepped outside. He locked his kitchen and storm door, then unlocked his car. Rocco opened the driver's door and plugged his cell phone into its charger. He tried to keep the charge near 100% at all times. He walked to the end of the drive and picked up his morning paper. He always waited to read it until after his morning serves, sitting leisurely with it, more coffee and his favorite breakfast, an Egg McMuffin.

He was halfway back to his car when he heard the vehicle approaching very slowly from the north side of his street. When he turned to look he noticed the headlights were off. He continued to watch, then was amazed to see it stop in front of him.

The front passenger window on the Charger rolled down to reveal a young, bald black male. Internal alarms began going off in Rocorro's mind. He put the paper in his left hand and made his right hand free. He was glad he was wearing his gun belt.

"Mornin'" Luther said.

"Morning," Rocorro answered.

"I got a message fo' you."

The only sound was the Charger idling, along with a bird chirp here and there. The sun had not yet risen so the only light was a street lamp some thirty feet away.

"A message?" Rocorro said. "You sure you got the right guy?"

"You know," Luther said, "you an old man. Old men do shit like read to their grandchildren, play golf, shit like that. If I was you that's what I'd do. Maybe even move to Florida, stop asking all these questions. Questions that'll get you hurt. Know what I'm sayin'?"

More alarms. Rocorro eyed the man carefully, trying to memorize as much as he could about his face and clothes. And about the car. "And you are?"

Luther laughed. "See? There you go, still asking questions. Who I am jus' don't matter, do it? All you need to know is what I jus' told you. It ain't hard. Stop asking questions. That's all."

Rocorro decided to roll the dice. "Message delivered. Now, here's my answer. You tell Tyrone that while he doesn't scare me, I apparently scare him. Otherwise, why's he sending punks like you to speak for him?"

Luther looked puzzled. "Tyrone?" He looked over at the driver, "Do you know Tyrone?" The driver shook his head. Luther looked back at Rocorro. "Tyrone who?"

"Get off my street," Rocorro said, "and tell your boss what I said."

"Shame about your friend," Luther said.

Rocorro froze. "What did you say?"

The man shook his head sadly. "Cryin' shame! Really was. What *was* his name, now?" He snapped his fingers. "Bo! That's it. Musician dude. Really and truly, a cryin' shame."

"What did you do to Bo?" Rocorro shouted as he started towards the car, his hand wrapped around the grip of his pistol. A younger Rocorro would have already drawn the weapon. The older Rocorro did not.

Luther, however, did.

This time he used a silenced semi-automatic. The first bullet struck Rocorro in his chest, the second just below his neck. Both were fired quickly and efficiently. Rocorro immediately went down, just a few feet from the end of his drive.

Luther stared at Rocorro for a moment, then, satisfied he was dead, said, "You shouldn't have messed with The Family, old man." He then said to the driver, "Let's go."

****

Angela Harwell bolted upright in her bed. She looked around, confused for a moment. Then she whispered a single word.

"Grandpa!"

She grabbed her cell phone off the night stand next to her bed and quickly dialed his number. It went to his voicemail.

She was out of bed and had her clothes on in less than 30 seconds. She hit "redial" and again it went to his voicemail.

Oh my God! Oh my God!

She grabbed her 9 mm and badge and flew out her door. She ran down the concrete steps and was in her cruiser, turning the ignition key with one hand and hitting "redial" with the other.

"You have reached Rocco. Leave a message..."

She threw the phone down on the passenger seat, backed out of her space then squealed out towards the complex exit. In the eternity it took for the gate to open, she dialed his number one more time.

Voicemail.

She turned the lights and siren on as soon as she was through the gate. Tears rolled down her cheeks as she tried again to call her grandfather.

Voicemail.

She hit 120 as she drove down Highway 64, which turned into Stage Road when it crossed over Highway 70. Less than a mile later, she turned right onto Charles Bryan.

At first, she couldn't tell anything was wrong. The house was dark and his car was underneath the carport. She used her floodlight to scan the yard and carport. Then she saw him. He had crawled back up the driveway in an attempt to get to his phone. He'd nearly made it. There was a trail of blood that he left along the way.

"Oh, Grandpa," she whispered.

Harwell got on her radio and had her dispatch contact Bartlett PD and Paramedics. She'd used the "officer down" urgency to expedite the response. Then, grabbing a towel she kept in the car, and her weapon, she opened her door and got out.

She held her gun at the ready, carefully aiming it from side to side as she walked towards him, watching, listening, ready for anything or anyone who may be hiding in the shadows. She resisted the urge to run.

Finally, she reached him, and knelt down. She placed her gun next to him, then sat up on her knees and placed her hands over her mouth, unsure what to do. He was facedown, and unmoving. With a quivering voice, she said, "Grandpa?" She laid a hand on his shoulder, and gently shook. There was no response. Trembling, she felt for a pulse. She didn't detect one. She took his hand and placed it open-palmed against her face. She needed to do *something,* but was afraid to move him. She finally laid herself against his body, put her hand in his, cried softly and said tearfully, "It's all my fault. It's all my fault." She could hear the sirens in the distance; suddenly she felt his hand squeeze hers ever so gently. She quickly sat up.

"Grandpa?" She leaned closer. "Grandpa! Can you hear me?"

He weakly attempted a smile, then blinked his eyes open. "Hi, Angel," he whispered, then coughed. A small trail of blood drained from one corner of his mouth. "What are *you* doing here?"

"Oh, Grandpa," she said, "an ambulance is on the way. You're going to be okay." She used a corner of the towel to dab at the blood coming from his mouth. "It's all my fault, Grandpa. I'm so sorry." She began to sob, and her hands shook as she made the futile attempt at doctoring him.

"Angel," he managed, "Shhh. Not your fault. Black... Charger. Tyrone's..." He coughed again, then said, "Tyrone's boys. Shooter... black male. Bald. Maybe killed..." He coughed again. "Bo."

She gently turned her grandfather over. She tore open his bloodied shirt and gasped when she saw the wounds. She placed the towel across his chest and neck and pressed against each bullet hole. As she pushed down, she cried, "You can't die, Grandpa. Not yet. I need you. Don't you dare die!"

"Angel," he said in a barely audible voice, "Listen to me." Harwell became quiet, the sirens louder. She leaned into him, and placed her ear next to his face. He said, "Attic. Look..." He paused, tried to swallow, then said, "... in the attic."

Harwell sat up, bewildered. "Look in the attic?" He nodded. "Why, Grandpa?" He didn't answer. She wiped quickly at her eyes, then immediately reapplied pressure against the wounds. She couldn't help but notice, however, that there was little new blood. She knew what that meant. While her heart was breaking, his was barely beating.

With the ambulance pulling up, she said, "I love you, Grandpa. So, so much."

She saw a barely perceptible nod, then he mouthed, "Love you... too." It was the first time he'd ever told her that, and they would be his last words. His eyes closed and his face fell to the side. Despite heroic attempts by Bartlett's finest, she lost the only family she had left in the world.

She managed to stumble back to her car. She opened her police laptop and entered "Bo Sanders." The details of his murder earlier that morning quickly appeared. That was all she needed to know. This was The Family. This was Tyrone.

She had one more, long cry in her.

She cried until she had no more tears left. She vaguely remembered answering questions. They put out an APB on the Charger. Harwell knew they'd never find it. She watched them load her grandfather into an ambulance.

She then watched it drive away.

As she watched, Harwell recalled one question they'd asked her very clearly.

"Did your grandfather say anything about who may have shot him?"

She looked the investigator in the eye, then said, "No."

Harwell knew she lied.

And she knew why.

Chapter Ten

Dear Diary:

Grandpa is gone.

For the first time since I was a little girl, I feel all alone. I have no one left. My heart is broken, a piece of it gone with him.

Perhaps the cruelest thing of all is the way he died. He was taken from me by someone who has no heart, who has no conscience and who has no sense of right or wrong. The complete opposite of Grandpa. Grandpa's murderer is a coward, a bully picking on someone older and weaker. Perhaps he felt threatened by Grandpa. He should. Because a part of Grandpa lives within me. Tyrone has, at last, made a mistake.

War has been declared.

I will miss so many things about him. Our ballgames, his smile and his phone calls. I'll miss the sound of his voice, his love, guidance and his encouragement. I will miss his strength and especially his wisdom. I relied on that so much.

I don't imagine I will ever eat barbecued nachos again.

I keep asking myself, "What would Grandpa do?"

His favorite movie was Wyatt Earp. There was a very powerful scene where Doc Holiday asks Wyatt what he was going to do after his brother was gunned down in an ambush. Wyatt didn't hesitate:

"Kill 'em all."

It was the law of the land then. It seems appropriate now.

I will bury Grandpa according to his wishes. After that, my life will have but one purpose:

Bury Tyrone.

Harwell saved the entry, then turned off the screen. She sat alone in her apartment, in total darkness. She pushed Tyrone out of her mind for now and thought only of her grandfather.

She felt the tears returning.

She did not try to stop them.

****

Danny Sullivan re-read the text that he'd received from Tyrone earlier that morning: *Party. 10:00 tonight. Be on time.*

It wasn't a party. It was a meeting. It wouldn't start at 10 either. The *Be on time* was three words. Therefore the actual time to meet was three hours past 10, or at 1:00 am. Since there wasn't a location listed, the meeting would take place at Tyrone's home and not one of the safe houses. Apparently Tyrone had gotten his alibi and Danny suspected that holding a meeting this quickly meant something important was on the agenda.

He helped Jasmine load up the last of the suitcases into her Lexus, then secured both boys in their car seats. He gave both a long hug. "Ronnie, Donnie, you be good for your momma and Auntie Carla, you hear me?" They smiled, then said, "Okay, Daddy," nearly simultaneously.

Danny faced Jasmine. She was clearly worried. "Come here, Jas," he said, wrapping his arms around her. She'd told herself she wouldn't cry, but she sobbed into his shoulder anyway. "Shhh, Jas," he said, "don't let the boys see you cry. Everything's gonna work out fine."

Jasmine moved her face from side to side, wiping the tears into his shirt, then regained her composure and leaned back against his arms to face him. "Are you *sure* this is the best way?"

Danny nodded. "It's the only way, baby. Now we got this, okay? We talked about it. You do everything I told you and we'll have a chance. You and the boys aren't safe here. You go stay with Carla for a while and lay low and let me take care of things here. Do exactly what I told you to do as soon as you get there. I'll call you every day, make sure you and Donnie and Ronnie and," he paused, looked down and rubbed her belly, "little what's her name are doing okay."

That made Jasmine smile. She placed her hand on his. "Oh, it's a 'her' huh? How do you know that?"

"Call it..." he said, pausing a moment, "a father's intuition. Besides, it isn't fair that you're the prettiest girl in the family, seeing as how you're the only girl. You need some competition. Keep you on your toes."

She smiled, then kissed him. "I'll miss you."

"Damn right you will. I mean, look at me. All this man, fine as hell."

She laughed, then held his face tenderly. "You're right," she said, "you are fine. And when my phone rings, it better be you telling me that everything else is fine as well." She suddenly squeezed him, and said, "I can't lose you, Danny, I just can't. Me and the boys need you. And so does Isabella."

Danny paused. Isabella. That was his mother's name. He hadn't heard it in a very long time.

"I... really like that name," he said.

"I had a feeling you would. Of course, it could also be Lonnie."

"That's right," he said, "spoil the moment."

A few minutes later, he watched as she drove away and began the five-hour trip to a friend's house in Gordonsville, a little town about a hour or so east of Nashville. He would be due at the meeting about the same time as she would arrive there. She'd gotten a month's leave of absence from her job.

Danny had a month.

He hoped he wouldn't need that long.

****

Special Warfare Officer, and Navy SEAL, David Joseph Sanders watched his CO sign the emergency leave request. They were in an office on a base in Little Creek, Virginia, home of Navy SEAL Teams 2, 4, 10 and 18. He was in his dress uniform, and had already packed for the unplanned trip home. It was nearly midnight. DJ and his team had been on maneuvers and it had taken that long to get word to DJ about his father and get paperwork rushed through that granted him time off.

His Commanding Officer stood, picking up the paper as he did. DJ immediately got out of his own chair, stood rigidly at attention, and waited. He seemed shorter than his actual 5'11", probably because he had little neck between his bald head and broad shoulders. His muscled frame and narrow waist gave him a commanding physical presence.

"At ease, son," his CO said. He stood half a foot taller than DJ and had earned his SEAL trident about the time DJ was born. The only sign of aging he showed, however, was graying hair and a wrinkle here and there. DJ stood at ease, and the officer handed the paper to him. "I'm sorry to hear about your father, DJ. I remember meeting him last year. Will thirty days be enough?"

"Yes, sir."

"I understand he was killed. Murdered. Do they know who did it?"

DJ's face contorted for a brief moment, and his eyes became moist. He was horrified he would cry in front of his CO. He blinked, then regained his composure. "I don't know, sir. I don't believe so."

"You know, son, we are Navy SEALs. But we're also human. I don't mind telling you I cried when my father died. And I still do, sometimes, when I remember him and what he meant to me. I wouldn't be here if not for him. I imagine you feel the same way about your father."

DJ nodded, and a tear made its way down his cheek. "Absolutely, sir."

"It doesn't make you less of a man, son. Nor does it make you less of a SEAL. Now, go bury your father. Spend some time with your family. Then remember you have a family here as well. If you need us for anything, I mean *anything*, all you have to do is call."

He extended his hand, and DJ grasped it. DJ then stepped back, saluted, and the CO returned the salute. "Thank you, sir," DJ said, then turned to leave.

"DJ," his CO said. DJ stopped and faced him. "I didn't know your father well, but there's one thing I remember clearly."

"What's that, sir?" DJ asked.

"He was mighty proud of you. Mighty proud. Maybe that will give you some comfort over the next few days."

DJ nodded. "Yes, sir. It will, sir. Thank you again, sir."

****

Danny didn't drive to the meeting.

Instead, at around a quarter to one that morning, he threw a large duffle bag into the back seat of his newly-acquired, ten-year-old Dodge minivan, complete with a luggage rack, dark tinted windows and wood-grain panels on both sides. Despite more than 170,000 miles on the odometer, it was in reasonably good shape and would serve his purpose. The engine had been rebuilt only 20,000 miles ago and Danny was confident it would get him where he wanted to go.

Danny knew Tyrone would be looking for his Malibu. He'd traded it for the van at a dealership in Little Rock the day before and still had the drive-out tag taped to the back window. He used an old address, a rental that he owned, which would pass scrutiny should the tags be checked.

His new cell suddenly vibrated. It was a text from Jasmine. It said simply, "Arrived safely at Carla's. Everyone's fine. Already did what you asked with the Lexus." He texted back, "Good. Don't worry. ILY." Then, she answered, "ILY2." He smiled, thought about keeping the conversation going, then decided against it. He'd call her tomorrow. He'd bought two pay-as-you-go cells with pre-paid minutes for each of them. When the minutes were used on one they'd switch to the other. He thought, perhaps, he was being a tad overly cautious, but that was fine. Vigilance could not be stressed enough if he was to have any chance of his plan working.

Earlier, he'd sealed his "company" cell phone inside a padded pre-paid envelope and put it into a FedEx drop box near his home. He addressed it to a phone recycling center in California. He knew that Tyrone had a GPS chip installed to track his movements. He toyed with the idea of destroying it but that would give Tyrone knowledge that something was wrong sooner rather than later. Danny needed later. He could also check his messages for a day or two should anyone leave one.

He backed out of his garage, then stopped at the end of the drive. He felt sad knowing his house would be empty for some time. His mail was being forwarded to a private box at a UPS Store. He'd stopped the paper. He kept the utilities on in order to keep the video surveillance up and operating. He'd instructed the alarm company to immediately notify police should they detect any activity whatsoever - unless he informed them ahead of time - for the foreseeable future. He assigned a new password, known only to them, himself and Jasmine.

The first real break Danny had gotten so far was when Jasmine brought up Timecia's information on her work station computer and, lo and behold, there was Harwell's address and cell number, listed under one of her emergency contacts. He hadn't made any attempt to contact her thus far, however. The news of her grandfather's killing, as well as Sanders, had been the top story throughout the day. She'd be too preoccupied with that to deal with him, but contact had to be made soon. He was sure Tyrone was involved and Danny had no intention of dirtying himself with these murders. It merely rushed his and Jasmine's plans, but he was good with that. This way, there'd be no second-guessing, no over-thinking. When the bell rang, you had to get up and face your opponent.

No more talk. Come out swinging.

Still in the driveway, Danny briefly toyed with the idea to call Harwell then and there, but decided it would be better if their first contact was face to face. He backed into the street and began the nearly 30 mile trip from his Whitehaven home to her Lakeland apartment. He had no idea what to expect, especially since he'd never met her. But Jasmine talked to some nurses, and also to a few officers she knew well, and was able to find things out about Harwell that Danny liked. Assets that could prove useful in the field of battle. She was skilled in martial arts and an expert marksman. She was as strong as most men and passionate about her job and the department she worked for. And, by killing her grandfather, Tyrone had just added revenge to her motivation.

The murder of Harwell's grandfather furthered Danny's conviction that nothing, and no one, was off limits. Including Joyce and his children. And knowing this could actually work to Danny's advantage.

He glanced at the time and knew Tyrone would now be wondering where in the hell he was. He was never late for a meeting because Tyrone wouldn't stand for it. It infuriated him to wait, on anything. Whether it was sitting in traffic, waiting on a meal or beginning a meeting - he liked for things to move when he wanted them to move. You learned being on time meant arriving 15 minutes early. Tyrone used to love to say, "If you're on time, you're late as far as I'm concerned. If you get to a meeting exactly when it's supposed to start, you're telling me you didn't want to spend any more time with me than you absolutely had to. That hurts my feelings. And if you're late, you're sending a message that my time isn't important to you. If that happens, God help you."

He could sure use God's help right now.

Thirty-three minutes later, Danny arrived at Harwell's complex. To his great relief, the gate was open. It was a large complex with many streets and he was glad he had GPS technology. He was soon in front of her building. As Danny zeroed in on an empty parking space he saw a white Crown Vic with Government tags. As he got closer, he also observed there were blue lights on the front dash and rear window, as well as maneuverable floodlights mounted on both sides. It was surely Harwell's car. He was glad he wouldn't have to wait another day to meet her.

He parked, got out and pushed the door closed, not bothering to lock it. Carrying a sealed manila envelope, he noiselessly climbed the stairs to the 2nd floor. He didn't have the luxury of darkness despite the hour because, besides the floodlit entrances, every door had a light burning beside it. He could've unscrewed the bulb, but that would do little good. If someone was looking for him, they would've already seen him. He didn't imagine that Tyrone would have anyone watching Harwell's apartment, at least not yet, but he couldn't assume anything. He would just have to take his chances.

He knocked on apartment #6.

Round one had begun.

****

"Where the *fuck* is he?"

Tyrone swore to himself, not expecting an answer. In his private office with him was Rod Man, Luther and Joe. There were nine others in Tyrone's den waiting for a meeting that was supposed to have begun thirty minutes earlier. Tyrone called this meeting to discuss a matter of incredible importance to The Family, and it actually had nothing to do with the two shootings. Rico had, in fact, finally come through and obtained everything Tyrone needed to provide an air-tight alibi on the afternoon Timecia was assaulted, and that made this meeting possible. But it was now 1:30, and that meant Danny was thirty minutes late and counting. Tyrone angrily redialed Danny's number and, as he did the previous eleven times, got his voicemail. He looked at the phone in disbelief, then calmly ended the call without leaving a message. He dialed another number. This time his call was answered.

"Do you have any idea what time it is?" an irritated voice said.

"Not now, Rico. I am *not* in the mood. I need you to do something for me."

"What now?" Rico said. "I sent you everything you needed, didn't I? You should've gotten it, what? Eighteen hours ago? I received confirmation that one of your goons signed for it."

"Rico, did you not fucking hear what I said? Shut up and listen for once. This won't take long. Now, I pay you a lot of money. It's time to earn it. I need you to do something for me right now."

"What do you want, Tyrone? I'll give you two minutes."

"Won't take that long. Turn your computer on and run a location on a phone for me."

Rico sighed. "Hold on a minute."

Tyrone could hear Rico get out of bed and move around. He heard a door open. A minute or so later, Rico said, "Okay, Tyrone, what's the number?"

"It's the one ending in 7993," Tyrone said.

Tyrone waited while Rico ran the trace. "Got it," he said. "It's in Whitehaven, and right now it's not moving. Imagine that. Probably because it's the middle of the fucking night!"

Tyrone let the sarcasm slide. "Where in Whitehaven?"

"I don't know," a sleepy and exasperated Rico answered. "You want the latitude and longitude for Christ sake? Hang on, let me zoom in some." Tyrone waited. "It's somewhere near the airport. Hang on." Tyrone waited. "Yeah, he's at the airport, or at least his phone is. Tell you what, if it starts moving I'll let you know. Okay? Can I go back to bed now?"

He disconnected before Tyrone could answer.

Tyrone dropped the phone from his ear, tapped the screen and then dropped it on his desk in front of him. He thought out loud. "The airport? Why would Danny...?"

Tyrone made a decision. "Luther," he said calmly, "go to

Danny's house. See if he's home."

Luther stood immediately and started towards the door. "Luther!" Tyrone said again. Luther stopped turned to face Tyrone. "Take Joe with you. And, Luther," Tyrone said, "do you think you might be able to control yourself and not shoot anybody this time?"

"Tyrone, I tol' you, man. I had no choice. He said your name. He went for his gun..."

"YOU KILLED A GOD-DAMNED COP!" Tyrone screamed. He forced himself to calm down. "A *cop*, Luther. Or at least he used to be. You *know* how I feel about that. Do you know the kind of manpower they'll use to find out who did this? You should've just gotten the hell out of there." He got off the couch and walked over to Luther. He got right in his face. "Listen to me very carefully. We don't kill cops, or people that used to be cops, and *especially* former cops whose goddamned daughter *is* a cop! Period! And I swear to God, Luther, if word gets out that I had anything to do with this..."

"No one saw us, Tyrone. You heard the news. There ain't no witnesses."

"They got your car on a neighbor's security tape, Luther. They tied it in with the Sander's murder. The cops know it's the same car."

"The cap on Sanders was an accident, Tyrone. I wasn't going to kill him. I tol' you how that happened. And that Charger is in a thousand pieces by now, including the plate. They can look for it all they want."

Tyrone laughed. "You still don't get it, do you? You killed Detective... *Detective* Angela Harwell's grandfather. He was the only family she had. And she's no ordinary cop, Luther. It's hard to explain... she'll *know* I had something to do with it. She wanted my ass *before* this happened. How bad do you think she wants it now?"

Luther looked him in the eye, then said evenly, "You afraid of a woman *cop*? *That's* what this is about?" He snorted in derision.

"Jus' fix it, Tyrone. You always been able to fix it. This is jus' another thing. 'Sides, she can't put you there 'cause you *wasn't* there."

Tyrone stared at Luther, and Luther stared back. Finally, Tyrone said, "You've been with me a long time, Luther. I love you like a brother. But don't think for a minute that I wouldn't kill you."

Luther broke into a wide grin. "I know you would, T."

"Now, go get Danny. I need Danny."

Before the door closed behind Luther and Joe, Tyrone was already dialing Danny's cell again. He knew what would happen before he dialed it, and it did. He didn't leave another message. But Danny's unexplained absence, along with the past few day's events, made Tyrone wonder if they might somehow be connected. He didn't believe in coincidences. He refused to be lulled into a false sense of security. He hoped Luther and Joe would find Danny home, having merely fallen asleep, and they'd bring him back here. Then things would improve immensely. But he didn't believe that would happen. Not with Danny's phone being at the airport.

An unfamiliar ache in his gut began. And with it a feeling that something was very wrong.

It stubbornly refused to go away. And it only served to make him more wary than ever.

Especially now, when he needed things to be running perfectly.

He needed no distractions. No hint that anything was wrong in The Family.

Because it could ruin everything.

Chapter Eleven

As Harwell stood in her grandfather's attic and looked around, it was as if she'd been swept back in time.

She spent the better part of an hour wandering around and reminiscing. The memories were nearly overwhelming. There were clothes that were worn by her grandmother that were supposed to have been given away. She thumbed through the vintage albums her grandfather loved, and she recalled the silly dance moves they did together as the golden oldies vibrated from needle to speakers. The old games, movies and pieces of furniture here and there were all but worthless to others, but priceless to her.

What moved her to tears, however, was their Christmas tree, standing in one corner, surrounded by boxes of ornaments and decorations. The only real Christmases she could remember had been in this house and they'd been insanely happy ones. It would begin every year the day after Thanksgiving. The artificial tree would come downstairs and she and her grandmother would decorate it while her grandfather put lights up outside. Three stockings hung over the fireplace and dozens of treasured holiday decorations were lovingly placed all around the house. Beautifully wrapped presents would soon find themselves under the tree and not a Christmas went by that Harwell wasn't completely spoiled.

She could still hear, as plain as day, her grandfather's voice saying, "I saw Santa Claus!" as the door to her room swung open. This was how every Christmas morning began. Even after she'd moved into her apartment, he'd call and say those same words as soon as she answered the phone, normally a couple of hours earlier than she would've preferred.

All of these traditions continued even after her grandmother's death.

It saddened her to know it would never happen again.

But there was also an old footlocker, placed front and center where it couldn't be missed, that she couldn't remember ever seeing before. An envelope was taped to the top, and, in her grandfather's handwriting, were the words *Angel - To be opened upon my death.*

She decided to delay opening it until she was back in her apartment. She'd waited until everyone had left her grandfather's home before she hauled it down from the attic. She easily carried it to her car, and then upstairs to her apartment. She took it to her bedroom and set it on the floor at the foot of her bed.

She opened the envelope carefully. There was a letter inside. She unfolded the paper, then began to read.

Hello Angel,

If you're reading this it means we are no longer together and I know you must be sad. But we have to be realistic. Death is inevitable, and unless something awful happens, you will long outlive me.

In this locker you will not only find my last will and testament and important legal papers, but other items that I hope you will treasure, as I have.

I'd like to think that, one day, we will all be together again, including your mother and your father. Boy, won't we have some stories to share! Until that happens, I want you to know just how much your grandmother and I loved you. I am so very, very proud of the woman you have become. Everything that has happened has only made you stronger. I took every opportunity I had to say to anyone who would listen, "That's my granddaughter!"

Don't mourn me. I had a wonderful life. Cremate me and scatter my ashes in left field at the stadium Then, every time you go to a game, tilt one back for me and know that I am there, with you as always.

We had a good run, you and I. You were the reason I was able to keep going after Grandma died. You always had time for an old man and that was most special, indeed. Keep your generous nature, your fighting spirit and your sense of right and wrong.

Allow yourself some happiness, whatever that may be, wherever you may find it. Follow your instincts. They'll never let you down.

Finally, Angel, if you ever find yourself in a bind, listen carefully. I'll be putting in to be your new guardian angel. I'll let you know whether to duck or jump.

I do so love you, Angel. Next to your Grandma, more than anyone. I wished I'd been able to say it more. To both of you.

Grandpa

Harwell allowed a sad smile, then whispered a prayer of thanks for this unexpected gift. She set the letter aside, knelt down beside the locker and unbuckled the straps. Upon opening it, the first thing she saw was a thick, brown leather binder, zippered on three sides. She unzipped it and found his will, the deed to his house, his investment portfolio, a savings account book and a sheet of paper which contained all of his user ID's and passwords that he used online for his credit and debit cards. She also found the title to his car and a life insurance policy. She replaced all the items, zipped it back and set it aside. She wasn't the least bit interested with what she was about to inherit.

The next items she pulled from the locker were a bundle of sealed Manila envelopes, rubber-banded together, each marked with a different year. She opened the first one. Inside she found old ticket stubs. She poured them out onto her bed and stared at them. They were the stubs to every ballgame she, her grandfather and grandmother had attended that year. On each stub he'd written the score, and whether the Birds had won or lost. She picked up a random ticket. It was from a few years ago and they'd won, 8-3. She closed her eyes and tried to remember, but it was impossible. She would have been 14 at the time, skinny and still jumping at the slightest noises in the night, real or imagined. Sometimes they would make her scream, often without her even knowing it, and she would suddenly find her grandpa in her room, holding her, soothing her, whispering that he was there and no one could hurt her, until she was able to sleep again.

Who will hold me now? she wondered.

His high school baseball glove came out next. He played shortstop and lettered every year beginning with his sophomore year. She held the glove next to her chest and tried to imagine her grandfather as a young boy, no more than 15 or 16, grabbing this glove from a locker and running out onto a baseball field, his whole life still in front of him. He'd told her many times that he could have played college ball and then who knows? But he decided to take a year off first, and then a letter from Uncle Sam changed his plans.

She took his Army fatigue shirt from the locker next, and put it on. She looked at herself in the dresser mirror, lifted her right arm and fingered the hole in the shirt just below her armpit. She remembered the story. He'd been wading through a chest-deep swamp, more afraid of snakes than snipers, holding his weapon high above his head when the bullet tore through the shirt. It scared him far more than it hurt him. It was little more than a flesh wound, but there was a lot of blood and it burned like hell. It also earned him a Purple Heart, but he gave little credence to his deserving what he considered a badge of honor designated for those who were truly wounded.

Wearing the shirt, Harwell recalled the many times he'd told her how the thirteen months he'd spent in Vietnam had been the most important in his life. He'd witnessed cruelty and oppression unimaginable to him before he'd been drafted. Hunger, poverty, disease and war were all rampant in an otherwise beautiful country. He made a vow: he'd dedicate his life to try and level the playing field, to protect the weak from those who would take advantage.

He, of course, chose law enforcement.

His police badge was next. How many times had she seen him proudly wear it? She polished it against the green cotton fabric of the fatigue shirt and it shone as brightly as it had the first day he took the oath to protect and serve. He'd told her often that, as a baby, she'd been fascinated with it.

She still was.

Then Harwell retrieved a large photo album from the locker. She took it to her kitchen table and sat down. The first picture was of her grandfather and grandmother on their wedding day. In this picture time stood still. They were both young, healthy, happy and obviously thrilled to have just taken their vows. Their life together could be measured in mere hours at that moment, hours that would turn into days, days into weeks, weeks into months and months into years. Harwell looked at the date on the picture and realized when her grandmother died, they'd been married twice as long as she'd been alive, yet their love for each other never diminished. Up until the very end, Harwell remembered her grandfather coming home, sneaking up behind his wife, wrapping her in a bear hug and then kissing her neck playfully until she'd finally make him stop. He'd then walk away, occasionally smacking her behind as he left, grinning and whistling.

Harwell asked her once, "Grandma, does it bother you when he does that?"

"Honey," she answered, "it would bother me if he didn't." And then she smiled, and winked.

The next page was another wedding picture, but this one was her mother and father. Harwell had never seen it before, didn't even know it existed. Her mother's gown was stunning, and her father looked almost fairy-tale handsome in his Marine dress uniform. What struck Harwell most of all, though, was how sublimely happy her mother looked. Harwell had never seen that look before. There was a light in her mother's eyes that, apparently, was extinguished forever after her father's death. Harwell silently wished she could have brought some sort of joy to her mother. She wondered what she'd done wrong, what she might have done differently, but then she remembered her grandfather's words to her, spoken many times:

What happened was not your fault, Angel. Never, ever think it was. Your mother did what she thought she had to do to protect you. Whether or not it was right or wrong doesn't matter now.

What you have to remember, what you <u>must</u> remember, is that she loved you very much, enough to give you the kind of life she wanted you to have, the only way she knew how.

There were more pictures, the majority of Harwell with her grandparents on different trips, vacations, birthday parties, Christmases, Halloweens, cookouts and other special occasions, and in every one Harwell was smiling. And as she looked through the album, she realized that her grandfather had been right. She'd had a wonderful life and her mother *knew* it would be this way. And with this realization she felt a weight lift from her that, until that moment, she didn't even know she carried. This weight had been with her ever since her grandfather took her away from the trailer that horrible night. It was the reason she was always pushing herself to be stronger, faster and never being satisfied. She knew now these invisible demons were likely what made her so afraid of getting close to anyone. *Maybe now there would be room for someone.*

She spent more than an hour looking through the snapshots. She laughed, and she remembered, and she sighed. Now and then, a tear fell. At last she closed the book, and went back to the locker. She laughed again when she looked inside. There were two bottles of Samuel Adams Lager, one marked *Angel* and the other *Grandpa - One for the road.* She took them to her fridge, knowing exactly when she would retrieve them.

There was one item left. It was wrapped in tissue paper. When she finished taking off the paper, she sat on the bed and clutched her childhood friend close to her heart for a long, long time. Finally, she held it out in front of her, and smiled.

"Oh, Tigger," she whispered, "we're going to be okay now." Harwell took the stuffed animal and laid him next to her pillow. It was late, and she was exhausted. She laid down next to him, and with her lights still on, fell asleep.

She was awoken by a knock at her door. In seconds, she had the Glock in her hand and had turned out the lights.

Luther and Joe slowly rolled up to Danny's house, and stopped the Mustang in front just past the driveway. The two men stayed put at first, content to watch the house, looking for any movement or signs of life such as a light turning on in any of the windows. Nothing happened of course. But they had no way of knowing that they had missed Danny by about an hour.

Luther lit a cigarette. Joe fanned the smoke and complained, "You have to do that now? You can't wait?"

Luther laughed. "You wanna know somethin' Joe? You been a real asshole since you quit smokin'. A real asshole. You don't like it? Go outside, check the house. See if you can wake Danny up. Otherwise, shut the fuck up. You hear me?"

Joe shook his head, then opened the passenger door and got out. He slammed the door in a show of meager defiance, but he was smart enough not to push Luther too far. Luther outranked him, and was the guy next in line should anything happen to Tyrone. He was also very aware that Luther was quite willing to kill and completely unafraid to die. He seemed more machine than human. Joe imagined him as his friend, but knew that a bullet through his head from Luther's gun was but a split-second from reality. He had a very short fuse. Luther never hesitated. Joe knew of at least a dozen killings by Luther's hand, most ordered by Tyrone. There were likely more.

Joe, however, wasn't the stereotypical gangster. He wasn't particularly violent. Like Danny, he was in it for the money. Joe actually had killed only one human being in his life, a rival gang member, and it was self-defense. The teen had been sent to kill a Family member, any Family member, and had fired first, putting a bullet into Joe's leg before Joe returned fire. He hated killing - it had actually made him physically ill. Luther had laughed when he saw him puking afterwards. Pulling the trigger had no affect on Luther whatsoever. In his mind, a man - or woman - who deserved killing, deserved killing. He lived the credo of the only book he'd ever read, Jack London's *Call of the Wild*. Eat or be eaten. Kill or be killed. So very simple.

Joe walked warily around the house, keeping a distance of about 10 feet at all times. The back yard was fenced and Joe wasn't about to go through the gate. He had an intense fear of Pit Bulls, or any large breed, and had learned the hard way that just because you didn't hear a dog didn't mean that one wasn't around. Especially when there was a sign like Danny had on the gate that warned: *Beware of Dog.*

He made his way back to the front of Danny's house, then decided to ring the doorbell. He clearly heard the two-tone chime inside. After a few seconds he rang it again, then knocked on the door. "Danny?" he said, and knocked again, louder this time. "Danny? You home?" Getting no response, he went back to the car.

He got in, then looked over at Luther. He had finished his cigarette, but the inside still smelled like smoke. Joe lowered his window a few inches, then said, "I don't think he's home, Luther."

Luther used the control on his side to lower Joe's window the rest of the way. He stared at the house for a time, then said, "You know somethin' Joe? Danny Boy sure does keep a nice yard, doesn't he? You see what I'm sayin'? That there is pride in where you live."

Joe looked over, then said, "Yeah, Luther, it's real nice. What do you want to do now?"

Luther shook his head. "I don' know. You wanna go in? Look around?"

"Don't see why. If Danny was home he'd have come to the door. Besides, could be a dog in there."

Luther laughed. "You afraid of dogs, Joe?"

"I'm afraid of teeth, Luther."

"Well, even if there ain't a dog there's bound to be an alarm." Luther took his phone, tapped it twice, then held it up to his ear. Almost immediately, he said, "He ain't home, Tyrone. Don't look like anyone is." He listened for a few seconds, then said, "Okay, T.

On our way." He dropped the phone in the console, then said to Joe, "Looks like we gonna have the meetin' without Danny Boy."

Joe said, "You have any idea what this meeting's all about?"

Luther shook his head. "All I know is that it's somethin' big. What T tol' me, the biggest thing The Family's ever done. I ain't never seen him so anxious to get back to work."

"You think Danny actually took off like Tyrone said?"

Luther glanced over his shoulder, then roared away from the curb. "Don' know, but I tell you somethin' Joe. I sho' wouldn't want to be in his shoes right now."

****

Danny knocked again, and waited. He held both his hands out to his sides, in plain view, so that Detective Harwell would be able to clearly see them, even through the peep hole on her door. He eyed the outside light, and again resisted the urge to unscrew the bulb that made him such an easy target. Impatient, he knocked again. "Come on, Detective," he said out loud, "please be home."

"Oh, I'm home. Now, who the hell are you?"

Startled, Danny looked to his left, and was shocked to see Harwell climbing the last step on the rear stairwell. Her Glock was leveled straight at him, and he slowly turned to face her, careful to keep his hands in plain view. He was dressed in shorts and tank so there would be no mistake that he was unarmed. Danny looked down and saw that the laser from her weapon was locked on his heart and the beam was steady. He may have been nervous, but she obviously wasn't. He slowly raised his hands without being asked.

Danny cocked his head toward the door. "Were you inside when I knocked?"

She nodded. "I was."

"How did you...?"

"I'm light on my feet," she answered. She walked towards him, and said, "Now, turn around, very, very slowly." When he hesitated, she said, "Look, I'm in a bad mood. You really need to do what I tell you." He turned around, then, satisfied he was indeed unarmed, she said, "Okay, turn around and face me."

Danny did as he was asked, then said, "I'm here for a very good reason, Detective Harwell. And I know you're hurting. I'm sorry about your grandfather."

Harwell gripped her weapon tighter. Sweat formed on her forehead. "You better start making sense. Who the hell are you, how do you know me and why are you knocking on my door?"

"My name is Danny Sullivan, Detective. Timecia Harrison gave me your name."

"Timi..." she stopped, and lowered her weapon for just a split second. She quickly re-aimed it and said, "How do you know Timi?"

Danny took a deep breath, then exhaled it. "Detective, I'm not comfortable outside here in all this light. Can we please...?"

"How the *hell* do you know Timecia?" Harwell spat the words at Danny, and the laser moved to the middle of his forehead. His hands involuntarily raised even higher.

"Detective," he said softly, "I was there when Tyrone beat her up." He nodded towards the envelope. "It's all here. Every detail."

Harwell let that sink in. "You were there...?" She paused, swallowed, then said angrily, "Were you also there this morning, at my grandfather's house?"

He shook his head. "No. But I have a pretty good idea who was."

She eyed the envelope in his hand. "But you *were* there with Timecia? And you didn't *help* her? What kind of a man *are* you?"

Danny's eyes searched for the right words. "A man with a family, Detective. My boys need their dad. I didn't want to make my pregnant wife a single mom. Believe me when I tell you there was nothing I could do. But that's why I'm here now. I want to help her. And I want to help you."

She motioned her gun towards the parking lot, then said, "Go away, Danny. I don't need any help."

"Detective, please," Danny pleaded, "I know things, things that may help. I walked away from The Family tonight. I'm supposed to be at a meeting right now. You don't let me in your apartment, you tell me to leave, I'm as good as dead. I sent my wife and kids out of town so they would be safe, but I stayed. You can't fight Tyrone alone. I can't fight him alone. But, maybe together..."

Harwell mulled that over. "Why should I trust you?"

"Because," Danny said, dropping his arms, "you can't trust anyone else." Before she could say anything, he said, "Detective, I believe The Family killed your grandfather."

She lowered her gun completely. She said, softly, "Before he died, he described a black male, bald, riding in a black Charger. Said he was one of Tyrone's boys."

Danny nodded. "Luther. I was pretty sure it was him. Please, let me help you Detective. I want this as bad as you do."

She looked into his eyes. She decided he was telling the truth. Maybe there was room for one more. "What are our chances, Danny Sullivan?"

He hesitated, became suddenly thoughtful, then pretended to run figures through his head. "Well," he said, "if everything goes in our favor, and we're very, very lucky, maybe, just maybe, one snowball's chance in hell."

She nodded. "I've faced worse." Then she said, "What have you got in mind?"

"That meeting tonight," he said. "Something's about to go down. We've got to find out what. I may know a way to do that, but we don't have much time."

She nodded, turned and started down the steps. Over her shoulder she said, "Give me a minute." After about one minute the locks on her door unlocked, the door opened and Harwell motioned him inside.

"I gotta know how you do that," he said as he went in, and then the door closed behind them.

Chapter Twelve

Tyrone stood, and everyone knew the meeting was about to begin. It was long past the scheduled start, and Tyrone ordinarily wouldn't be happy. This meeting should have been over by now. But he was too excited to dwell on that.

"Gentlemen," he said to the twelve men seated around him, "I have big news. No longer will I be satisfied remaining within the limits of the city we all call home. The Family is about to expand."

He paused, letting his words sink in. "I have ambition," Tyrone continued. "We *all* have ambition. You, my most trusted Family members, have served me well for a long time. Your reward for that loyalty is about to pay off in ways you cannot imagine."

Tyrone was a polished speaker, particularly when it came to motivation. A few of the men allowed themselves to smile. Others sat emotionless, wanting to hear more before believing what sounded too good to be true.

"Why, gentlemen?" Tyrone asked, "*Why* should we allow rival gangs in say, Nashville, Atlanta and other major markets easily within our reach, make a fortune on product that we could provide? Especially if ours was better quality, cheaper and, most importantly, available?" He made eye contact with a few of his men. "Luther? Tyler? Josh? Any reason at all?"

Luther spoke. "Lotta miles, T. We're spread pretty thin now. How we gonna manage all this extra territory?"

"Luther!" Tyrone scolded, "have you no faith in me? Have I ever let you down? Gentlemen," he continued, "I have been *busy!*"

Tyrone's growing excitement was contagious. He had their attention.

"I've been doing the math, gentlemen. See if y'all come to the same conclusions I have." The room was pin-drop quiet now. They were the students and Tyrone the professor, and they hung on every word.

"When a kilo of powder arrives in Mexico from Colombia, it costs around 12 G's. By the time it gets to us, it's been cut down from about 85% pure to about 60% - if we're lucky - and yet it *increases* in price another 25%, give or take. In essence, all the middlemen between Colombia and Memphis are taking money from The Family! Money that rightfully belongs to me and to all of you! Does that seem fair?"

No one answered. They didn't have to.

"Now, what if I were to tell you that I'd be able to ship that same product from Mexico, directly to here, with zero middlemen, at Colombian purity, at a substantial discount and enough quantity that when it's all said and done, when it's all sold, I will make every man in this room," he paused, then finished, "a millionaire."

That last word had the desired result. The men were hooked.

"Y'all heard right." Tyrone said. "There's no mistake. I told you I had big news. And I challenge any man to come up with one single reason why you shouldn't believe every word I just said. Anyone?" No one made a sound. "Seriously now, you can speak up. Y'all got nothing to fear. Have I *ever* lied to you?"

Luther loudly cleared his throat. Tyrone looked at him. "Luther? You want to say something?"

"Well, boss, there was that time in New Orleans when you told me you had three beautiful ladies in your hotel room with you. What I heard was, there was only two and one of them was bow-legged."

Tyrone looked at Luther, and feigned anger. Then, barely suppressing a smile, said, "Let me tell you something, Luther. She wasn't bow-legged until *after* she got T-Boned." He and Luther burst out laughing, then the rest of the men joined in. When it died down, Tyrone said, "Ok, Luther. You got me. And gentlemen, laughing is good. I like to laugh. And since we're all in a good mood now, allow me to make it even better." He walked into an adjoining room and returned with a silver Halliburton briefcase. He placed it on a coffee table and opened it. He reached inside and pulled out stacks of banded, brand-new $100 bills. He began tossing them to his men, one at a time.

"This is ten grand for each of you, gentlemen," he announced as he threw the packets. "It's not a loan. It's yours free and clear. Let's call it a down payment. Better yet, a bonus. Count it if you want. I want you to remember this feeling." He paused, dramatically. "Now, imagine how it will be, how your life will change forever, when I give, to each of you, your very own briefcase with one hundred of these babies," Tyrone held up a packet up for all to see, then slapped it against his other hand, "placed inside. One million dollars. One... *million*."

No one said anything. It had yet to sink in.

"Well," Tyrone said, "doesn't anyone want to know any details?"

"You just tell us what you want us to do, Tyrone," one of the men said.

"What I want," Tyrone said, "is what you've all given so willingly over the years. I want. I *need*, your undying loyalty. I want you to understand that there is only one family and that is *The* Family." His voice grew louder and it drew them all in. "I want you to trust me and know, I mean *know*, that I will *never* let you down." He let his voice drop, but it remained filled with emotion. "Never forget this day, gentlemen, this historic moment. If we work together, as Family, *we will make history*." He stood where all the men could clearly see him. "Once Family?" he said, and thrust a fist in the air.

They all leapt to their feet, and with their own fists raised in solidarity, exclaimed, "Always Family!" They repeated, "Family!" again and again, giddy with the prospect of riches promised. Luther and Tyrone made eye contact, and shared a slight, knowing nod.

Just then Tyrone's phone rang. He looked at the caller ID, then declined the call. Putting the phone back in his pocket, he said, "Gentlemen, I need to make a call. That's all I have for you tonight anyway. Go home, get some sleep and take care of The

Family business the way you always do. Keep tonight open. I will be in touch."

They began to make their way out when Tyrone said, "Wait. One last thing." They all stopped. "I shouldn't have to mention how top, top secret all this is, but I will. No one can breathe a word about this to anyone, and gentlemen I mean anyone. Not to your newborn baby, not to your long dead great, great grandmother. If you do, you will find yourself buried next to her. Is that understood?" No one said anything, but the look in their eyes answered Tyrone's question. "Well, alright then." Tyrone looked at his watch. "Look for my call."

One of the men said, "When, Tyrone? I mean, how long before we all rich?"

"Why Anton? You in a hurry?"

"Well, I been poor a long time. Sure would like to know how rich feel." Everyone laughed, and a nearly simultaneous chorus of, "I know that's right!" filled the room.

Tyrone smiled. "Soon, Anton, very soon. Now y'all go home and dream about being able to buy everything you've ever wanted." As they began to file out, Tyrone said, "Luther, Joe, hold on a minute. I may have a job for you."

Luther and Joe sat back down, and as soon as the others had left Tyrone was back on his phone. "Sorry about that, Rico. What've you got?"

"Couple of things. One, your phone's on the move. It's somewhere over Arizona right now. Problem is, when I checked, there's no commercial airline that's flying over Arizona at this point in time."

"Then how the hell is Danny doing it?" asked Tyrone.

"He's not, Tyrone. Couldn't be. But his phone is."

"How's that possible?"

"If you were listening, you'd have heard me say there's no *commercial* airline flying over Arizona. There is, however, a FedEx jet on the way to California that should be, at this moment, over the state of Arizona. I seriously doubt Danny's on the plane.

He mailed the phone, Tyrone. Simple as that."

"Mother fucker!" Tyrone said. "I knew it! I got me a runner. And I don't need that. Not now. What do you got on the vehicles?"

"Now that," Rico said, "is also very interesting. The Malibu is sitting on a used car lot in North Little Rock, Arkansas. I looked up the VIN and the title's been transferred to an LLC. He apparently traded it for a used minivan, a 2003 Caravan. There is, of course, no chip on it. I can't trace it."

Tyrone swore again. "What about the Lexus?"

"He didn't sell it, or if he did the title hasn't been transferred yet. It's in a town called Gordonsville, Tennessee. It's on the other side of Nashville. I can put you within ten feet of it whenever you want."

Tyrone pondered that, then made a decision. "I'll call you back, Rico. And thanks. You may be a pain in the ass, but you are good."

"It's how I roll," Rico said, then hung up.

Tyrone looked at Luther and Joe. "Go get some sleep boys. Actually, sleep in one of the guest rooms here. I don't want you straying too far. Make sure the Mustang is all filled up. Gonna make a little road trip in a few hours."

"We goin' after Danny?" Luther asked.

"I don't know about Danny," said Tyrone, "but make sure you have a couple of those infant car seats strapped in the back seat before you leave. If he's done what I think he's done, you're going to need them."

"We gonna take his *kids*?" Joe asked.

"What you're going to *do*," Tyrone said, suddenly angry, "is what I *tell* you, Joe! Do you have a problem with that?"

"No problem at all, T," Luther answered quickly. "He's good. Let's go, Joe." He shoved Joe towards the door, and left Tyrone contemplating the ways he was going to make Danny pay for trying to walk away from The Family.

He would make him an example.

This time, Tyrone thought to himself, *when my gun is between his legs...*

****

Later that morning, Navy Seal DJ Sanders walked through the exit doors at Memphis International Airport to the pickup area for incoming flights. He soon found his sister waiting beside her red Impala, the trunk open. He was in uniform and she was able to immediately spot him. She ran to him, and he dropped his bag and hugged her for a long time. Finally, she stepped back and looked at him.

"Oh, DJ," she said, "I'm so glad you're here."

"How's Momma, Lucy?"

"Not good," Lucy answered, "but she'll be better now that you're home. She hasn't stopped crying since it happened. None of us have." Her voice broke and she dabbed at her eyes with a tissue. DJ fought, once again, to control his own emotions.

"It's good you were able to get to her so quickly," DJ said.

She took his arm and they walked toward her car. "Well, soon as I got the call, I threw some things in a bag and was in my car. I had a full tank, filled up the night before, thank God. I flew down the interstate; I had no idea how fast I was going. Had one cop pull me over when I was going through Jackson, but as soon as I mentioned Mr. Rocorro's name he escorted me right to Momma's front door. It was pretty much just me and her all day yesterday. It's been awful, DJ. Just awful."

DJ threw his bag into the open trunk, then closed the lid. "Who else is here?"

"You wouldn't believe it," she said as they both got into the car, DJ behind the wheel. "Earl closed the car lot for the whole day. All those guys are at the house. A bunch of his musician friends are there. They brought food, and coffee and I'm pretty sure I smelled liquor. They're all with Momma right now, which is good. I didn't have to leave her by herself. Family will be getting here pretty much all day today. That apartment's going to be full by tonight."

When they'd gotten buckled in, and just before he drove away, they looked at each other. Lucy said, "You look good, DJ. Really good."

DJ grinned at her. "You," he said, "are too skinny. Don't you eat?"

She hadn't laughed in two days, and it felt good. "Hard to eat when you're either in class or studying eighteen hours a day."

The ride to the apartment began, each lost in their own thoughts. Normally, they looked forward to coming home, but not this time. DJ's thoughts were interrupted when Lucy spoke.

"DJ? How long are you going to be home?"

"I've got 30 days leave," he said. "I guess it depends on how things are going. What about you?"

"I can't stay that long," she said. "I have to get back to school. Right after the funeral."

"Okay," he said, "I understand."

"DJ," she said again, then hesitated.

He looked at her. "What's on your mind, Lucy?"

She shook her head, and began crying. "I don't know," she said, "it's just that, well, I can't stand the thought that whoever did this to Daddy might get away with it. Okay? He, or they, whoever, just shot Daddy in the head and then dumped him out in the parking lot like he was a sack of fucking garbage!"

DJ stopped the car. He'd never heard her use that word before. He looked over to her and said, "I know, Lucy. I know. It's all I've thought about. I got this. Believe me, I got this. Okay?"

She nodded. "I'll never be happy until whoever did this to Daddy is found, DJ."

"Bin Laden couldn't hide from us, Lucy. Neither can they."

She looked at him. "I believe you, DJ. She took a business card out of her purse and handed it to him.

DJ took the card and read out loud, "Angela Harwell. Detective." He looked at Lucy. "Isn't that Mr. Rocorro's daughter?"

"It's his granddaughter."

"That's right, I remember now. She lived with him after her

mother was killed."

"It was actually suicide."

"Oh, no," DJ said, "I never knew."

"I didn't either until a couple of hours ago," Lucy said. "Momma told me. She also told me that Mr. Rocorro and Daddy met up at B.B.'s the very night it happened. She didn't know why they were meeting, but it was the first time in a couple of years. Then they're both murdered by someone in a black Charger not three hours apart. You may want to call her, DJ. See what she knows."

He put the card in his shirt pocket.

Calling Harwell would be a good place to start.

****

The doorbell woke Jennifer Riley from a fitful sleep. She'd not left her apartment since learning about the murder of her friend, Bo. When she'd gotten the news she was fearful that she'd played a part in his death. Then, when she heard that Rocorro had been killed that same morning, she was overwhelmed with guilt.

It was ripping her apart, almost as if she'd pulled the trigger herself. She'd had little to eat and had ignored dozens of calls on her cell. She ended up turning it off. She didn't want to talk to anyone until she could figure out what to do.

But when her doorbell rang she thought it might be her sister checking on her.

My sister might know what to do Jennifer thought. *She always knows what to do.*

She ran to the door in pajama pants and t-shirt, and looked through the peephole. Instead of her sister, however, she saw a black man in a dark suit. He looked professional and important.

The man noticed the peephole darken when Jennifer looked through. He said, "Jennifer Riley? MPD. Please open the door, ma'am. I need to talk to you." She was afraid to make a sound. "Miss Riley, please. There's nothing to be afraid of. It won't take long."

"Why do you want to talk to me? Am I in trouble?" Jennifer finally said.

"I'm an investigator, ma'am. And no, you're not in trouble."

Jennifer was petrified. "Do you have to come in? I mean, can't I just come down later and talk to you at the precinct or something?"

"No, ma'am," the voice said with authority, "we need to talk now. I have credentials. I'll hold them up so you can see. I won't keep you. It's just routine questions."

Jennifer looked through the peephole again and saw what appeared to be a legitimate badge and ID. She unlocked the deadbolt and opened her door until the chain caught. "Can I see your badge again?" He held it up for her. Convinced, but still nervous, she closed the door, unhooked the chain, and said, "Come in."

The man entered her apartment, and identified himself as Sergeant Malone. He declined her invitation to sit. He noticed she was shaking.

"Relax, ma'am," Malone said, "you're not in trouble. I'm investigating the two homicides that happened early yesterday morning, Mr. Sanders and Mr. Rocorro. We think they're related. We understand that both victims were at the club, at B.B. Kings, the evening before, and that you were working that night."

Jennifer sat down on her couch, and nodded. In a voice barely above a whisper, she said, "They were there."

"How well did you know the victims?"

"I... I didn't know Mr. Rocorro. I met him that night. Bobo was my friend." Her eyes filled with tears again.

"Miss Riley," Malone said, "one of your co-workers told us that you..."

Jennifer broke down at that point. She sobbed, "I'm so sorry. They told me they wouldn't hurt them. I didn't know. I swear to God, I didn't know!" She buried her face in her hands. Malone found a box of tissues and placed it beside her. She took one.

"Ma'am," Malone said, "what was it you didn't know? And

who are *they*?"

"Two men... came in right after Rocco, or Mr. Rocorro, went to talk to Bo. They gave me a phone number and $100 and said to call them when Mr. Rocorro left. I had no idea... I mean, I asked if they were going to hurt them. They laughed and said no, it was nothing like that, but that it was real important. When Mr. Rocorro left, I called them. And now they're both dead. I never should have trusted them."

"Do you remember what the men looked like?"

"Yeah, one was... shouldn't you be writing this down or something?'

There was just the slightest hesitation, then Malone patted his breast pocket and said, "I've got a digital recorder going. Much better than trying to write it all down. I've should have told you that right away. I'm sorry. Will you acknowledge that I'm recording you and that I have your permission to do so?"

"Oh, yeah, sure. That makes sense. You have my permission."

"Now," Malone said, "tell me about the two men."

"One was tall, bald, and had lots of tattoos all over him. He was probably 25 or so. The other was shorter and had long hair, dreadlocks I think, and a goatee. He might've been a little older. Hard to tell."

"Do you think you'd recognize them, like in a lineup or a mug shot?"

"Oh, yes, sir," she said emphatically. "I'd know them anywhere."

"Have you, uh, spoken to anyone else about these men?"

She looked puzzled by that question. "No, you're the only one. Shouldn't you know that?"

"Not necessarily, ma'am. We're not the only department looking into these homicides. Rocorro was former Bartlett PD, so their guys are looking. I heard the FBI was called in as well."

"I see. Okay."

"Let me ask you a very important question, ma'am. Do you think that number you called might still be on your cell phone?"

Jennifer brightened. "Hey," she said, "I never thought of that." She started to get up, then said, "But... how did you know I called from my cell?"

Malone shook his head condescendingly. "C'mon, Miss Riley. Give me some credit. Every young, pretty girl I know has a cell phone practically glued to her hand. And they'd use it to call someone in the next room. Now, am I right?"

Jennifer nodded. "You're right. Hang on, I'll go get it." She jumped off the couch, excited to think she might be able to help catch the guys. She stopped as soon as she was up and said, "What about the $100 bill? I still have it. Do you think you might be able to get a print or something from it?"

Malone smiled. "We just might. You know, you'd make a good detective. Tell you what, I'll check it out and then call you when you can get it back."

"I don't want it," she said as she walked down the hall to her bedroom. She found the cell, and the bill, and was scrolling through old calls while she walked back. Then, delighted, and just as she entered her living room, she said, "Hey! I think I found it!"

She held out the phone and the C-note to Malone. He took them from her, and she noticed that he'd put on latex gloves. "Why are you wearing those?" she asked.

He smiled at her. "You've just given me evidence," he said, putting the money and phone in his inside pocket. "How would it look if *my* prints were on them?"

She nodded. "Of course. Maybe I wouldn't be such a good detective after all, huh?"

Malone moved closer to Jennifer and placed a hand on her shoulder. "You're just upset, Miss Riley. It's understandable. You've been through a terrible ordeal."

The gesture was comforting to her. He had a nice face and very unusual eyes. She found she couldn't stop looking at them.

Malone then said, "Tell me, Miss Riley..."

"Jennifer," she said, then blushed. "Please, call me Jennifer."

He smiled again. The hand on her shoulder moved to her face.

"Tell me, Jennifer, are you alone?"

She was confused by the question. "Well, yeah, but why do you want to know that?"

"No reason." Then, ominously, he said, "You were right, you know."

"About... what?"

"You shouldn't have trusted the men at the club that night. In fact, you're much too trusting. Letting me in your apartment is another example. Big mistake." Before she could react, Malone put his hands around her neck, positioned his thumbs under her chin and easily lifted her off the floor. Her legs kicked wildly, and she desperately grabbed his forearm and tried to break free. It was futile. Malone was too strong.

"Far as I'm concerned, Jennifer, *you* killed those men."

She recognized suddenly what made his eyes so unusual. They were almost dead; cold and cruel. Jennifer managed a weak scream, but he quickly stifled it when his thumbs moved from her chin to her windpipe and he squeezed, tighter and tighter. He smiled as he watched her struggle.

"That's it," he said, "keep fighting. I like it when y'all fight."

As time passed and her kicks weakened, he squeezed still harder, effectively crushing her windpipe. Jennifer's vision of Malone was replaced with flashes of white light. She had the sensation of floating. Sound was muffled, but she could clearly hear her heart beating.

Bump bump. Bump bump. Bump bump.

His smile turned into a sadistic grin. When he sensed she was on the edge of death, he suddenly gave a brutal, practiced twist and broke the trusting hostess's neck. He tossed her to the floor like a broken doll.

Bump bump. Bump bump.

She landed in a motionless heap, and heard one final beat of her heart.

Bump bump.

****

Malone admired his work, then made a call.

"Hey, T. Got the phone... No, she hadn't talked to anyone... Yeah, I believed her... No, she's through talking... Okay, on my way."

He was whistling as he closed the door to Jennifer's apartment.

And there was one less witness for Tyrone to worry about.

Chapter Thirteen

Lt. Mitchell Matz was reviewing a report when Harwell walked into his office without knocking. He looked up at her and said, "Detective, you shouldn't be at work this soon."

Harwell stood there for a moment, then without a word, laid her badge on his desk. He glanced at the badge, set the report down, then looked back up at Harwell.

"What's this?" he asked.

Harwell found herself at a complete loss as to how to answer his question. He was more than her boss. He was a mentor, friend and the consummate example of a good cop and good human being. He'd been a lieutenant for five years, but had spent 15 before that cruising some of the roughest sections of the Bluff City and had earned his bars.

"Angela," he said again, eyeing the badge, "what are you doing?"

She closed the door, then faced him. "Mitch, I'm sorry, but I need some time."

"Of course you do," he said softly, "and I understand completely. But what does that have to do with you coming in here and putting your badge on my desk?"

Without a word, she turned around to leave. "Detective!" he said, more urgently, just as she had her hand on the door. She stopped but didn't turn around. "What the hell are you doing?"

"Please, Mitch," she said, "this is hard enough." She turned and faced him. "There are things I need to do. Things I may *have* to do." The look in Harwell's eyes told Matz he would not be able to change her mind. After a moment, she said, "I want to thank you for everything. You're a damn fine cop."

"As are you, Detective. I've never met a better one."

"There was one," she said. "My grandfather."

Matz nodded. "Listen," he said, "I don't know exactly what you have in mind, but I have an idea. I won't try to stop you. I honestly don't know what I'd do if I was in your shoes. Please keep in mind two things if you would. One, your badge will be right here, whenever you're ready to come back. Two, if you find yourself in a jam, I don't care when, or why, or where, you call me. Believe me, Detective, I will come running."

Harwell smiled, and nodded. "Thank you, Lieutenant," she said, "I will." The two officers shook hands, lingering longer than usual, and he wrapped both his hands around hers.

"Good luck, Angela," Matz said, and then she was gone.

****

DJ Sanders observed Harwell leave the building at 201 Poplar Ave. He noticed that she did not get back in her cruiser but rather in the passenger seat of an older model Dodge Caravan that pulled up just as she got to the street. As it continued west across 3rd street, the black Cadillac that he also had his eye on followed the van, just as he suspected it would. He put his full face motorcycle helmet on, started his bike, and fell in behind the Caddy.

****

Tyrone's phone rang at exactly at the pre-determined time.

"Buenos Dias, mi amigo," he answered gaily. The adrenaline was flowing. This was the phone call that he'd been waiting for.

It was about to begin.

"Good morning, my friend," Ricardo repeated to Tyrone. "I am happy to hear your voice again."

"And I am equally happy to hear yours as well, Ricardo," Tyrone said.

"As much as I enjoy speaking to you, Tyrone, I should like to make this call as brief as possible. Is everything arranged for tonight's little rehearsal?"

"Absolutely, Ricardo," Tyrone said. "Everything's ready,

everyone's on board. The runway is ours and so is the tower. Is the ETA the same as we discussed?"

"My pilots pride themselves on being punctual. We will be on time. I will welcome you aboard my family's humble Gulfstream and there we will finalize all the details. Does that sound satisfactory?"

"Very satisfactory, Ricardo. I look forward to the beginning of a beautiful business relationship."

"Until tonight, Tyrone, I bid you farewell."

Tyrone ended the call, placed the phone back on the night stand, then turned his attention to the sleepy brunette who lay beside him.

"Who was that?" she asked, her eyes yet to open. They'd been up late.

Tyrone brushed her hair away from her face. "Just business."

She nodded, then yawned. "Okay." His hand wandered. She grinned. "Really? Again? Don't you need any sleep at all?"

"Honey," he said, "that phone call was like an overdose of Viagra and caffeine. I may never sleep or wear a Speedo again."

She laughed, then moved closer to him. "Well, then, let me see if there's anything I might be able to do about both of your problems." She disappeared under the covers and Tyrone laid on his back and smiled.

Life was good.

****

Harwell had one more stop to make.

She knocked on the hospital room door and waited for an answer. Finally, someone said, "Come in." She pushed the door open and walked in to see Timecia sitting in a chair and her mother on the couch. When they saw who it was, both women relaxed and broke into smiles.

"Detective," her mother said, "come in and see how much better my baby is today!"

Harwell stopped just inside the door and was amazed to see the vast improvement in Timecia in such a short time. Her face was still bruised, but the bandages had been removed except for her nose. Her arm was in a sling and her fingers were still taped together, but otherwise she showed remarkable recovery. She heard the door close behind her and she turned to see who was there. There were two men, NFL front line sized and Harwell couldn't believe she'd missed them. She had been too focused on Timecia. Her hand automatically went for her weapon.

"Detective," her mother said, "I'd like you to meet two more of my babies. That there is Todd and Russell. Boys, meet Detective Angela Harwell." They nodded their greeting, and Harwell relaxed. She said, "I'm very glad to meet you guys. I'm glad you're here." She then turned back to Timecia. "Hey, Timi," she said, "you look great."

Timecia grinned, and said, "Hey, Angie. Where've you been? I've been looking for you."

"I know," she said, "I'm sorry." She walked up to her, then kneeled down. "How are you feeling? You okay?"

Timecia nodded. "I feel better every day," she said, "and especially today. Look who's here!" She nodded towards the door to her room, and Harwell heard a child's sweet voice exclaim, "Hi Aunt Angie!"

Harwell turned around, and there was Kristin. Her "bodyguards" had hidden her in the bathroom. She held her arms open and Kristen flew into them. "Kristin!" she said, "Oh, I have missed you so much!"

"I missed you, too, Aunt Angie," she said.

They hugged each other, then Harwell said, "I need to talk to your mommy now, okay sweetie? Why don't you go see Uncle Russell for a minute. I'll see you before I go."

Kristin went to her uncle, and Harwell turned her attention back to Timecia. "Timi," she said, "I..."

"Now, Detective, I know you told me not to bring Kristin to the hospital," her mother said, "but we were careful, and if you could've seen the look on Timi's face when that baby came into this room!"

"It's okay, Mrs. Harrison," Harwell said. "I'm pretty sure Tyrone's busy right now." Then she said to Timecia, "I may not be able to see you for a while, Timi. There's some things I have to do."

"I heard about your grandpa, Angie," Timecia said, "I sure am sorry."

"Terrible thing," her mother said. "I prayed for you all night long, child, I did for sure."

"Thank you," Harwell said, "that means a lot." Her phone suddenly buzzed, and she read the text. She had to hurry. She stood, and said, "Mrs. Harrison, I want to make sure you and your boys take good care of Timi and Kristin until I get back. I made you a promise a few days ago. I intend to keep it. The next time I see you, I'm going to say, to both of you, 'I got him, and he'll never hurt you or anyone else again.'"

A tear fell down Timecia's cheek. "You be careful, Angie. And thank you. For caring about me and my daughter."

Her mother struggled to stand, and when she did she took Harwell's hand and said, "May God be with you, child. I will pray for you every single day, I swear I will. Now you go get that bastard, and send him straight to hell!"

Harwell embraced her, then, very tenderly, Timecia. She kissed Kristin on the forehead and quickly left the room.

****

Through binoculars, Rod Man watched Harwell climb the steps to the Med and walk inside the hospital. He was far enough behind the Caravan to feel safe that he hadn't been made. He'd been on numerous tails and all had been successful. He'd been told merely to keep an eye on Harwell but something told him that whoever was driving the van might be important to Tyrone as well. When he called and described the van that Harwell had climbed into, Rod Man thought Tyrone would come through the phone.

It was Danny. It had to be. Keep both eyes on that van. He would call Luther and Joe to help. Wait for Luther and Joe, then bring him Danny. Preferably alive, but that was optional. If he did, there would be a generous bonus waiting for him.

Rod Man impatiently looked at his watch. It had been fifteen minutes since Tyrone had said his backup was on the way. He was growing afraid that their window of opportunity was closing. He desperately needed that bonus to pay off gambling debts that had gotten out of control. He owed men that even Tyrone stayed away from and they were growing impatient. The money from last night helped, but another packet would buy him time until the million dollar payout was in his hands.

Then he could start over. He would be smarter this time. He would pace himself. No more borrowing and paying their triple-digit interest. If he ran out of money, he'd leave and go home and not look back.

He looked at his watch one last time, then decided he could wait no longer. He got out of the Caddy and began a casual stroll towards the van. His gun remained in the shoulder holster hidden inside his sport coat. He was sweating profusely, both from the heat and anxiety. He and Danny were friends and had worked together for a long time. But this was business. Friendship had nothing to do with it. And while he struggled with it initially, when he remembered the men who would soon come calling for their money, Danny and the Sullivan family were forgotten.

He was able to blend in with a number of pedestrians who were going in the same direction he was. He had about a hundred yards to cover and the group was walking slower than he would have liked, but he forced himself to relax and appear casual. He kept a lookout for the Mustang Luther and Joe would be driving but didn't see it. When the group finally reached where Danny had parked, Rod Man joined the others who entered the lot.

The pre-pay lot was nearly full and there were enough vans and trucks that gave Rod Man plenty of cover. The van's tinted windows made it impossible to see inside but he figured Danny remained in the driver's seat. He decided to approach from the passenger side. A full size truck was behind Danny's van and Rod Man casually made his way behind it. He was sure Danny hadn't seen him. He dropped down and drew his weapon. Rod Man remained below window level until he was beside the van's front passenger door. He reached up, grabbed the handle, and pulled very, very slowly.

It was unlocked. He yanked the door open, stood and aimed his weapon directly at... no one. Rod Man was dumbfounded. He looked in the back, his weapon out in front of him, but the van was empty.

How was that possible?

He looked desperately around for any sign of Danny, but there was none. He put the weapon back in the holster and closed the door. He crossed over to the other side of the lot and waited a few minutes. Danny did not return. He could think of nothing to do except go back to the Cadillac and wait. He would not tell Tyrone he left his car.

To his horror, when Rod Man returned to the place he'd parked the Caddy, it was gone. Stunned, he pressed the appropriately named panic button on the remote, hoping he'd made a mistake about the exact place he parked. He knew it was in vain. He knew precisely where he parked it and it wasn't here. And he suddenly knew why.

"Fuck fuck fuck fuck FUCK!!!!" he screamed.

****

After exiting a door from behind the hospital, Harwell climbed into the waiting Cadillac.

"This is very nice!" she said as they pulled away.

"I like it," Danny said, "but I miss my Caravan."

"How'd you know he'd come for you?"

"I know Rod Man," he said. "Strong as an ox, about the same IQ. Very predictable. Right about, ummm... now, he's remembering I have keys to this baby."

"How long before Tyrone puts the trace out?"

"We got some time. No way in hell Rod Man's calling Tyrone with this piece of news, at least not right away."

She looked in the back and saw the duffle bag. "You even managed to get the bag. I'm impressed."

"God did not bless me with just looks, you know."

She rolled her eyes, then said, "Think we can make it to, say, Little Rock?"

"No, that would be pushing our luck. I figure we can hang on to this for maybe 15 minutes at the most. Why would we go to Little Rock, anyway?"

"We're not. I was kidding. Cross the bridge into West Memphis. I'll let you know when to exit." She looked into the side mirror. "You know," she said, "that motorcycle is still tailing us."

"I see him," Danny said, "but like I said, I don't think he works for Tyrone. Not his style. We should find out what he wants."

"Let's see if he follows us to our next stop. If he does, he's definitely not one of Tyrone's boys."

Who are you, easy rider? Harwell thought to herself.

Friend or foe?

Chapter Fourteen

"**Y**ou have GOT to be fucking KIDDING me!"

An enraged Tyrone was inches from Rod Man's face, and Rod Man was barely able to contain his bowels. He'd witnessed countless tirades from his boss over the years but his fury had never been unleashed on him. Not like this. He stood trembling in Tyrone's office, with Luther and Joe seated behind him.

Tyrone, dressed in his bathrobe, stepped back from Rod Man and angrily walked to his desk. He threw open a drawer and, much to Rod Man's relief, pulled out a cigarette. He lit it, took a deep draw, and exhaled. He glowered at Rod Man and said, "Tell me, first of all, how Danny was able to get out of the van without you knowing it."

'I don't know...'

"No!" Tyrone interrupted, infuriated. "Do *not* tell me you don't know. You were the only one there. You saw him park the fucking van. Did you look away? Did you go take a piss somewhere? Did you call your girlfriend? Your boyfriend? What?"

Rod Man tried to think, desperate to recall every second of his surveillance of Danny and the van, and of Harwell.

Harwell! Of course!

"It had to be when I was watching Detective Harwell, Tyrone. After she got out of the van, I kept the glasses on her until she went inside The Med.
I swear that was the only time I took my eyes off that van."

Tyrone took another drag from the cigarette. "Uh-huh," he said, "and what'd that take? Thirty seconds?"

"I guess," said Rod Man, "maybe about that."

Tyrone stabbed the cigarette out in an ashtray on his desk. "So what you're telling me is that Danny knew you'd followed him, and then figured out you'd watch Detective Harwell while she sashays into the hospital, giving him *maybe* a thirty second window to give you the slip. Is that what you're telling me?"

"I swear to God Tyrone, it's the only time my eyes weren't on the van."

Tyrone moved the ashtray, then sat on the edge of the desk, facing Rod Man. A smile slowly crept on his face. "Is Danny *really* that smart? I mean, I knew he was smart. It's why I hired him. But this is Houdini shit. It's like he read your mind. And like a trained dog, you did *exactly* what he needed you to do. How does that make you feel?"

Rod Man was afraid to answer. He shrugged his shoulders.

"But it gets even better," Tyrone continued. "Because then you thought you were smarter than *me!* I give you explicit instructions - oh, wait, I'm sorry. That's a big word. You may not know what *explicit* means. It means clear, Rod Man, as in crystal *fucking* clear. I give you crystal *fucking* clear instructions to wait on Luther and Joe before you make a move. But apparently, you hear Danny saying, 'Here, boy! C'mere Rod Man. Good doggy! Good boy!' Because you leave *my* Cadillac, and with your tail wagging up a storm, you try to take Danny Boy all by yourself."

Behind him, Luther laughed. Rod Man's face burned from embarrassment.

"And Danny's got the keys, doesn't he Rod Man?"

"Yes, sir."

"And, probably, my car."

"Yes, sir."

"Well, let's find out." Danny took a cell from his robe pocket and pressed a button. Almost immediately, he said, "Where's my car, Rico?"

"Well good morning to you, too," Rico said, "and the answer to your question is West Memphis."

"Did you kill the engine?"

"Didn't have to. It's parked."

"Where?"

"Oh, Tyrone," he said, "You are going to *love* this."

****

Harwell stood in the doorway of the Chief of Detective's office, at Police Headquarters on East Broadway Street in West Memphis, Arkansas.

"Hello, *Captain* Jessup McCaskey," Harwell said, and the graying man seated behind the desk glanced up, removed his reading glasses, and smiled. "Detective Harwell? Is that you?"

"It's me," Harwell answered.

McCaskey stood and immediately said, "Come in, come in. Sit down, please."

Harwell took a seat across from the desk. "I'm sorry to just show up like this."

"No, no, don't be," McCaskey said, "you're always welcome here. You know that."

Just over a year ago, Harwell had hand delivered a child abuse suspect to McCaskey who had fled into Memphis and had holed up in an uncle's apartment complex. Harwell had maintained surveillance outside of the apartment in an unmarked car for two days until the suspect finally ventured outside. Harwell instantly recognized him. As soon as her car door opened, he ran.

The chase lasted less than sixty seconds. Even with a head start of at least a hundred feet, he was no match for Harwell's speed and stamina. He was soon cuffed, stuffed and on his way back to West Memphis where he was charged and jailed. Harwell learned afterward the victim was McCaskey's niece. Since then they'd kept in touch professionally and even met at a few Redbirds games.

"When did you make Captain?" she asked.

"Six months ago," he said, "how about that?"

"Congratulations."

"Sorry to hear about your grandpa, Angela," he said sincerely, "I liked him and I know how close you two were."

"Thank you," she said.

"I've been checking but I haven't heard anything about a

funeral. There's a lot of folks here who'll be there."

"There won't be a funeral," she said. "My grandfather is being cremated. He didn't want a fuss made over him. I plan to honor his wishes."

McCaskey seemed stunned for a moment, then said, "Good enough. Now, what can I do for you?"

"You've told me more than once that if I ever needed anything to come see you. Does that still stand?"

"Still does. You just name it."

"I need a ride. For me and a friend of mine."

He nodded, then said, "Okay. Where to?"

"No, I mean I need a car, unmarked, but with dash lights."

"When?"

"As soon as possible. Right now, preferably."

"Can I ask why?"

"You can, but there's a couple of more things."

"And that would be?"

"There's a black Caddy parked out in front. Tinted windows. No idea how it got there. Pretty sure it's stolen, though. You should impound it."

"Tow truck'll be here in less than five. Don't reckon you know who it belongs to, do you?"

"I might. I think my grandfather did, too."

The implication was not lost on McCaskey. "I understand. What do you want me to do with whoever may come lookin' for it?"

"I want you to let him have it. Allow him to drive it away. Hassle him just enough so that whoever picks it up doesn't get suspicious. But if you would, please, install a GPS chip that will sync with a smart phone. I don't know if I'll need it, but if I do it'll come in mighty handy." She handed him a card. It had her name and private number on it. "I'll pay for it, of course."

"Nonsense," he said, "it's a police matter. We'll get it done for you. What else?"

"There's a guy across the street sitting on a motorcycle. Young, black male, blue jeans, white t-shirt. He's been following me for a while. I'd like to talk to him."

Understanding exactly what she meant, he picked up the phone on his desk, hit one number, then said, "Jill? Need you to do a couple of things for me."

****

Tyrone ended his call to Rico, then dropped the phone onto his desk. "Why?" he said, thinking out loud, "Why are Danny Boy and Detective Harwell together? And why did they drive to the West Memphis Police headquarters? Of all places?" He hopped off his desk, walked over to a solid oak file cabinet and opened the second drawer. He flipped through some files until he found the one he wanted, then drew out a single sheet of paper. He took it to Rod Man. It was the title to the Cadillac. "Go get my car, Rod Man," Tyrone instructed, "and take this with you. They may not let you have it without it. If they ask, tell them someone stole it and OnStar tracked it for us."

Rod Man took the title. "Yes, sir."

"Well, alright then, go take care of it. I want my car back." Tyrone walked around him to speak to Luther and Joe.

"Tyrone..." he started.

"What?" Tyrone answered, irritated.

"How do I get to West Memphis?"

"I don't *care* how you get there, Rod Man. Take a cab, take a bus, *walk* if you have to. You're goddamned lucky you're not being taken out of here in a goddamned *box*! You fucked up, boy, but I'm feeling benevolent. That means generous, your word for the day. I'm giving you another chance. Now, get out of my sight before my *benevolence* runs clean out. As soon as you get that done, you report back here to me. We got a big night coming up."

Rod Man left the room. Tyrone turned to Luther and Joe. "Boys," he said, "I'm going to take a shower. There's a lovely lady with blue eyes and a perfect ass in my bed at this moment who I hope will join me. If all goes well, I may be a while. Help yourselves to my kitchen. You're welcome to anything you can find. Don't touch anything containing alcohol. You're driving to the other side of Nashville soon and nothing, I mean *nothing*, can go wrong."

"Uh, boss?" said Luther.

"Yeah, Luther," Tyrone answered.

"If me and Joe are driving to Nashville this afternoon, there's no way we'll be back in time for this party you're throwin', is there?"

Tyrone shook his head. "No, Luther, probably not. Tonight's just the dress rehearsal, though. Believe me, you'll both be here for the real thing. I tell you what - before you leave, I will fill both of you in on every detail. I'm dying to tell somebody. I can trust you guys. You'll be the first to know." He turned to take his shower.

"Tyrone?"

"What, Luther?"

"I jus... Well, if your lady friend, you know, after you done and all, well if she still ain't satisfied, tell her I'll be in the kitchen."

Tyrone stared at him with an incredulous expression. Then he burst out laughing. They could still hear him laughing all the way to his bedroom.

****

After Capt. McCaskey had taken care of Harwell's requests, she gave him the short version of what she and Danny had planned. McCaskey listened without interrupting.

"So," she asked, "what do you think?"

"Awful lot of unknowns, detective. But then, I don't have to tell you that, do I?"

Harwell shook her head. "We know. But there's no other way."

"You got vests?"

She nodded. "I do of course, but Danny doesn't."

"We'll take care of him. What else?"

Harwell said, "I've got a duffle bag with almost everything I need, including weapons. But if you've got a spare box of nine mil and .38 cal ammo laying around, I wouldn't say no."

Captain McCaskey got up and walked over to a large metal cabinet, unlocked it and removed two 100-round boxes. He placed them on his desk directly in front of Harwell. She smiled. "You're a good man, Jessup."

McCaskey sat back down, seemed to mull over something, then opened the top drawer to his desk and grabbed a set of car keys. He threw them to Harwell. She caught them, and he said, "There's a blue Crown Vic right out front. It's my car. You're welcome to it. There's just one catch."

"What catch?"

"Where ever it goes, I go. I'm going with you."

Harwell shook her head. "This isn't your fight, Jessup."

"The *hell* it ain't. Tyrone's a cop killer. I'm a cop. That makes it my fight. Besides," he said, "I owe you one, Detective. A big one. I want to help, and right now you need all the help you can get."

Just then, there was a knock at the open door. Danny was there, and with him was DJ. "Detective," he said, "I'm sorry to interrupt, but I have someone here I want you to meet."

****

"What do you think?"

Tyrone was back in his office, seated at his desk and had just laid out every detail to Luther and Joe. Joe was completely awestruck, but Luther, as always, was emotionless.

"Two thousand keys, Tyrone? Over two *tons* of powder? My, my, *my*, son, that *is* ambitious."

"It's much more than that, Luther! It's unprecedented. It will make The Family invincible, un*touch*able! The profits from this one deal will enable us to buy anyone we want. We'll have police, politicians, DA's. Shit, man, we may even buy ourselves a governor."

Luther laughed. "Before we start pricin' governors, we got to pull this off first. Allow me to play devil's advocate, Tyrone.

Seems to me you might just be, I don' know, maybe a little... over confident? I mean, I know we the only ones that really know about this, but, just to be safe, shouldn't you make sure that Danny and that woman cop is, let's say, out of the picture before this thing goes down?"

Tyrone put his elbows on the desk, pressed his fingers against his forehead and closed his eyes. Then, very calmly, he said, "More than a year, Luther. That's how long I've been working on this." He opened his eyes, leaned back in his chair, and looked directly at Luther. "For over a *year* I have sweated, and planned and worked out every *conceivable* detail, every *possible* scenario. No stone was left unturned. And now, when it's less than two *days* from going down, Danny takes off on me, you kill Harwell's grandfather, and for some goddamn reason those two seemed to have hooked up."

Luther said, "Surely a couple of more *days* won't..."

Tyrone pounded the top of his desk with his fist. "No, goddammit, no! *Nothing* can stop this Luther, you hear me? *Nothing*! If I postpone this deal, Ricardo will think there are weaknesses in The Family. He'll cancel the whole thing. That's not going to happen. Not now. Not ever!" He got up and began pacing around the room. "This will be my finest hour. This will be my *legacy!* Everything I've done up to this point has been carefully calculated, always moving toward this... this zero hour if you will." He stopped in front of Luther. "I'm a General, Luther. I don't wear a uniform, but I'm a General just the same. The Family is my army. No," he said, "not two days. Not two hours. Not even two *minutes!*"

"Okay, boss. I get it. So what do we do once we get to Nashville?"

Instantly, Tyrone's demeanor changed to all business. "Rico tracked Jasmine's SUV. It's actually parked in a rural area near a town called Gordonsville, the other side of Nashville. Nothing but farmland, closest neighbor is a half-mile away. I guess Danny figured they'd be safe there. Maybe Danny's not as smart as he thinks he is. The house and land belongs to Jimmy and Carla Taylor, probably friends of Jasmine's. I'll text you the address. Use the GPS on your phone to find it. Rico said the Lexus hasn't moved since it arrived. Danny won't be there, I know that now, but Jasmine and his boys will be. If we get his family, we'll get Danny, and maybe even Harwell. Wait until after dark, get inside that house. You bring me Jasmine. You bring me his boys. Do your best not to hurt them, but bring them to me no matter what. If anyone else sees you, kill them."

Luther nodded. "Okay, Tyrone. We got this. Just another thing."

"Boys," Tyrone said, "you get this done, and that packet of bills you got the other night will seem like chicken feed."

****

At that moment, a Crown Vic with blue lights flashing sped down an interstate, headed towards a destination where anything could happen.

McCaskey, driving, broke a long silence when he said to Harwell, "You sure you're ready for this? I mean, so soon after what happened to your grandfather?"

Harwell, beside him, didn't hesitate. "I've never been more ready for anything in my whole life, Jessup."

"I've been thinking," Danny said from the back. "I mean, check this out. We're like the A-Team. The four of us, all bad-ass, going against the odds."

"Really?" DJ said. "And which one are you?"

"Me? Isn't is obvious? I'm Mr. T."

DJ laughed and shook his head.

"What's so funny?" Danny asked. "If I had a Mohawk and some bling? Spittin' image and just as bad-ass."

"You're dreaming," DJ retorted. "You couldn't box Mr. T's shadow."

"Oh, is that right Navy boy? And you could?"

"I'm a United States Navy SEAL, Danny. And you're goddamn

right I could."

Danny was willing to concede. "I respect that, DJ. You can be Mr. T."

Then, a couple of seconds later, added, "I guess that means I'm the brains of this operation."

Harwell looked over her shoulder and said, "Really? *You're* the brains?"

After that, nothing more was said.

It didn't matter who was who, or who was in charge.

The danger was the same for all of them.

Chapter Fifteen

Luther and Joe had a perfect night for surveillance.

As a light rain fell from an overcast sky, the house went completely dark just after ten o'clock. In the two hours they'd been watching the house, they'd seen neither the Lexus nor Jasmine and the twins. But the garage hadn't opened and there had definitely been activity inside the house. Rico had assured Tyrone that the Lexus hadn't moved from this location and this is where they would find it. Jasmine had surely parked inside the safe confines of the garage, out of sight to everything except GPS satellites and Rico's computers.

The two men had parked about a quarter-mile from the Taylor farm. After some searching they'd found an old barn just off a gravel road, the same road which led them to their current location. They hid the car behind the barn, waited until dusk, then made a wide circle on foot around the property to try and find the best vantage point. They happened upon an old shed, empty and barely standing. It was perfectly situated on higher ground, far enough away to be inconspicuous, especially at night, but close enough for easy surveillance with binoculars. Despite a leaky roof, it provided adequate shelter and Luther and Joe were glad they'd be able to stay dry while they watched and waited.

They were also pleased that, while the front porch light remained on, the back porch light was extinguished, allowing for an easy approach in nearly total darkness. There was also a back door to the garage, and they decided to enter the house from there. Luther made a wide sweep with his binoculars, searching for any movement, man or beast. Satisfied there was none, he removed the glasses from his eyes.

"It's nice out here, ain't it Joe? It's like Tyrone said, guess they figured they safe way out here in the country. Almost seems a shame we got to show them they ain't."

"How long you want to wait?" asked Joe.

"We'll give 'em an hour, make sure they all asleep," Luther answered. "Around eleven or so, we'll wake they ass up." He continued to gaze through the binoculars, then said, "I sure hope Danny Boy's pretty wife is in there. Got somethin' special planned for her. Hate to drive all this way for nothin'."

****

Greg Brunson had been the night shift Air Traffic Controller at the Millington Private Jetport for nearly five years. It was easy work. Very little traffic either took off or landed during his shift from 8 pm until 2 am, which was when the tower actually closed until the morning shift reopened at 5:30. There was only one major runway, 8,000 feet long and 200 feet wide. They catered mostly to small corporate and private jet owners, and offered refueling and maintenance should it be needed. There were a couple of hangers for those who wanted overnight shelter for their aircraft.

Brunson had a regular gig at Memphis International as well, but he had two kids in college and one other in a private high school. The combined tuitions were breaking him and when this slot opened up, he grabbed it.

He worked the second job for yet another reason. His wife and some of her girlfriends enjoyed weekly, and sometimes bi-weekly, trips to the nearby Mississippi casinos. It was bleeding him dry but he didn't have the heart to tell her they couldn't afford it any longer. He doubted she'd quit even if he did.

Dollar slots, though she would never admit it, were as addictive as any drug.

And just as expensive.

Brunson could barely believe his luck when he was approached about a month ago just after he closed the tower and was walking to his car. A black Cadillac had parked next to him. As Brunson unlocked his car, the Caddy's window rolled down, and the person inside asked him if he'd be interested in making a lot of money -

all cash and risk free? Very simple and above board. Just land one small jet for maintenance while the tower was open, then let it take off again. The next night the plane would land after the tower closed, and he didn't need to know why. Just light up the runway until the jet landed and taxied.

Then the man told him how much money he would make. It was two year's salary.

For that much money, Brunson told the man, he would land the plane, wash and wax it and have pizza brought in for the pilots and passengers.

He was told that wouldn't be necessary.

Just land the plane, ask no questions and make very, very sure there'd be no record of the second landing anywhere. No log. No recording. No nothing.

Do this, and he'd get half the first night, and half the second.

Tonight was the first night.

He actually smiled when his wife texted, only an hour ago, *Lost everything. On my way home.*

****

Luther lit a cigarette, then glanced at his watch as he exhaled the smoke. "Only fifteen more minutes." He put the binoculars against his face and scanned the house again. Nothing had changed, and there was no sign of any sort of movement. The house remained completely dark and quiet.

"Luther," said Joe, "how we gonna handle this?"

He took the glasses off his eyes and looked at Joe. "What do you mean?"

"I mean, shit Luther, these are little boys we supposed to get, not more than, what? Two or three years old? I ain't used to this, you know? We sell dope, that's one thing. They're all grown people, making choices. But these are kids, and they're Danny's kids. I don't like it, is all."

Luther took a deep draw off the cigarette, then looked at Joe with contempt. "You're pathetic, Joe," he said, smoke curling from his lips as he spoke. "Why'd Tyrone even send you with me? I'd be better off alone."

"I'm not pathetic, Luther. I just know how I'd feel if they were my kids."

"See, that's another thing. You talk about folks makin' choices? You don't think Danny knew what he was doin' when he took off? When he sent his wife and kids out here? He knew. You damn straight he knew. You run from The Family, that's the risk you take. That was *his* choice. Whatever happens now, he asked for it."

"So what're we gonna do? When we get inside?"

"We gonna *do* whatever the fuck we *have* to do, Joe. We gonna get Jasmine and the boys and take 'em back to Tyrone just like he told us to. Now you get comfortable with that and be ready to help me, or so help me I'll shoot you jus' as dead as anyone else who gets in my way. Now jus' shut the fuck up 'til it's time for us to move."

Joe did as he was told.

But he felt sick inside.

****

Tyrone's men were on time, as he knew they would be. When he had them all gathered around him, he said, "Okay, boys, follow me."

He took them to his garage. There were four double garage doors, and behind each were large bays, clean and brightly lit with multiple high-output fluorescent bulbs. There was also a massive workshop, well equipped with tools and a large workbench set against the back wall. A ten horsepower air compressor stood ready to use and there was even a hydraulic lift installed in the floor.

What stood out most of all, however, in the center of each bay there were four identical, brand-new, full size cargo vans, each fitted with United States Marshal door decals and full law-enforcement lights across the top.

The men, naturally, were impressed.

"Gentlemen," Tyrone said, "May I have your attention?" They became quiet and waited for Tyrone to speak. He walked over to one of the vans and opened the dual doors at the rear. "Gather 'round, please. It's time for a little show and tell. And what I'm about to show and tell you, will blow your minds."

****

A few minutes before eleven o'clock, Luther stood, took one long, last draw of his cigarette and inhaled deeply. He dropped the butt, not bothering to stomp it out. "C'mon, Joe," he said. "It's time."

Joe hesitated, then stood. Luther noticed. "Joe," he said, "I'm only gonna ask you this once, and I mean only once. You ready to go or not?" He removed his .38 semi-automatic from the rear waistband of his jeans. He pulled back the slide, and a round was ejected from the chamber. He caught the bullet in mid-air and showed it to Joe. "Because if we get inside, and you don't do your job, I'm savin' this one for you." He put the round in his pocket and waited.

"I'm fine, Luther," Joe said, "let's just get this over with."

They both put on thin latex gloves and then full face ski masks. With weapons drawn, the men started down the hill towards the house. The rain had stopped but the ground was still wet. They took their time on the slippery grass, careful not to fall and make any unnecessary noise. They reached the back door and were confident they'd not been seen or heard. There was no window to look through. Luther grabbed the doorknob, and turned. When it stopped, he very slowly pushed against the door. It opened a couple of inches.

Surprisingly, it was unlocked!

The men froze until they were sure there was no alarm. After about a minute, Luther quietly released the doorknob, then whispered to Joe, "I'm goin' to take a look around, see if I can find them. You wait here until I get back, in case anyone comes home that we ain't expectin'."

Joe nodded that he understood and Luther pulled a small penlight from his front pocket. He turned it on and put it in his mouth. He slowly pushed the door open until it was just wide enough for him to get through. He looked at Joe and nodded once. Joe returned the nod. Luther slipped inside.

He slowly turned his head and let the light shine around the room. His gun moved with it. It was just bright enough for him to see, but that would improve once his eyes adjusted to the darkness. He felt a surge of excitement when his light shone on the Lexus. He was pleased as well to discover the Lexus was the only vehicle there. As he panned his light towards the door to the house he was startled to see two sets of eyes shining back at him, no more than three feet away. Before he could react, he heard someone whisper a single word.

"Ready."

Instantly, he heard growls that were far too deep and menacing to belong to anything small. For the first time in his life, Luther was frozen with fear.

A pounding heartbeat later, the same voice said, "Go!"

****

"These vans, these *Prisoner Transport Vans*, are identical," a smiling Tyrone bragged to his men. "Note the government tags. Notice the wall which separates the front from the back, equipped with a window which easily slides open and closed for easy communication with your prisoner. Notice also the stainless steel, uncomfortable looking bench, complete with a seatbelt. They are authentic down to the last detail!"

Tyrone walked around and opened the driver's door. "In each van, two of you will sit in the front and become U.S. Marshals, with all the proper ID's, badges and credentials. The other will be dressed, much more appropriately I might add, in a prison jumpsuit and will sit, cuffed if the circumstances call for it, in the back. And in the extremely unlikely event that any of you are pulled over by area law enforcement," he continued as he reached inside and pulled a large, sealed plastic envelope with "U.S. Marshal" printed on it in large, black letters, "you will have the paperwork which shows who your prisoner is, complete with picture, where your prisoner was picked up, and where he is going."

Tyrone leaned against the van and waited. He knew a question was coming. The wait was short.

"Where in the hell did you steal *these* Tyrone?" one of the men asked. "Surely they lookin' for 'em."

"*Steal* them?" Tyrone asked incredulously, "you think I *stole* these beauties? No, gentlemen, I am *not* a thief! I bought these vans right off a lot and brought 'em back here. Then I had a genius mechanic friend I know convert 'em right here in my little garage. No one's looking for them. They are legally mine." He waited again, then said, "Go ahead. Ask me anything. I love talking about this."

"How'd you get all that other stuff?" another man asked. "The lights and badges and stuff? You can't just order that shit from Amazon, can you?"

"Great question!" Tyrone said, "And no, you can't. But my good friend Rico can. It cost me a fortune, but if everything goes according to plan - and it will, gentlemen - we will make ten fortunes. Always remember this," he said, then paused for dramatic effect, "you have to spend money to make money."

"I'm guessing," said yet another man, "that we gonna be movin' more than just a prisoner. So where we puttin' the product, boss? Just right there in the back?"

Tyrone stared at the man. "Really, Anton? What kind of a question is that?" Anton struggled to say something, but Tyrone stopped him. "It's a *great* question! It's one of the ones I was waiting for someone to ask. Allow me, gentlemen."

He walked over to the work bench and picked up one of four cordless drills, equipped with a Phillips head screwdriver bit. He climbed into the back of the van and squatted down beside the bench. He removed six 3" long machine screws from the floor on each side of the bench. He wiggled the bench to show that it had been loosened.

"Josh, Tyler," he said, "get in here and take this bench out." The men did as they were told. Along with the bench, a section of the floor, welded to the legs, came out with it. Tyrone followed, then made his way to the driver's door. He opened it, reached inside and said, "Gentlemen, it's time for the main event."

With the flick of a switch, four servomotors began to hum, causing the van to vibrate. With an audible *whoosh!* the rear floor suddenly separated, down the middle from front to back. The men watched as four output shafts pushed the two halves of the floor up and against the side walls of the van. The humming stopped and each section remained solidly in place, revealing a spacious, hidden cavity.

One man said it all when he whispered, "Damn."

"I know," Tyrone said from behind them. "I *know*! I told you my friend's a genius It's a custom made storage compartment, gentlemen, eight feet by four feet by twenty-four inches and both it and the floor are lined with a quarter inch of the finest synthetic rubber made. It's operated by the switch that turns on the inside lights. When the bench is in place, it activates a micro switch that interrupts the signal to the motors, so only the lights work. When it's removed, it closes the circuit so that both the lights *and* the floor works. Turn off the switch up front, the motors reverse. Then, once the floor has closed, and as soon as the bench is replaced, the compartment is automatically vacuum sealed. The seam in the middle becomes virtually invisible. It's more than genius," he boasted reverently, "it's fucking foolproof."

"Tyrone? Being vacuum sealed and all, could one of them drug sniffin' dogs find the stuff once it's closed up?" Josh asked.

Tyrone smiled. "Let's hope we never have to find out. But, let's assume they can. For that to happen, someone would have to have reason to suspect there were drugs in this van. With cover like this, why would any cop, anywhere, be suspicious?"

At that moment, any doubt about Tyrone's claim of a foolproof plan disappeared. The men could feel it, certain their days of just envying those with money would soon come to an end.

"Where we pickin' it up, T? Four vans, all that room? You're talkin' about some serious quantity. That much powder just don't fall out of the sky, you know?" asked Anton.

"And that," said a gleeful Tyrone, "is the other question I was waiting on. And, believe it or not, you're a lot closer than you know. It will, gentlemen, quite literally fall out of the sky."

"When, Tyrone?" Tyler asked.

"Soon, Tyler, soon. For now though," he said, and was now addressing the entire group, "I want you men to divide up into groups of two or three and spend the next hour or so practicing. Pick a van, grab a drill. Remove the benches, get used to opening and closing the floors. Put the benches back in. Get it down to a science. Let me know if anything malfunctions. Gentlemen!" he said, and everyone stopped moving and the room became whisper quiet. "We roll in ninety minutes. We're gonna do a little run through. I'll brief you just before we leave, but I will tell you this right now. It has got to be perfect. No mistakes, no playing around. Total professionalism. Does everyone understand?"

They all nodded.

"Alright then," Tyrone said, and looked at his watch. "Get to it."

He and Rod Man went back into the house, and soon the sounds of drills could be heard in each of the vans. Tyrone looked at his phone as they walked. There was still no word. He swore.

"It's way after eleven, Rod Man. What is Luther *doing*?"

****

The first pit bull leapt and found Luther's gun hand. Luther fired wildly, but was unable to aim and each round slammed harmlessly into the ceiling and walls of the garage. The dogs were undeterred by the gunshots. Rather, they had the opposite effect. The one on his hand bit even harder and caused Luther to drop his pistol. The other went low and clamped his jaws on Luther's ankle, crushing it. Waves of pain engulfed Luther, and he immediately went down. He tried frantically to flee, kicking his way backwards with his free leg, and screaming maniacally, "Get 'em off! Get 'em off! Help! Help me, Joe!" He'd dropped his penlight, and his terror magnified in the blackness. The brutes sank their teeth into whatever part of Luther they could find, instinctively shaking their heads violently from side to side, giving their prey no chance to fight back.

As shock set in, and with his strength depleted, Luther's screams diminished to quiet whimpers. Somehow, perhaps it was a final surge of survivor adrenaline, Luther swung, and connected, just as one of the pits located his throat.

The punch proved ineffective; there was nothing behind it. As time slowed to a trickle, Luther gave up and accepted his fate. He didn't blame the dogs. He understood them for they were much alike. They did as they were told, asked no questions and felt no remorse. He was now dying by his own credo. Eat or be eaten. Kill or be killed. The beast on his throat shook, and the rest of Luther followed.

And then he was gone.

His final minute of life was just as he'd lived, in a world ruled by chaos and violence.

It was a fitting end.

Outside, Joe was frantic. As soon as he heard the dogs he pulled the door closed and retreated. As he backed away, he was torn by Luther's frantic cries for help. He wanted to run. He knew he should help Luther, but for the life of him, he could not bring himself to open the door. Twice he came back to the door and reached for the knob, and twice he changed his mind. When Luther's tortured screams abated, then stopped completely, Joe made his decision. Luther was a goner. He could only save himself. He turned to run.

As soon as he did he was seized by the throat and slammed up against the house next to the door. At the same instant, he felt his weapon being easily wrenched away. Joe frantically clutched at the hands around his neck, but he was no match for the sheer strength and leverage of whoever was holding him. He stared wildly into the eyes of DJ Sanders. Behind him was Harwell and McCaskey, guns drawn and aimed at his head. DJ's grip around Joe's neck was relentless, and Joe felt himself about to lose consciousness. Harwell approached and put a hand on DJ's shoulder.

"DJ," she said, "we need him alive, remember?"

Reluctantly, DJ loosened his hold and allowed the man to fall to the ground. Joe, now on hands and knees, coughed and gasped as his brain screamed for him to resume breathing. Harwell walked over to him and waited a moment while he recovered. She then took her foot and flipped him over onto his back. She stepped on his shoulder and pointed her Glock directly between his eyes. She leaned over and yanked his ski mask off.

"Hi there," she said, "I'm thinking this isn't one of your better days, huh? Sore throat, trouble breathing. I imagine we've made it kind of bad for you, haven't we? I mean, you've got to somehow tell Tyrone - and that's assuming you live to see him again - that not only did you leave your partner in there to deal with those two pits all by himself, but that he's dead and your little mission here this evening was a total failure."

She pressed her foot down even harder on his shoulder. Joe started to grab her leg, but caught himself.

"Oh, please, *please* try," Harwell said, "it would *so* make my day." Joe quickly put his arms back down by his side.

"Now, Joe - I mean, you are Joe, right? See, we all heard your friend in there calling you to help him, but I'm guessing you're afraid of dogs?" Joe nodded. "Yeah, that's what I thought. So tell me Joe, do you have any other weapons on you, *anywhere* on you, besides the gun you let DJ take from you? Because I don't want to touch you in any of those places where you may try to hide something." This time, he shook his head. "Good. Now, I have only a couple more questions for you. Is there *any* doubt in your mind right now who's in charge? Or what we're willing to do in order to find out what we need to know?"

"No ma'am," Joe said, softly, "you made your point. You're in charge." He then looked her over, head to toe. He squinted, then said, "Do I know you?"

"We've never been formally introduced," she said. "Why? Do I look familiar?"

"Not sure," he said.

"It'll come to you," Harwell said, "now get up."

Harwell stood back while Joe struggled to stand. When he was finally on his feet, McCaskey stepped up and took his turn with the gangster. He frisked him for weapons and, finding none, cuffed him.

"You're under arrest, son," he said, "so allow me tell you your rights, Arkansas style. You got the right to remain silent, but I wouldn't recommend it. You done made a lot of people mad and I'm thinkin' you oughta answer every question they ask. You got the right to an attorney, but I just don't see how you're gonna find one way the hell out here. You got the right to make peace with God, and if I was in your shoes that's probably the *first* thing I'd do. Finally, anything you say better be the goddamn truth 'cause otherwise you just might end up as dog chow like your friend in there. Actually, your *former* friend. Now," he said, "do you understand these rights?"

Joe nodded. Sweat poured down his face and his breaths were raspy from the chokehold DJ had put on him. He tried to blink the sweat out of his eyes and began to look at his captors, as if for the first time. "You guys..." he panted, "... are *cops*?"

Suddenly DJ pushed past McCaskey, grabbed Joe's sweat soaked tee shirt with both hands and shoved him against the house. His face was inches from Joe's. "First question," he said, his voice even and emotionless, "did you kill my father?" Joe's eyes were wide with fear and confusion. When there was no immediate response, DJ pulled Joe back away from the house, then slammed him violently back into the siding. "ANSWER ME MOTHER

FUCKER! DID YOU KILL MY FATHER?"

McCaskey said, "Now son, that there's one of them questions I was talkin' about. And to make matters even worse for you, the man askin' is a You-ni-ted States Navy SEAL. I'm thinkin' you best come up with some answers mighty quick."

Joe suddenly realized who they were. He should have known right away who Harwell was. The crazed man who looked ready to kill him had to be the musician's son. He shook his head. "No!" he said, desperate for them to believe him, "No! I didn't kill anyone. It was Luther. I swear."

Harwell stepped up. "He's telling the truth, DJ. We know Luther killed my grandfather. I'd lay odds he was the shooter on your father as well. I don't think Joe here is man enough to have stood up to either one of them." She looked at him disdainfully. "He was there, though. Why don't you let him go and then we'll find out what he knows?"

DJ flexed his hands on the frightened man's shirt, trying to decide what to do. Once again, he grabbed Joe's neck with one of his powerful hands, then said through clenched teeth, "I hope you give me a reason, mother fucker, to rip your goddamn head off!" He squeezed even harder. "Please. Just one reason." He then let Joe fall to the wet ground.

McCaskey casually walked over, reached down and helped the traumatized gangster to his feet. "You got to watch your step around here," he said. "You keep trippin' like that you might hurt yourself." He turned Joe towards the door. "Now, why don't we all go inside where it's cooler, and then maybe you can answer a few more questions."

Joe frantically tried to break free from McCaskey's grip. "No!" he said, "there's dogs in there, man! There's pit bulls in there!"

"Pit bulls? You worried about a couple of Pit Bulls?" He turned Joe around to face DJ and Harwell. "Take a good look, Joe. This so-called piece of shit *family* you belong to killed his father, her grandfather and my friend. Them pits are the very least of your worries. In fact, I'm guessin' I'm the only reason you're still breathin'." He turned Joe back around. "So I figure that makes me the good cop. But don't imagine for one second we're bosom buddies or anything like that because so help me God, the first time you move funny, or stutter, or say the wrong thing? I'll come back out here, and I'll just drive away. And when I'm gone, and it's just you and them and those cranky ol' puppies in there, no matter how loud you scream, I promise ya, no one'll hear. You understand that, *Family boy?*" Joe nodded. "Good. Now *move!*"

And as he opened the door, McCaskey snorted. "Pit Bulls! Hell, son, I'm from Arkansas. You can *marry* a pit bull in my state!"

****

Tyrone looked at his watch. He couldn't wait any longer. "Rod Man, go tell the boys to wrap it up. Put all the benches back in. Get the vans ready to roll. Each van carries a drill and an extra battery. Three men to a van. We'll have to go with three vans tonight. Do a radio check and make sure each van is on the same channel. Do it now. We roll in twenty."

Rod Man left and Tyrone found himself alone in his office. He looked at his phone as if trying to will it to ring. Luther should've contacted him by now. Something must have gone wrong. He dialed the number to Luther's phone and very nearly pressed "send." He changed his mind and dialed another number.

"Rico," he said, "has the Lexus moved?"

"Jesus Christ, Tyrone," Rico said angrily from the other end, "do the hours nine to five mean *anything* to you?"

"Rico," Tyrone said, "this is important, and I mean really goddamned important. Has the Lexus moved?"

"Hold on." After thirty seconds, Rico was back on. "No, it's where it's always been. I told you I would let you know if it did. Don't you trust me?"

"I'm not in the mood, Rico. What about the Mustang?"

"Still there as well, Tyrone, just south of the Lexus."

Tyrone thought of something. "Could they have somehow

removed the chips? Off the Lexus I mean?"

"I guess," Rico said, "but I don't see how they'd have known about both of them. If they found one, seems to me they'd be happy and not even consider there might be a second chip. You're being paranoid. It's there, Tyrone. And from now on, you call me after midnight, my rates double."

The line went dead. Tyrone was sure something was wrong, but there was nothing he could do about it tonight. He had an appointment he couldn't miss.

He would deal with it tomorrow. He'd fix it. Besides, Luther was his most trusted and capable lieutenant. He'd *never* let him down. There was a reason why he hadn't called. A good reason.

Convinced, he put it out of his mind, then got up, straightened his jacket and adjusted his tie. He had to look his best. His rendezvous with destiny would not, *could* not wait.

He turned out the lights as he left the room, and closed the door. As he strolled toward the garage, he began whistling the theme song to the movie *Patton.* He was suddenly filled with confidence.

No bastard ever won a war by dying for his country. He won it by making the other poor dumb bastard die for his country.

He smiled as he remembered those lines from the movie.

But, unlike Patton, he would not be disgraced.

Chapter Sixteen

The dogs began growling as soon as Joe entered the dark garage which only intensified his anxiety. His mind was suddenly flooded with horrific memories of his New Orleans childhood home when he was no more than four or five.

Joe's father owned a pit bull named Cong, after the Viet Cong his father fought before Joe was even born. Cong was an undefeated champion in illegal dog fights and a legend in the darkest corners of the Ninth Ward. The dog was solid black, mean and nasty, with eyes Joe knew belonged to the devil himself. He vividly recalled the way the animal smelled and the same choking odor filled his nostrils yet again. This memory awakened the helplessness he felt when his father allowed Cong to strain at his leash, snarling and snapping within inches of his son. Joe would cower in a corner and beg his father to stop. Occasionally Cong would make contact with Joe's clothing, and sometimes even his skin. But the laughter from his father as he tortured his son was far more painful.

"Yeah, you cry boy," his father would say in his Cajun accent, "like a goddamn baby you cry. Just like you mama. But you mama ain't here no more, is she? You keep cryin' and maybe you won't be either. You be a man, boy, face this dog, or maybe one time I let him go."

Then one day his father left with Cong, and neither one ever came back. He'd heard later the dog fight ring was raided, Cong was destroyed and his father went to prison. Joe didn't care about either of them. His grandmother came and got him and that was that. His inherent fear of dogs, any dog, however, stayed with him.

And right now all the fear he'd felt as a child slammed into him like a train, and the ache in his gut caused him to double over. Then, when the lights came on, the first thing he saw was Luther's mauled corpse, and that was all it took. The contents in Joe's stomach erupted. McCaskey kept him from falling, and they all waited patiently until he finished.

"Oh you are *so* going to clean that up."

It was a new voice, but one that Joe recognized. He slowly looked up and saw Danny, standing beside an open door which led into the kitchen. Two brown and white, fully-grown American Pit Bull Terriers sat beside him, now silent and unmoving.

"Hello, Joe," Danny said. "Long time no see. I'd invite you in but you're kind of nasty. I see you've met my friends, all but these two beside me. Luther met them a few minutes ago. Didn't really hit it off though, but now they're anxious to meet you. To my right is Bonnie, and this is Clyde. They're brother and sister. Jasmine brought them with her the other night." He kneeled down, and the two dogs began to lick his face and playfully paw at him. Danny put his arms around both of them.

"They're just the cutest things, really. Had 'em since they were puppies, just part of the family now. My two boys ride 'em around like they're horses. Wouldn't harm a flea. That is, unless I say two words. And one of those words is," he paused, then said, "'ready.'"

The animals immediately stopped licking Danny and began the growling again. They stood eager, willing, muscles taut against their skin, their partially open mouths revealing glistening, white teeth, and an occasional drop of drool fell to the floor. Joe felt his heart hit another gear, and his breathing accelerated.

"DJ, Detective, Captain," Danny said, "it might be safer if y'all joined me up here. Wouldn't want y'all to get mixed up in all the carnage and stuff that's about to happen. Sometimes my puppies get a little carried away. Wouldn't want 'em to rip apart one of the good guys." They left Joe alone, and filed into the kitchen, fearlessly walking past the two pits. Joe retreated backwards, trying to put as much space between him and the dogs as he could. He slipped on the mess he'd just made and went down hard onto the concrete. His feet flailed and pushed against the floor until his back was, literally, against the wall.

"Where you going, Joe?" asked Danny.

"Danny, please," Joe pleaded, "not the dogs."

"Don't you want to know what the second word is?"

"No!"

"Actually," Danny said, "that's close. It rhymes with no. Same number of letters. Would you like to try again?"

Joe frantically shook his head.

"What's the matter, Joe? You afraid? A member of The *Family*? All you been through, and you're scared of a couple of canines?" Joe didn't answer. Danny looked down at his dogs, and said, "Sit!" Immediately the dogs did what they were told, and Danny stepped out of the kitchen and into the garage. Bonnie and Clyde remained where they were. He picked up a lawn chair and set it beside Joe, then hauled him to his feet. He grabbed a handful of dreadlocks and pulled until Joe winced in pain. "You didn't know I was here, therefore it stands to reason you and Luther came after my wife, my *pregnant* wife, and my kids. *My two-year-old boys*, Joe! How scared do you think *they* would have been?"

Danny threw Joe down onto the chair, then gripped the front of Joe's shirt and tore it open, revealing his chest and *The Family* tattoo. "Family!" he hissed. "What a joke. Do you actually believe that Tyrone considers you *family*? That he gives a shit about what happens to you? Tyrone will do whatever Tyrone has to, to make sure *he* remains on top. And Joe," he said, "that means he would go after your woman and your kids, the same way he sent you after mine, if he thought for *one second* you crossed him. Don't you know that?"

Joe looked down at the floor, and nodded.

"Of course," Danny said, and began walking back towards the kitchen, "I guess none of that matters if you're dead, does it?"

"Danny, wait," Joe pleaded, and Danny stopped. He turned and faced Joe. "I'm sorry, man." Joe said. "I didn't want to do this, I swear to God I didn't. I even told Luther that. But he threatened to kill me if I didn't help. He woulda done it, too. You know he would. The same way he killed the old man and the musician. I was there, but *he* killed 'em." He actually seemed remorseful. "I wouldn't have hurt your kids, Danny, or your wife, no way. No way in hell. You gotta believe me."

"If that's true," said Harwell from the doorway, "then why were you outside with a gun in your hand?"

Joe looked at her. "I told you. Luther would've killed me. I had no choice."

Danny walked over and stood next to the gangster. "Okay, Joe," he said, "let's see how badly you want to live."

****

Tyrone walked into his garage and found his men standing in a semi-circle, waiting on him. He felt a rush of adrenaline as he approached them, knowing they were depending on him to lead them into this historic quest, and with it the reward he'd promised them. For almost thirteen months he had planned and worked out every detail, all the while keeping it a secret and continuing with routine Family business. Finally, it was all coming to fruition. He fought to calm himself. The men looked at Tyrone expectantly as they waited for him to speak.

"Gentlemen," he began, "listen up. I am about to reveal all."

****

Danny whistled, and Bonnie and Clyde scampered to him. He positioned one on each side of Joe, then gave the order to sit. Harwell, DJ and McCaskey joined Danny and Joe in the garage. Joe started to tremble. The dogs were inches away and the evidence of Luther's ghastly death remained in front of him.

"It's all up to you, Joe," Danny said. "You tell the truth, you live. You try to lie and the last thing you'll hear is me saying that second word."

Joe's leg was twitching when he asked anxiously, "What if I tell the truth, but it's not what you want to hear?"

Harwell approached and knelt down in front of Joe. "Look at me, Joe," she said. When they had eye contact, she said, "I have a gift. I know when people lie. So let's play a game. I'll ask you some simple questions, sometimes you tell the truth, sometimes you lie. Okay?" Joe nodded. "How old are you?"

Joe hesitated. "23.".

Harwell shook her head. "Too easy. That was a lie. Try again."

"24."

She nodded this time. "That time you told the truth. Okay. Where were you born?"

"New Orleans."

"Product of Mardi Gras, huh? How'd you end up in Memphis?"

"My grandmother died when I was fifteen, left me by myself. All I had in New Orleans was bad memories. I had an uncle in Memphis."

"How many people have you killed?"

"I... I haven't killed anybody."

She looked at Danny. Danny understood. He said, "Ready." The dogs stood and began growling. Joe stiffened, then said, "Okay! Okay. One. I killed one dude, but only because he tried to kill me first. I got sick after, sick as hell. God is my witness it was self-defense. I'm no killer like Luther. I had no choice."

Harwell searched his eyes. She was satisfied. "That's better. It's fine, Danny."

Danny called his dogs off, and the growling stopped. Harwell turned back to Joe. "Why did Luther kill Bo Sanders? What did he do?"

"The musician?"

"Yeah."

Joe's head fell. "He didn't do nothin'. We didn't set out to kill him. He wouldn't tell Luther why the old man came to see him. Luther put a gun to his head to try and scare him." He looked at DJ. "I guess your father just panicked or something 'cause he tried to take the gun away. It went off."

No one said anything for several seconds. DJ had his eyes

closed. Then Harwell said, "Why did Luther kill my grandfather?"

Joe began shaking his head. "I don't know," he said, "I don't know. We should have just driven off. But the old man said Tyrone's name, then kind of made a move for his gun and... and Luther just shot him. Tyrone was furious. He always told us to never hurt a cop."

Harwell let that pass, then said. "Why were you following them in the first place?"

"Tyrone had us keep an eye on you after he..." He hesitated.

"I was there when he nearly killed Timecia," Danny said. "She knows."

Joe nodded. "He knew you and Timecia were tight so he had us follow you. We saw you go to the ballgame with the old man, so Tyrone had us follow him as well. We gave Tyrone his license plate, found out he was your grandfather, an ex-cop, where he worked, where he lived, everything. We were able to tail him to B.B.'s, then we paid a girl to let us know who he talked to. She gave us Bo's name. Tyrone told us to follow him and try to find out what was up between him and the old man."

He looked up at DJ. "I swear we never meant to hurt your father, had no reason to. All we wanted to know is what he and the old man talked about. That's all. But he wouldn't say. He had a lotta guts."

Harwell got up and walked over to DJ. She stood in front of him and tried to speak. Her eyes were moist. DJ said, "Don't say it, Detective. Do not blame yourself. This is not your fault. My father and your grandfather were friends. My father died honorably, as did your grandfather. The Family killed them. The Family is who I blame. The Family is who will be held accountable."

She nodded, not needing to say anything.

"Joe," said Danny, "were you at the meeting?"

Joe nodded.

"Who else was there?"

"Rod Man. Tyler, Josh. Me and Luther of course. All the front line guys."

Danny whistled, which got the attention of his dogs. "That's impressive," he said, "must have been important." He waited for Joe to speak. When that didn't happen right away, he said, "We don't have all night Joe. What was the meeting about?"

"If I tell you that," Joe said, "I'm dead."

Danny kneeled down in front of Joe and got inches from his face. "Now see, you got that exactly backwards. If you *don't* tell us, you're dead. You'll join Luther over there on the floor. Instead of one burglar who made the mistake of breaking and entering, there'll be two. Police here won't hardly even be bothered, both of y'all being lifetime criminals with records, not to mention gentlemen of color. The only thing they may be confused on is why y'all so far from home. Now," he said, "you got five seconds before I cut my dogs loose."

"How do I know you won't do that anyway, Danny? If I talk, I mean. You didn't give Luther no chance to say nothin'."

Danny nodded, then said, "You're right, Joe, we didn't. Thing is, we're up against The Family, so we have to be smart. Trying to take Luther alive wouldn't have been easy. He'd rather die and try to take us with him. So I said to myself, 'How do you fight an animal?'"

Joe knew the obvious answer, but left it unsaid. Instead, he asked, "How'd you know he'd go in alone? Leave me outside?"

"Gut feeling." Danny answered, then pulled Joe's hair again, nearly tipping the chair over. "And your time's up." He glanced towards his dogs. "Bonnie. Clyde!"

Joe's reacted immediately. "NO! Please, Danny, you win. I'll tell you what I know. Everything Tyrone told us, at least everything I can remember." Danny let go of his hair, and called his dogs off. "But I want y'all to know somethin' first. Y'all lucky."

"Lucky?" Danny said. "How the hell do you figure that?"

"Because," Joe said, "y'all may not be blood, but you more family than I ever had."

He dropped his head, and closed his eyes. The room was quiet. Even the dogs were silent. Joe then locked eyes with Danny.

"I'll talk. I'll help y'all any way I can."

"You do that," Harwell said, "and you just might live to be an old man." She placed her recorder on the hood of the Lexus and hit the record button. The red LED began blinking.

"Alright, Joe," Danny said, "start talking."

****

"Tonight," Tyrone said, "we drive these vans to a small airport in Millington. At 1:15 AM a corporate jet will land and taxi to one of the hangers to check out some flight 'computer issues.'" He mimicked quotation marks with his fingers. "You will then follow me into that hanger, at which point the doors will close and we will have complete privacy. While you all go through the motions of removing your bench and opening the floor, I will enter the jet and go over any last-minute details."

****

"And that's all that happens tonight," said Joe.

They had removed his cuffs, and he'd been given a glass of cold water and a clean towel. He was feeling much better.

"No product tonight?" asked Harwell.

"No," Joe answered, "not tonight. That happens tomorrow."

"Where's the jet coming from?"

"I'm not sure..."

"Mexico," interrupted Danny, "I'd bet on it. I was with Tyrone last year when he met with a guy just outside of Juarez. It's beginning to make sense now. Guy's name was Ricardo, I think. Yeah, it was Ricardo. Reeked of money. And I don't mean just a lot of money. It was more like Bill Gates rich. This guy could afford a whole fleet of jets. Had guys with AK's guarding the gate and the mansion. Had to be Cartel. Has to be connected to this."

McCaskey, quiet up to this point, finally had a question.

"Just how much cocaine are we talking about?"

****

"Two thousand kilos," Tyrone said. "And the best part? It's almost 90% pure."

He allowed his men to absorb that bit of information before continuing. "Tomorrow night, each van will be transporting 500 kilos from the airport, back to here. Once we are back inside the safe confines of this garage, we will cut the cocaine to 45%, effectively doubling our quantity and still remaining far above the average street purity of less than 30%. By eliminating the middleman, gentlemen, we will have four thousand kilos of product for the price of one. We will develop a loyal clientele who will prefer our product because of its purity. Our competition will be unable to compete."

No one moved. No one spoke.

"Each van will carry 1000 kilos of the newly cut product, each one traveling to five specific cities that I will have mapped out for you. I've already made the contacts and arranged the meeting places. They're expecting you. Each one will purchase 200 keys. They'll all pay cash. You shouldn't have to stop for anything except maybe to take a whiz. Where the cocaine was hidden, you will replace with cash. And I warn you, gentlemen, I will count it down to the last dollar. Don't be tempted. You won't get away with it. Besides," he said, "as soon as all this is said and done, you will all be millionaires. For every delivery made, each and every time that jet lands, you will each be paid one million dollars. Not bad for a few days work. And I challenge anyone to find a flaw in my plan."

Naturally, the men all agreed. There didn't seem to be any risk.

****

"He's all but eliminated the risk," Joe said.

Harwell, DJ, Danny and McCaskey all stared at Joe, mesmerized by his story. Despite what they thought of Tyrone personally, they admired the genius of his plan.

McCaskey broke the silence. "I gotta say something here," said McCaskey, "anybody done the math on this? Ya'll got any idea the kind of money we're talking about?" No one said anything.

"One hundred million dollars," Joe volunteered. "Tyrone just kept on sayin' it." The shock value was instant.

"Are you serious?" said Danny.

"That's more or less the figure I had," said McCaskey. "A kilo of good coke will normally fetch about twenty-five g's, and each van is moving a thousand keys. That means, when the coke is sold and the vans return, each one will be carrying twenty-five mill back to Tyrone. No wonder he can afford to pay his cronies so well."

"I wonder," said Danny, "if he'll call it off when Luther and Joe don't show up? Are you guys that important, Joe?"

"I don't know," Joe said. "Tyrone was fanatical about this thing goin' down tomorrow, like it was now or never. I ain't never seen him like this. I'm not sure if anything would stop it. It's like this would guarantee his legacy, or somethin' like that."

McCaskey spoke up. "Could tilt the odds in our favor," he said. "We could get with Millington Police or Shelby County Sheriffs and..."

"No!" Harwell interrupted. "No one local, not the FBI, not even the DEA. Nothing so obvious. You don't know Tyrone like I do, Jessup. He's got paid snitches everywhere. You try to sneak up behind him, suddenly he's not there. He can smell trouble. He'll know if we contact anyone, and I don't care what Joe says, I guarantee you he'd stop it then. He'd never take a chance getting busted with that much coke."

Danny said, "Detective, we're good, but we wouldn't have a prayer against Tyrone and twelve members of The Family. And don't forget about the Cartel who'll be on the jet, all armed to the teeth with AK's. If they're anything like the guys I met in Juarez, they're not afraid to pull a trigger, either. So as much as I admire our abilities, if we're going to stop Tyrone, we need help."

"I'm not saying that we go in and shoot it out with all those other guns," Harwell said, "I'm not suicidal. No, the best way is to let him think that everything is perfect. Let him load the cocaine, take it back to his mansion and cut it up, and then let those guys roll out of there like they don't have a care in the world."

DJ said, "Why would we do that? Why not once he's home with the coke, we call the Calvary, surround the house and go in and get him?"

"Because he'll fight, DJ, like a trapped rat. We don't know what sort of firepower he has in his vans or his home, but I'll wager it's major."

"You have no idea," Joe said. "Tryin' to get in is no easy thing. His house is like a goddamn fortress."

"Exactly," said Harwell. "and the last thing I want is one of our guys hurt or killed at the hands of that scumbag. But, if we watch, and wait until the vans roll, his ability to fight back will be substantially diminished. Textbook divide and conquer. And, he'll be committed at that point. Once those vans are on the road, there's no turning back."

"She's right," Danny said. "Until they're in uniform and rolling tomorrow morning, they'll remain on high alert. Once they're on the way, they'll let their guard down. But if you don't want to get MPD or anyone local involved, then who?"

She looked at McCaskey. "Jessup? Any chance Tyrone has connections to any of your good ol' boys in Arkansas? And I don't mean West Memphis or Little Rock. I mean from way back in the hills, from towns where even WalMart won't go."

McCaskey grinned. "You give me fifteen minutes on the phone Detective and I'll have all the home-grown, gun-totin' inbreds we'll need, all wearing badges and uniforms and who'll make them boys from *Deliverance* look like girl scouts."

She smiled back. "I can't wait to meet 'em." She looked at Joe.

"You ever hear Tyrone putting anyone in Arkansas on his payroll?"

He shrugged. "I never heard anything," he said, "but that don't mean nothin' really 'cause he don't tell me much. You're giving me way too much credit."

"He couldn't get to these boys," McCaskey said. "Trust me. They're God-fearing, flag waving lawmen who despise gangs and drugs and who just love a good fight."

"No more than I do," said DJ.

Harwell smiled. "I'm glad to hear that, DJ, because I'll need you to make a call or two as well."

DJ nodded. "You just tell me what you need."

"Detective," Danny said, "I still say we have one problem. We've got one killed in action and one prisoner and Tyrone is waiting to hear from both of them. And he knows that *they* know everything. I imagine he's wondering just what in the hell is taking them so long to check in. And the more time that passes, the more nervous he'll get."

"I agree," she said. "I just don't know what to do about it. I wish we could come up with a way to make him relax."

"The ideal situation is for me and you to join Luther on the casualty list. If he thinks we're out of the way, he may let his guard down completely. There's no way he'd shut it down then."

"You have my attention," she said. "I take it you have a plan."

"I might," he said. "I just might."

****

"Okay, gentlemen," Tyrone said, "your driver has the keys and you each know what van you're assigned to. This is a dress rehearsal so put on your uniforms and make sure you have your ID's and paperwork." He looked at his watch. "We roll in five. We'll only be taking three vans tonight since Luther and Joe aren't here. Are there any questions?"

No one said anything, but just then Tyrone's phone vibrated. He immediately pulled it from his pocket and saw that it was Joe. "Get in your vans and wait, gentlemen," he quickly said, "I've got to take this." He turned and ran from the garage and hit the "answer" icon as soon as he was inside his house.

"Joe!" he said, "talk to me."

"Tyrone," Joe said, sounding distraught and out of breath, "it's bad, man. It's really bad."

"Where's Luther?"

"He's dead, Tyrone. They were waitin' on us. Danny and the old man's granddaughter. It was a trap. They knew we were comin'."

There was a long silence on Tyrone's end. Finally, Joe said, "You there Tyrone?"

"How, Joe? How did he die? How the hell is Luther dead and you're alive?"

"He went in first, Tyrone. He told me to wait outside while he looked around. There was two dogs. They tore him up somethin' awful. There was nothin' I could do."

Tyrone removed the phone from his ear and was barely able to stop himself from throwing it across the room. He managed to calm himself enough to continue talking to Joe. "No!" he said, "No, Joe, this can't be right. Luther's not dead. Do NOT tell me Luther's dead."

"I don't... I mean, what do you want me to say?"

"Where are you now?"

"I'm in the car, Tyrone. I ran back to the car. I didn't know what else to do."

"What about Danny?"

"I shot him, Tyrone, him and the bitch cop. They didn't know I was outside. They never saw me. When they dragged Luther outside I was right there. When I saw him, I freaked. I just started shooting as fast as I could pull the trigger."

"Really," he said, more a statement than a question. "And they're dead?"

"Oh, they dead. They weren't movin' after I dropped 'em, but I put an extra bullet in each of 'em just to make sure. I... I..." Tyrone heard unmistakable sounds of Joe retching. Joe came back on, breathing heavily, and panic-stricken. "What do you want me to do now, Tyrone? You want me to come back to Memphis? Without Luther? I can't go back to the house. Lights were coming on all over the place. That's why I ran back..."

Tyrone didn't let him finish. "Why didn't you help Luther?"

"Tyrone, I swear to God I'd have helped him if I could. He didn't do hardly no yellin' at all. It was over so quick. If I would've gone in there, they'd of gotten me, too. And besides, if I'd gone in I never would've been able to kill Danny or the cop."

Something wasn't quite right but Tyrone couldn't put his finger on it. Suddenly he knew. "What's wrong with your voice, Joe? You sound like you have a cold or something."

Joe hesitated, trying to think. "I'm... I'm just upset, Tyrone. Luther was my friend, man. It was horrible how he looked. Like a whole pack of lions just ripped him apart. But I couldn't... "

He suddenly stopped talking. Tyrone said, "Joe? You there? Did I lose you?"

Joe whispered frantically, "I thought I heard something. Wait..."

Just then, Tyrone heard, in the background, someone yell, "Police! Police officers. Let me see your hands! Let me see your hands!"

"Oh, shit, Tyrone!" Joe said, "they found me. What do I do?"

Tyrone screamed into the phone, "Get out of there, Joe! Get out! Go! Go! Go!"

This time, more than one voice, much closer now, screamed, "Drop your weapon! Drop it now!"

"No place to go, Tyrone," Joe said, "they're right outside the window. Oh, shit! Mother fucker! I'm gonna try and run, Tyrone. I can't go to jail for no life. Oh, God, please don't shoot!"

Tyrone heard Joe start the motor. Then, an almost hysterical, "Don't do it! Don't do it!!"

Finally, multiple gunshots.

Tyrone listened in horror at what was surely Joe's last moments on earth. Eventually, he heard a car door open, and then a voice came over his phone, one he didn't recognize. "Who the hell is this? Identify yourself!"

Tyrone ended the call. He quickly dialed another number. "Rico," he said, "could you please change the number to this phone? Yes, immediately. Just text me the new number when you get it and inform the appropriate people. I don't care, Rico. Charge whatever you want."

He walked over to a chair, and sat down heavily. He wanted to grieve Luther's death, and even Joe's, but he didn't have time. He might try to arrange to have their bodies brought back to Memphis. When everything was over. He was now ready for it to be over. The price, he suddenly felt, may have just gone too high.

At least, he told himself, at the very least, Danny Boy and Detective Harwell were out of the picture. He never would have traded Luther's and Joe's life for theirs, but there was nothing he could do about that now. Patton's armies never fought a battle without casualties. And, like Patton, if he was to be a great leader, he would have to learn to deal with that inevitability.

He lifted himself from the chair and went back into the garage. He pulled himself together, and said, "Let's roll, gentlemen.

"Let's not keep the man waiting."

****

"Think it worked?"

McCaskey was reloading his clip and had directed his question to Harwell. Harwell looked at Danny. "What do you think, Danny? I thought it sounded pretty authentic." McCaskey and DJ had been the policemen. They couldn't take a chance on Tyrone recognizing Harwell's and Danny's voices.

Danny began clapping, then said, "And the Academy Award goes to..."

"There's one way to tell," Joe said. "Call Tyrone again. If he changed his number we probably pulled it off. If he answers, pretend you're the police again."

"He can change his phone number this fast?" asked McCaskey.

Joe nodded. "He can. He's got this guy named Rico. Man's a goddamn genius. Do almost anything like that."

McCaskey hit redial, ready to go back into angry policeman mode if he needed to. Instead, after listening a few seconds, he looked at Joe, amazed. "It's changed alright. That's weird he can do that. Why isn't this Rico working for us good guys?"

"I think maybe Tyrone can afford to pay him more than good guys can," offered Harwell. "Gentlemen, that was amazing. Tyrone now thinks Danny and I are dead and he doesn't even know about DJ and Jessup. Advantage good guys."

Joe said, "That still leaves me." They all looked at Joe. "What are y'all gonna do with me?"

"Frankly," Harwell said, "I wasn't sure you'd be alive at this point. What do you want to do with him, Jessup?"

Before McCaskey could answer, Joe said, "You could just let me go. Pretend you never knew me."

"Or," McCaskey said, "I could take you back to Arkansas, throw you in jail and charge you with murder, attempted murder, drug trafficking..."

"C'mon, man," Joe said, interrupting McCaskey. "I told you that dude left me no choice. He's been dead a long time and ain't no one cryin' for him. You'd never prove anything; I didn't even know his name. I done told y'all I was against this, didn't want to do it at all. And I just helped y'all in makin' Tyrone think everyone here took a bullet. Look, I got a brother in California, runs a construction business. Tyrone ain't gonna be lookin' for me. My brother'll give me a job. My girlfriend will bring my kids there if I tell her to. I can start over. Make an honest living for a change. Always wanted to try that."

"Or," McCaskey said, "as soon as we head back to Memphis, you can call Tyrone and warn him. You must think we're idiots."

"Don't know Tyrone's number now, remember? Even if I did I wouldn't call it. I don't owe Tyrone shit. And think about it, man. How much is my life worth if Tyrone finds out all that was play actin' and I'm still alive? Even if I was to tell him you all was on the way? Tyrone hates weakness. He believes in all that 'death before dishonor' shit when it comes to The Family. Well, I don't want to die. And I don't want to go to jail. I want to change my name and live a normal life with my family. Teach my kids that drugs and guns and gangs ain't the way to go. Maybe even help other kids. Do some good for once in my life. You guys can make that happen."

Harwell studied him. "I believe you," she said, "but it's not up to us. Tell you what. We'll put in a good word for you to the DA. Let him know what you did here. Who knows? You testify against Tyrone, anything could happen. But right now, we got too many other things to worry about."

****

Ricardo loved his jet.

It was a Gulfstream G280 and it was his pride and joy. It easily had the range to make the trip from Juarez to Millington and back with fuel to spare. It could seat ten passengers, but this evening, other than the flight crew, there was only Ricardo and two of his bodyguards.

There was no baggage since the trip was merely a practice run and they'd return to Mexico immediately after. Ricardo was finishing a late dinner of steak and potatoes, not a traditional Mexican dish but one of his favorites. He spent much of his time in the United States, especially Las Vegas, and he'd acquired a taste for American food.

He was savoring the last swallow of an expensive dinner wine when the pilot's voice came over the intercom.

"We're twenty minutes from our destination, sir."

He pressed an overhead button and immediately a lovely flight attendant appeared and cleared his dishes.

"Will there be anything else, sir?" Her voice was low and fluid, distinctly British, professional and non-suggestive.

"No, thank you, Amanda," he said. "You may remain up front for now. I won't need you again until sometime after we land. Be ready."

"Very good, sir."

Ricardo checked his Rolex and saw they would arrive precisely on time. He looked at the bodyguard closest to him and said, "Carlos. Come over here, please."

Carlos shouldered the AK-47 and maneuvered his way to Ricardo. Without a word, he waited for his boss to speak.

"After we land, we will taxi to a hanger. Tyrone will be waiting inside the hanger. I would like for you to open the door, locate him and show him inside. Then, go outside and observe. If there is anything that makes you even a little suspicious, I wish to know immediately. Tell Jorge to maintain his position inside."

Carlos nodded, then walked over to Jorge. He spoke in low Spanish to the similarly armed guard, who also nodded. Carlos then stood by the cabin door.

Minutes later, the pilot spoke into his headset. "Millington tower, this is November 216 golf sierra, handoff from Memphis approach currently over Dyersburg, established on the ILS runway two two approach, full stop. We appear to have a navigation computer issue we'd like to handle on the ground."

This was exactly what Greg Brunson, was expecting, and he was ready. "November 216 golf sierra, Millington Tower, report final approach fix with gear. Confirm you are declaring an emergency?"

"Tower, November 216 golf sierra, Negative emergency, thank you. We will report final approach fix, gear in transit."

"November 216 golf sierra, roger."

After a few minutes, the pilot spoke again.

"Tower, November 216 golf sierra, six miles over final approach fix, gear down and locked."

"November 216 golf sierra, roger. Runway two two. Wind two one zero at one niner, cleared to land."

"November 216 golf sierra, runway two two. Thank you, Millington. Appreciate the help."

Tyrone, who was standing behind Brunson, patted him on the back, then placed a small satchel on the floor beside the controller. He immediately exited the tower and ran back to his Cadillac where Rod Man waited.

Brunson eyed the satchel hungrily, knowing what was in it, but almost afraid to look. Slowly, he reached down and picked it up. Just as the jet touched down, he opened the satchel.

It was loaded with cash. He inhaled a sudden and relieved breath of air. It was there. It was all there. And there'd be another one tomorrow.

His troubles were over. At long last, his troubles were over.

Chapter Seventeen

Tyrone was escorted into the cabin of the Gulfstream by Carlos, and as soon as Ricardo saw him he rose from his seat, held out his arms and smiled.

"Tyrone," he said, "it's been too long."

The two men embraced, and Tyrone said, "Welcome to Tennessee, Ricardo. This is truly an historic day."

"And tomorrow," Ricardo said, "even more historic. Please, have a seat. Make yourself comfortable. May I offer you a drink? Perhaps something to eat?"

"I would like a drink," he said cheerfully. "Do you have bourbon?"

"Yes, of course." He pushed the call button, and Amanda immediately entered the cabin. "Two bourbons, my dear, on ice." Looking at Tyrone, he asked, "Do you have a preference?"

"We *are* in Tennessee," Tyrone answered, "How about Gentleman Jack?"

Ricardo smiled his approval. "Excellent choice. Amanda, two Jacks, please." She disappeared through the curtain.

Tyrone admired the spacious and luxurious cabin. "This is some airplane, Ricardo."

Ricardo smiled. "It gets me, how do you say? From A to B?"

Tyrone laughed. "I know it does. I think, very soon now, I will also own one of these." Just then, Carlos reentered the cabin and approached. He whispered in Ricardo's ear, then returned outside. Ricardo's beaming expression changed to concern. "Carlos informs me there are only three vans in the hanger with us. I am sure we discussed there would be four vans. Has something gone wrong?"

Before Tyrone could answer, Amanda returned with their drinks. She put them gracefully on the table in front of the men, then asked, "Will that be all, sir?"

"For now, Amanda. I will call you if I need you." She smiled, then left. Each man took their drinks, and Ricardo said, "To a long and prosperous life."

Tyrone added, "Very long and *very* prosperous." The glasses clinked, and each took a swallow.

"Now, to my question," Ricardo said, "and I'm sure it is nothing. But why only three vans?"

Tyrone forced himself to smile, then said, "Two of my men had to go out of town. Business. Couldn't be helped. Don't worry, Ricardo. All four vans will be here tomorrow night."

Ricardo looked deeply into Tyrone's eyes. "If you feel it is better, we could..."

"No!" Tyrone interrupted, a little too fast and a little too loud. Ricardo pulled back slightly in response, and Jorge stepped toward the men. Tyrone quickly regained control of his emotions. "It's fine. Everything's fine." Ricardo held a hand up, signaling Jorge to stand down. "I have everything in place," Tyrone assured him. "We will be full strength tomorrow. I have eyes and ears everywhere. *Everywhere*! If there's the slightest possibility that something may go wrong, I'll know about it. If that happens, we'll postpone. But," he said, downing his drink, "not until then."

Ricardo studied Tyrone carefully, then nodded. "As you wish, my friend. Nothing changes." Once again he pushed the call button. When Amanda appeared at the curtain, he said, "The papers, please." Moments later, she laid a two-page document in front of him. "Thank you, my dear," he said, dismissing her with a subtle motion of his hand.

"What's this?" asked Tyrone.

"This is a contract," Ricardo answered. "A very simple one. It merely states that I will provide you with 2,000 kilos of sugar. Very expensive sugar. You, in turn, will pay me twenty-four million in U.S. dollars, within five days of its receipt, by wire to the account we've already discussed. I would like you to sign it, please." He pulled a gold Urso pen from his pocket and twisted the top, revealing the tip. He handed the pen to Tyrone, then slid the contract to him. "You will sign the line on page two that has your name underneath it. I will then sign the other line."

Tyrone picked up the first page of the contract and read. It was exactly as Ricardo said. "I'm not sure I understand," he said.

"What is there to not understand, Tyrone?"

"This contract. What's it mean? You can't exactly take me to court on this."

Ricardo's expression turned suddenly cold. "Jorge!" His guard walked from the back of the jet and stood facing his boss. Ricardo gave a slight nod toward Tyrone. In an instant, Tyrone felt the barrel of the AK pressed against his temple. He didn't dare move.

"My judge," said Ricardo. "My jury. My court. I never lose. This is all you need to understand, Tyrone. From this moment on, we are no longer friends. I do not conduct business with friends because, from time to time, I am forced to hold accountable a business acquaintance who imagines he does not have to pay his debts. Of course, if you do not wish to sign, there will be no hard feelings. I will sell my sugar to someone else and we will resume our friendship." He waved his hand and Jorge lifted his AK and walked back to his post. "It is entirely up to you."

Tyrone stared uncomfortably at Ricardo. He wasn't used to being intimidated, or told what to do. He realized it was good he was unarmed. With all that had happened over the last few hours he may have acted irrationally. Reluctantly, he picked up the pen and signed. His new business acquaintance did the same.

"Would you like another drink?" asked Ricardo.

"Please."

Nothing else was said between them until after Amanda had refreshed Tyrone's drink. Then Tyrone asked, "Was all this really necessary?"

Ricardo shrugged. "Perhaps. Perhaps not. Allow me to explain something to you. My country is very poor. Where I was born, the poverty and disease we suffered daily was something the majority of Americans simply could never conceive of, no matter how destitute they imagine themselves. I watched two brothers and a sister die from starvation and cholera. This would never happen in your country. But now, the people in my birth village are prosperous and healthy, because I share much of the profits of my business. My money is therefore very important to me. Tyrone, I have seen what a lot of money can do to people. They believe, because they are rich, they are untouchable. They are always surprised when I find them with my judge and jury. They are found guilty, and then they die. I wish to make sure this does not happen to you."

Tyrone drained his drink in one swallow. "I understand, Ricardo. And I admire what you do for your people. You will have your money."

"Excellent. Then our business here tonight is finished." He stood and Tyrone stood with him. The two men shook hands, this time with no embrace.

"One final thing, Tyrone," said Ricardo. "You boast of your 'eyes and ears' watching for you. See that they are very vigilant. I sense in you that things may not be exactly the way you claim. I hope I am wrong."

Tyrone willed himself to appear confident. "My organization is ready. Our plan is flawless. Will I see you tomorrow?"

"No, I have business elsewhere. I will send in my place a most trusted associate. He will see to every detail."

"We will meet again then, one day," Tyrone said, extending his hand a final time. They shook, and he departed the plane.

"I hope so," Ricardo said softly to himself. "I sincerely hope so."

****

Harwell, DJ, Danny and McCaskey rolled west on I-40, blue lights on and making excellent time in the light pre-dawn traffic. They were anxious to return, ready to fine-tune and put their plan into motion. They'd left Joe with Nashville authorities for booking and eventual transport back to Memphis.

Harwell drove, and she and DJ were in front while Danny and McCaskey snoozed in the back. Harwell, despite having been up all night, wasn't remotely sleepy, and DJ, trained to go extended periods without sleep, was wide awake as well. DJ finally completed a lengthy text, hit 'send' then dropped his hands to his lap.

"Your CO?" Harwell asked.

DJ nodded. "Brought him up to date. Let him know what we needed."

"You think he can do it."

"I do. He can, and he will."

A few minutes passed. She said, "Have you spoken to your family since we left?"

DJ shook his head. "No. But I'll see them before the funeral. You?"

She also shook her head. "My family died with my grandfather. I don't have anyone else."

"I'm sorry."

"I'm sorry, too," she said. "For your loss." Then, "When's your father's funeral?"

"I'm not sure. Still a few days off I imagine. Black folks don't bury their dead right away. We give family plenty of time to travel from out of town. When's your grandfather's?"

"There won't be a funeral. He's being cremated. Probably be a memorial service at some point. Haven't really thought about it."

"What are you going to do after all this is over?"

Harwell thought that one over for a while. "I imagine, once I get my grandfather's affairs in order, I'll go back to being a cop. It's all that's left, all I care about anyway. There is joy in making a difference, you know?"

He nodded. "It's why I became a SEAL. Detective, my whole life Dad talked about your grandfather, and how he'd made a difference in his life. He loved Mr. Rocorro. That's why he wouldn't tell Luther anything. He'd do it again, the same way, if he had the chance."

They were silent after that, mentally preparing for what lay ahead. Without even realizing it, Harwell pushed on the accelerator just a little harder. The adrenalin was flowing.

They had much to do. They had less than 24 hours.

But they would be ready.

They would not be denied.

****

At precisely 1:55 AM the following morning, Tyrone was back in the tower at Millington Jetport. He watched as Brunson hit the switch that illuminated the runway lights. In just five minutes, the long anticipated sequence of events that would make him a very rich man would begin.

All four vans were in place and ready to begin loading the cocaine the jet would be bringing him. He'd replaced Luther and Joe and even managed to get US Marshal ID's and new paperwork made for the replacements. It had cost him more than all of the other fake credentials combined because of the short notice, but it was worth it. Compared to the profit he was about to enjoy, it was peanuts.

He had everything in his garage ready to begin cutting the cocaine immediately upon returning. He had the tables set up, the bags ready to fill and the flour standing by. His men were all well versed in cutting powder for profit and he anticipated the process would run quickly and efficiently. In addition, he had brought in more than a dozen others from his organization to help. He anticipated the vans would all be reloaded and on the road by sunup.

The weather was nearly perfect for the touchdown, the unload and subsequent takeoff. Clouds lingered in the area and this would allow the jet to sneak in almost invisibly. Memphis would pick it up on her radar of course, and there might be an inquiry, but no one would know anything about a landing at an airport that had been closed, theoretically, for nearly an hour. There would be no radio traffic, and the jet, and Tyrone and his vans, would be long gone before anyone arrived to investigate.

"There she is," Brunson said as he pointed to his radar. Sure enough, there was a blip moving towards the jetport.

"That's her! That's our plane," exclaimed Tyrone. He put the second satchel of money down, the same way he'd put the first the night before. This time, though, before he left to join his men, he said to Brunson, "I want to emphasize something again, just to make sure there is no misunderstanding." He deftly laid the barrel of his weapon against Brunson's throat. "No one can know about this. We were never here. You don't know me. You never met me. Tonight you were home in bed at this time."

Brunson couldn't take his mind off the gun. "I understand. I won't tell anyone. I swear."

"Because if you do, you know what'll happen, right?"

Brunson swallowed. "I imagine you'll kill me."

"That's right. But I'll kill you *last*. See, I know where your kids go to school. You got two pretty little girls in college that my men would enjoy, over and over, *before* they killed them. You have a son yet to finish high school. Wouldn't it be a shame for him to get this close and then not be there to get his diploma? And we know that little wife of yours just loves to gamble. We know where she gets her hair done, where she shops and where she meets her girlfriends for lunch. Do I make myself clear?"

Brunson couldn't speak. He nodded.

"Good. Now, as soon as that plane lands, shut off the lights and go on home."

****

Minutes later, the jet touched down. As soon as it did, Brunson shut down the runway lights.

DJ, dressed in fatigues, sat on a hill overlooking the jetport a safe half-mile away. He looked thru his binoculars, observed the landing, then keyed a button on a walkie-talkie. "Fox One to Fox Two. The Eagle has landed. I say again, the Eagle has landed. Will advise when the groceries are loaded."

Everyone on his team had secure military walkie-talkies, compliments of DJ's CO. Even Rico had no access to these frequencies.

Immediately, Harwell sent the confirmation. "Copy Fox One. The Eagle has landed. Standing by for groceries are loaded call."

DJ replaced the binoculars, and continued his surveillance.

****

Unloading didn't take long.

As soon as the jet had taxied into the hanger, Tyrone's men slid the large hanger doors closed and the work began. Tyrone's men lined up and formed an assembly line, handing the packaged bundles from one man to the next, filling up one van and then moving on to the next while others closed the floor and replaced the bench. Less than twenty minutes was required to complete the task.

"That was poetry," Tyrone said to Rod Man. "Pure poetry."

While the last bench was being screwed down to the floor, the rear hanger doors were opened, the jet taxied out and rolled quickly to the end of the runway. The pilots didn't need the runway lights to take off. The jet's lights were sufficient. The whine of her rear-mounted engines filled the air, and seconds later she was airborne.

"Let's go, gentlemen!" Tyrone said to his men. "Start your engines! Head it up and move it out! We still have work to do!"

One by one, the vans drove out of the hanger, with Tyrone and Rod Man in the Cadillac following close behind.

****

DJ watched the procession leave, then keyed the microphone on his radio. "Fox One to SEAL One. The Eagle has launched. I say again, the Eagle has launched."

"Copy Fox One. The Eagle has launched. SEAL One will monitor movement and make sure they park where we think they will. Stay safe over there."

DJ switched channels, then keyed the mic once more. "Fox Two, this is Fox One. The groceries are loaded and the family has left the store. I say again, the groceries are loaded and the family has left the store."

Harwell answered, "Copy Fox One. The groceries are loaded and the family has left the store. See you soon."

"Fox One to Fox Two. On my way."

****

McCaskey stood in front of twenty officers seated in a seldom used room of the West Memphis police station. They'd been recruited from the Arkansas towns of Lepanto, Marked Tree, Gilmore, Tyronza and Truman, and were all willing volunteers. They'd never done anything quite like this, and were anxious to prove they were up to the task.

"Gentlemen, we've been over this, but I'm gonna go over it again. There'll be two cruisers and one motorcycle for each van. Two men to a car and one on the bike. That's five men per van and that should be enough."

A Truman officer raised his hand. "Uh, Capm'? Question?"

"Okay," said McCaskey, "go ahead."

"I was jes' wonderin', what do you want them other boys to do while I make the arrests?"

Laughter all around.

McCaskey waited until the room was silent again. "Son, while I like your confidence, keep in mind that these are big-city gangsters and they will shoot you *without hesitation* if you give 'em the chance. I want zero casualties. That's the reason we're doin' it this way. They'll be relaxed. Their guards'll be down, hopefully, until it's too late. They're figgerin' their plan is perfect. But you boys, and the great state of Arkansas, is gonna show them that ain't the fuckin' case!"

The men both laughed and clapped. McCaskey continued, "That being said, this is serious. They got real guns and real bullets, and they'll use 'em to keep from going to jail. Make no mistake. This ain't no training exercise. This ain't no game. Use of deadly force is authorized and probable."

The room settled down, then McCaskey continued the briefing. "There's four main avenues out of Memphis. East and west on I-40, and north and south on 55. We figger that's the most likely way they'll go. You've all been assigned one of these avenues. Soon as it's been established they left the house, we move. Each officer will be armed with a sidearm and a shotgun, and one of you will carry an extra shotgun for the man on the bike. Each of you should be able to make eye contact with your designated van within 20 minutes after leaving here. Make every effort to do so. Tell you what, let's add five just to be sure. Exactly 25 minutes after we go, everyone make your stop. Pull up beside them. One of their tires are low. You want to help 'em out. I want the stops to appear friendly - just wondering who they're transporting, just shootin' the shit, bein' neighborly. The designated officer will then decide when it's safe, and he'll say, 'We got to go now'. Let me repeat that. 'We got to go now.' I want all three suspects in sight before the go words are spoken. Then take 'em down quick and clean. Is that clear?"

No one said anything. McCaskey took that as a yes.

"Boys, this is likely the most important thing you'll ever do as a police officer. You'll be taking a shit-load of drugs off the street, maybe save a few teens from taking that first hit. I have full confidence that you will succeed. Take no chances, keep your eyes open and let's everybody come back home."

"When do you think we'll move, sir?"

"Don't know. Pretty soon, I reckon."

"Why can't we go now. Get a head start. Find a place to hide and wait on 'em?"

"Tyrone may have people watching for exactly that. Can't take the chance. Once he moves, though, he won't be able to call it off. Then we'll take 'em down."

"You sure it'll be today?"

"We ain't *sure* of anything. We strongly *suspect* it'll be today. He'll be anxious to move this powder as fast as he can. They been cutting the cocaine for a few hours now. Sun'll be up before long. We got people watching the house. As soon as I get the word, we move. We'll run with lights and sirens until we hit the interstates, then we run silent. Meantime, make sure the tanks are full, your weapons are loaded and your minds are right. If you gotta piss do it now. Remember also that we maintain radio silence unless I contact you or if you're in grave danger and need backup. You all know your call signs. If the vans don't go where we think they will, I will contact you and let you know. Otherwise, stay the course. Good hunting, gentlemen. Smoke 'em if you got 'em."

The men all got up and filed out of the room.

****

"What time is it?"

Harwell looked at her watch. "It's almost 5:30." She looked at Danny, then said, "You've got a watch. Why didn't you just look at it?"

"Too tired," he said. "I can't lift my arm." He made a show of barely lifting his arm a few inches before he gave up and let it drop. "See?"

"You're weak," DJ said. He'd joined them in an empty foreclosed property, less than a quarter mile from Tyrone's mansion. It had been simple to enter. The upstairs bedroom window gave them a perfect, and private, view of the main gate and drive leading into the garages. Harwell was taking her turn with the binoculars.

"I'm what?"

"You're weak," DJ repeated. "She's not complaining. I'm wide awake. You sure you're up for this? Maybe we should leave you here and let you get your little nap in."

Danny sat up. "Hold on a minute, Navy boy. You don't know who you're talking to. You think I'm weak? Why don't we put on some gloves and get in a ring. Then we'll see who's weak."

DJ looked at Danny and grinned. "Anytime, big man."

"Hush!" Harwell said suddenly. "The gate's opening."

"It's about time," said DJ. He picked up his radio. "Do you see the vans?"

Harwell kept her eyes on the gate. "Not yet... wait! There they are. All four. Let 'em know."

DJ was ready. "Fox One to Fox Three."

McCaskey instantly answered, the excitement in his voice obvious. "Go ahead Fox One."

"The kids are moving, I say again, the kids are moving. Roll the sitters."

"Copy Fox One, the kids are on the move. Rolling the sitters."

"Fox One to Falcons One, Two, Three and Four. The kids are on the move. I say again, the kids are on the move."

"Copy Fox One, the kids are on the move. Wheels up time now."

Harwell looked at DJ. "I still can't believe you were able to get four Navy choppers to help us out."

"Funniest coincidence, Detective. My team just happened to be conducting their Sensor Management Training Exercise this very morning. Besides," DJ continued, "it's what we do. When one of our team calls for help, you answer the call."

****

Just as the Seahawk helicopters were lifting off from the Naval Air Station at Millington, the two Gulfstream pilots were wrapping up their extensive post-flight checklist from their hanger at Juarez International. Their passengers had disembarked more than an hour earlier, just after they landed. The pilots envied them. They were likely already home and sound asleep. It had been two long nights in a row and the pilots looked forward to a hot breakfast and then a warm bed.

The cabin door opened and the steps unfolded. They walked down and onto the floor of the hanger Ricardo rented. Ordinarily, the maintenance crew would already be busy, going over every square inch of the plane with a fine-toothed comb, but not today. They were alone and that seemed strange. Still, they reasoned, it was early and this particular flight was shrouded in secrecy. Perhaps the crew had not yet been informed. No matter - it was not their problem.

They opened the hanger's exit door to blazing sunshine and they were temporarily blinded. They raised a hand to block the sun, and were shocked to see that the hanger was surrounded by a SWAT team, with weapons drawn and aimed directly at them.

"Ho-la, amigos! Got - DAMN it's about time. How you guys doing?" A large American in an ill-fitting two-piece suit approached the pilots, walking quickly with his credentials open and in plain view. A gold badge glinted, and he was followed closely by two armed agents, weapons drawn and aimed.

Once in front of the pilots, he said, "I'm Scott Jenkins, DEA, USA. What took y'all so long? I mean, Mexico's hotter'n *hell!* I thought I was gonna pass out!" He flipped the wallet closed and put it in his jacket pocket. "Y'all under arrest, in case you was wondering."

The shocked pilots stared at Jenkins, dumbfounded. Finally, one of them recovered and said, "What's this all about? Why are you arresting us?"

Jenkins smile wryly. "Really Pedro? You want to go there? Okay. We're just gonna ask you some questions. See if we got our facts straight."

"About what?" the other pilot asked.

"Oh, hell, Pancho, it ain't all that big a deal. Let's see... Y'all took a ride without filing a flight plan. You landed in a closed airport. The FAA wants to discuss that tidbit with you *and* that air traffic controller." He turned to the men covering him and said, "Guys, what am I forgetting? Maybe it's the sun, but wasn't there something else?" He snapped his fingers. "Oh, yeah! There's a little matter of 2,000 kilos of cocaine, delivered to Millington, Tennessee, to some thug named Tyrone, so that *your* boss can get rich making kids in *my* country addicts! And that's what *I* wanted to talk to *you* about. Now, turn around so my boys with their guns here can make sure you don't have guns."

"You're making a big mistake. Do you know who we work for?"

"Ooh, hang on. I *love* these games. Is it Ricardo fucking Montalban? Is Tattoo gonna come waddling out and start yelling, 'De plane! De plane!'? Listen, I don't give a fuck who signs your paycheck. Assume the position *pendejos,*" he turned around and, grinning, explained to his men, "That means 'assholes' in Mexican," then, facing the pilots again continued, "or end up face down on this hot-ass tarmac. Comprende? And, by the way, your little jet now belongs to the United States Government. You got the keys?"

****

McCaskey ran outside to his men and began yelling. "Move out! Move out!"

The cruisers and motorcycles immediately began rolling, lights on and sirens blaring. McCaskey got into his own cruiser and followed. His heart was racing. Two days ago he didn't know Tyrone existed. Now he was in the throes of the biggest bust of his career.

"Fox Three to Fox One."

DJ answered, "Go ahead Fox Three."

"Be advised, twenty-five minutes from now, the children *will* be grounded."

"Copy Fox Three. Twenty-five minutes."

"Fox Three to Fox One, confirm Falcons are flying?"

"Roger that, Fox Three. Falcons are in the sky."

****

The first call from one of the choppers came in almost immediately.

"Falcon One to Fox One."

"Fox One to Falcon One. Send it."

"Falcon one is contact, Van One headed east on Interstate Four Zero. I'll continue to follow and advise when kids are grounded."

"Fox One copies."

A few minutes later.

"Falcon Two to Fox One."

"Go ahead Falcon Two."

"Falcon Two and Three is contact Vans Two and Three moving west along Interstate Four Zero. Falcon Four is contact with Van Four headed south on Interstate Five Five. Falcon Two and Three will follow to the west, Falcon Four will follow southern route."

"Copy Falcon Two, yourself and Falcon Three following vans to the west, Falcon Four will monitor mover to the south."

Five minutes later.

"Falcon Two to Fox One."

"Send it Falcon Two."

"The two vans moving west along Interstate Four Zero crossed the river and have now split. Falcon Two following Van Two moving west along Interstate Four Zero, Falcon Three following Van Three traveling north on Interstate Five Five."

"Fox One copies, Falcons Two and Three continue to monitor, advise any changes. Fox One to Falcon Four. Update status."

"Falcon Four to Fox One, Van Four is continuing southbound on Interstate Five Five and has just crossed into Mississippi."

"Roger that, Falcon Four, Van Four has entered Mississippi on Interstate Five Five. Advise any changes."

DJ dropped the radio and expelled a big breath. "Well," he said, "in ten minutes, all hell breaks loose."

"After that," Harwell said, "We go after Satan himself."

Chapter Eighteen
The Last Chapter

Tyler was headed west on Interstate 40 towards their first stop in Little Rock, just over two hours away. Josh was beside him and Anton was in the back, and all three were swaying to loud hip hop music that poured out of the van's speakers. They were all in a great mood. They didn't have a care in the world. They would soon be rich.

Per Tyrone's instructions, the cruise control was set to two miles per hour over the posted speed limit. Even though there was little chance of being pulled over - they were U.S. Marshals after all - taking unnecessary risks made no sense considering what was hidden underneath the rear floor.

Tyler noticed the motorcycle cop first. He immediately reached over and turned down the music.

"Why'd you do that, Tyler?" Josh was about to turn it back up but Tyler grabbed his hand.

"Look behind us, man. Cops."

Josh looked over at his side mirror. He saw the cop. He relaxed when he noticed there were no lights on. "So what, man? We ain't doin' nothin' wrong. He got no reason to pull us over. Turn the music back up."

Just then, the lights on the motorcycle lit up, and he pulled alongside the van. At that point, Tyler noticed the two cruisers. A deep, sick feeling began to form in his gut. When the bike was beside him, the officer motioned for Tyler to roll his window down. Tyler complied.

The officer lifted the shield on his helmet. He yelled over the noise of the wind, "Hey there, Marshal! Where you headed?"

"Little Rock!" Tyler answered. "Prisoner transfer!"

The officer on the motorcycle pointed a thumb back over his shoulder. "You got a low tire! No way in hell you'll make Little

Rock! Got some guys with me! Pull over and we'll help you take care of it!"

"What are you going to do, Tyler?" asked Josh nervously.

"I'd better do what he says. We got all the paperwork. Just don't panic. They probably won't even check."

He slowly pulled into the emergency lane and the motorcycle remained beside him as he stopped. Suddenly, one cruiser passed and moved over in front of the van while the other pulled in close behind. They'd effectively blocked the van in, their lights were on, and Josh was close to losing it.

"What the hell, Tyler? Where'd those other cops come from? Why are their lights on? What the fuck they doin'?"

"Relax, Josh. Be cool man or they gonna suspect somethin' is wrong . Remember we're cops just like they are."

The two officers in the cruiser in front of the van got out and approached the rattled men. Josh hadn't rolled his window down at that point, and the officer on his side had to tap on the glass before he did.

"Mornin' Marshals," he said, "What y'all got here?"

"Prisoner transfer," said Josh, trying desperately not to sound nervous. "We got the paperwork. You want to see it?"

The officer spit out the toothpick he'd been chewing on, and said, "Nah. We don't need to see all that." He made a show of checking out their vehicle. "Damn! You federal guys get *all* the big money. *Look* at this van! Ain't this *somethin'* Marv?"

The officer on Tyler's side said, "It is a sweet ride, I do declare. Newer 'n anything *we* got. Say, can we take a look at y'all's prisoner? See what the back of this lawman limousine looks like?"

Tyler said, "I guess that'll be alright. Go ahead."

"Now wait a minute," Marv laughed, "I don't want to open that door. He might decide to make a run for it, scare the shit outta me. How 'bout you come on, open up the door for us." He looked at Josh. "You, too, uh, *Marshal*, if'n you don't mind."

The two patrolmen opened the doors and waited as Josh and Tyler uneasily exited the van. The motorcycle officer had squatted down near the back of the van. Josh looked in disbelief at a completely flat tire. The officer noticed the look, and said, "I told ya it was low. I had no idea it'd gone flat. Must've picked up a nail somewhere. Real shame - brand new tire. No reason to fret, though. We got a truck on the way to fix it. Be back on the road in no time. Meantime," he said as he stood up, "let's open up that back door."

As Josh and Tyler stood at the rear of the van, all five patrolmen were gathered with them, shotguns over their shoulders. When the door was opened, Anton was seated on the bench, cuffed and looking frightened. It wasn't an act.

"Look at that rabbit, boys," Marv said, shaking his head. "Scared shitless! He must have heard about our Arkansas jails. Well, hell, that's enough fun for one day. You can close the door. We got to go now." Relieved, Tyler reached for the door.

"Yep," Marv said, then repeated, "we got to go now."

Two officers grabbed Josh and threw him against the van, holding him there with their shotguns. Two others tackled Tyler, and he was quickly cuffed. The fifth leveled his shotgun on Anton. He said, "I don't believe for one second that those cuffs are secure. You so much as scratch your nose and double-ought buckshot will splatter you all over this purty van. You understand me, boy?"

Anton leaned back against the wall, closed his eyes, sighed and nodded.

****

"Falcon Three to Fox One. The kids are grounded. I say again, the kids are grounded."

DJ excitedly answered. "Copy Falcon Three. The kids are grounded. Thank you."

They received similar calls, almost immediately, from Falcons Two and Four. Falcon One, however, had yet to check in.

"Fox One to Falcon One. Update status."

"Falcon One to Fox One. Van One is still headed east on

Interstate Four Zero and is not pulling over. Stand by."

"Copy Falcon One. Standing by."

****

Chad, the driver of that van, had been informed of the low tire, same as the others.

The difference was, he wasn't buying it.

"You gonna pull over, man?" asked his partner.

Chad shook his head. "I don't know. Something don't sound right to me. There ain't shit wrong with our tire. Call one of the others. See if they're okay. Do it quick."

His partner dialed a number. "There's no answer. Fuck!" He dialed another. Then another. "No one's answering, Chad. What the fuck's going on?"

Chad didn't answer. Instead, he slammed his foot on the accelerator and swerved hard left. The patrolman was barely able to avoid being hit and somehow kept the bike upright.

"Oh, no you didn't!" he said to himself. Lights and siren were activated. The two cars followed suit.

The chase was on.

****

Tyrone was online in his office, pricing private jets, when his cell phone rang. It was the cell in Chad's van. He thought it odd that they would be calling so soon.

He answered it, saying, "Talk to me."

"Tyrone!" a frantic voice said. "It's no good. They're chasing us."

The words, at first, didn't register. "What? Wait, *who's* chasing you?"

"The *cops*! The fucking cops! Two cars and a motorcycle. None of the others answer their phones. They... Jesus Christ look out!

Mother *fucker!*"

His brain would not accept this. "This is a joke, right?"

"Does it *sound* like a fucking joke, Tyrone? Do you not hear the sirens?"

He did hear them, but he had no answer. For the first time in his tenure as head of The Family, his mind went blank. It wasn't real. It couldn't be real.

"TYRONE! Did you fucking hear me? The cops know, man! We're fucking busted! What the fuck do you want us to do?"

"I... I don't know. Where are you?"

"Where ARE we? We're on the fucking expressway, going about 120! Rickey's in the back getting beat to shit! We..." There was a pause. Then, "Oh my god, Tyrone, this is fucked up!"

"What?" he said.

"There's a goddamn helicopter up the road. It's... I think it's a fucking *military* helicopter, flying low as shit." There was a pause. "Is he... have they got the goddamn *military* after us? Tyrone, he's heading right toward us! It's like a game of fucking chicken! Chad, stop man! Pull over! What the fuck are you *doing*? Chad! CHAD!"

There was a prolonged, terrible noise, then the line went dead.

Tyrone dialed the other three phones. Nothing.

It was unthinkable. His mind refused to grasp that he'd just fallen from the top of the world and into an empty pit. He watched as the Gulfstream jet on his screen began to fade; the irony was not lost on him. A fortune - *his* fortune - had just vanished into thin air. And with it, his empire. As he began to recover, his disbelief turned into anger, and he switched into survivor mode. He wasn't beaten yet.

He dialed another number. "Rod Man! Get in here. Hurry!"

He went to his safe and, with shaking hands, managed to open it. He stuffed his pockets with cash. When his pockets were full, he opened his briefcase, emptied the contents on his desk, then put the rest of the cash in it. As he closed the lid, his phone buzzed. It was a text from one of his moles.

Five MPD unmarks right outside your gate. They're looking for you T.

He sat down heavily and stared at the screen. *"Fuck!"* Tyrone said out loud. Then, "Think! *Think* Tyrone!" Just then, Rod Man rushed in. All at once, Tyrone knew what he would do.

"Grab the keys, Rod Man. We got to go. We got to go *right* now. I'll meet you in the Caddy."

Rod Man looked at him, baffled.

"NOW, Rod Man!"

****

"Falcon One to Fox One."

"Fox One to Falcon One. Go ahead."

"Be advised, Van One is down. I say again, Van One is down. I had a civilian aircraft enter my airspace. Was forced to deconflict and drop altitude. I guess I may have gotten a little too close. Driver panicked and hit a guard rail. Vehicle exited the road and is now upside down. Multiple rollovers. No other vehicles are involved. Suggest emergency responders be notified."

"Copy, Falcon One. Van One is down and requires medical attention. Glad no civilians were involved. Thanks for the help."

"Not a problem Fox One. Exercise is complete. All Falcons, off station and RTB at this time."

"Okay," said DJ, "they're returning to base. All the bad guys are accounted for."

"Not all of them," Harwell said. "We got the kids. Now I want Daddy."

****

Tyrone was on the phone as he got into the back of the car. "Charlie? Tyrone. I need you at your plane right now. What? Charlie, I don't care. I'm in a real bind. This is an emergency."

Just then, Rod Man got behind the wheel.

"Hang... hang on, Charlie." He muted his phone, then looked at Rod Man in the rear view mirror. "Get us to the airfield, Rod Man. Go out the back way. Don't waste any time. I'm trying to keep us out of prison. Get moving."

Rod Man started the car and gunned the engine. He veered off the main drive, onto the lawn and into the back yard. He threaded the caddy through large oak trees that covered the last hundred yards of his property. Rod Man knew exactly where he was going. He'd practiced this escape route until he could navigate it with his eyes closed.

Tyrone un-muted the phone. "Charlie, you still there?" He was barely able to keep the phone against his ear due to the speed and uneven terrain. "I know, Charlie, you already told me. But what if I was to offer you fifty thousand? Yeah, you heard right. In cash. Yes, up front. Good. I thought that might change your mind. I'll see you at the field. Have the doors open when we arrive and you be inside and ready to go. I don't know where we're going yet. The only thing I do know is that we're in one hell of a hurry."

They soon approached a wrought iron gate which Rod Man opened with a remote. He swung the Caddy right onto a side road and quickly accelerated on the smooth asphalt.

"We've just got a huge break. Charlie's already at the field, getting ready to take a friend's kid up. He's waiting on us."

"What's going on, Tyrone?" asked Rod Man.

"Not now, Rod Man. I have to think. Just get us to the plane."

The Caddy sped on.

****

Harwell's attention was drawn to the screen on her phone. Excitedly, she said, "He's on the move." She quickly grabbed another phone and dialed. "Lt. Matz? Detective Harwell. He's rolling. Are you in position?"

"We are, Detective," Matz said, "We have the gate covered. As soon as he's through, we'll get him."

"I want him alive," Harwell said, "if at all possible."

"Understood, Detective."

Harwell looked thru her binoculars and focused her attention on the gate. When it didn't open right away, she said, "Come on, Tyrone, we're waiting for you." More seconds ticked by. "What the hell are you waiting on?"

Suddenly DJ said, "Detective! Look at this." He showed her the phone that was tracking Tyrone.

"Son of a *bitch*!" Harwell said. She redialed Matz. "Lieutenant, there was another way out. He's on the streets. I'll radio his position as soon as I'm in the car." She looked at DJ. "See if Jessup's here, DJ. Hurry."

DJ spoke into the radio. "Fox One to Fox Three."

McCaskey's voice crackled over the air. "Fox One, go ahead."

"Daddy is running. Are you in position?"

"Right outside and waiting. What's going on?"

"Daddy snuck out a back door. We got to roll." They were in McCaskey's cruiser in seconds. "Alright, boys," Harwell said. "He's got a head start. Let's catch up."

****

Harwell was up front with McCaskey, keeping track of the Caddy. "Where're you going, Tyrone?" She studied the screen. "Okay, he's about a half mile ahead of us, headed south on Highway 51. I bet he's going over the bridge into Arkansas." She grabbed the microphone, ready to radio Matz, then hesitated. "Wait a minute." She studied the phone's map. "Get in the right lane, quick Jessup. He just turned west onto Whitney. Why would he do that?"

Danny spoke up from the back seat. "Oh, man, why didn't I think of that? He's going to the airfield."

"He's going where?" asked Harwell.

"There's a small airfield on Second Street and he's headed right for it. It's where we flew from when we went to El Paso. He's got a pilot on call that he uses all the time, keeps his plane there. He's almost there. We need to hurry."

Harwell grabbed the microphone on McCaskey's police radio. "Lieutenant Matz, this is Harwell. You copy?"

The answer was immediate. "Copy, Detective."

"Suspect is on Whitney headed west, almost to North Second Street. He's going to an airfield there where a plane might be waiting on him. We're right on his tail. We'll continue to monitor and advise. Have your units form a perimeter when you get there, have a chopper on standby and, just in case, an ambulance as well."

"Will do, Detective."

Harwell replaced the microphone. She looked at the phone. "Tyrone's absolutely flying. We can't lose him now. How fast can you drive?"

"Fast enough," McCaskey answered, then gunned the cruiser.

"But safely, right Captain?" Danny said, tightening his seat belt. "Arrive alive and all that?"

DJ shook his head. "You are such a baby."

"Now, see, there you go again. First I'm weak, and now I'm a baby. You just lucky we ain't in no ring."

DJ laughed. "Like I said before, anytime big man."

****

The Cadillac screamed to a halt next to the Beechcraft Baron G58, a twin engine beauty known for its speed and range. It was already out of the hanger, doors open and ready for boarding. Charlie was in the pilot's seat and was prepared to crank the engines and take off as soon as his passengers were seat belted in.

Tyrone's door opened even before they had come to a complete stop. As soon as he got out of the car, a man approached him. He'd been waiting by the plane, a young child was with him.

"Are you the son-of-a-bitch who kicked my son off this plane?"

he said angrily, "My six-year-old son?"

"Get away from me, man," Tyrone said, tossing his briefcase into the plane. "I don't have time for you." Unafraid, the man continued to berate Tyrone.

"Today's his birthday, asshole. I've been promising him his first ride in this plane for a week, and then..."

As Rod Man joined him, Tyrone pulled a pistol from his jacket and aimed it at the man's head. "You want to die? Do you want to watch your boy grow up, or do you want to die?" The man threw his hands up and backed off, protectively stepping in front of his son as he did. At that moment, Tyrone saw McCaskey's cruiser pull into the airfield. He swore. He'd run out of time and options.

"Boss," Rod Man said, drawing his gun and crouching behind the Caddy. "We got company."

"No shit, Rod Man," Tyrone said sarcastically. Making a snap decision, Tyrone ran over, threw the father to the ground, then reached down and snatched up the frightened boy. As the desperate gangster carried the struggling lad towards the plane, the horrified father yelled, "Hey, man, what are you *doing*?" He got up and started to run towards Tyrone. Tyrone calmly turned, and put a bullet into the man's shoulder. The boy watched his father go down and began hysterically shouting, "Daddy! Daddy, help!"

Tyrone lifted the boy by his arm until their faces were even. "Shut up, you little fuck!" he screamed. "Do you *hear* me? Shut the fuck up!" The boy's father tried to get up, but Tyrone turned his gun on him again. "Stay down," he said, "or the next one's in your head.

"Rod Man!" Tyrone screamed, "get ready to move!"

****

Harwell and the rest watched in horror as the scene unfolded. She immediately grabbed the microphone. "Lt. Matz, this is Harwell. Stand down! I repeat, instruct all cars to stand down! We now have a hostage situation involving a child. We have one gunshot victim at this time. Wait for my instructions."

"Copy detective. We will stand down. Be careful Angela."

Harwell had only one last instruction as the cruiser screamed towards the hanger.

"Tyrone is mine. You all need to understand that. If it works out, get out of my way."

****

Using his hostage as a living shield, Tyrone remained out in the open and defiantly faced McCaskey's cruiser as it approached. He shoved his pistol against the boy's ear and waited. The cruiser stopped some thirty yards away, and the four occupants quickly piled out the opposite side. Remaining behind the car for cover, they drew their weapons.

"Tyrone!" Harwell said, "Good to see you again. It's been a long time."

Tyrone's face looked puzzled for a moment. Then there was recognition, followed by disbelief.

"What's the matter, Tyrone," Harwell asked. "You look like you're seeing a couple of ghosts."

Tyrone smiled, then briefly laughed. "Hello Detective. Danny. Good to see y'all alive and well. I take it Joe and Luther have also made a miraculous recovery?"

"Yeah, those country doctors in Gordonsville are *really* good," Danny said. "Joe actually wanted to be here for this, this *Family* reunion, but he's at the DA's office right now. Can't shut that guy up, you know? But Luther, well, he's not saying much. Kinda hard to talk without a throat, and the rest of him in so many chunks and pieces."

Tyrone tried to appear in control "Who're your friends, Danny Boy?"

"I'm sorry," Danny said. "Where are my manners? You know Detective Harwell of course. This is DJ Sanders. As you recall, Luther killed his father so he traveled all the way from his Navy

SEAL base in Virginia just to meet you. And over here is Captain Jessup McCaskey. He's from Arkansas. His boys met your boys a little while ago. They sort of messed up your plans, didn't they?"

Tyrone turned suddenly livid. "You goddamn traitor. You're as good as dead, Danny Boy."

Harwell spoke again. "Let the child go, Tyrone."

Tyrone wasn't listening. He was too focused on Danny. "I treated you good, Danny Boy. Paid you well. What happened? Why would you walk away from The Family? Turn against us?"

"*Why?* Because *my* family was *way* more important. But that doesn't matter now. You can't win, Tyrone. Put the boy down and let's call it a day. No one else gets hurt."

"Well, Danny Boy, that's a nice offer, but I don't think so," Tyrone said. He still had his gun against the boy's ear. "I will shoot this child, so help me. You think I'm done? Not by a long shot." He quickly looked over his shoulder at his pilot. "Charlie! Get ready to leave *now*!"

"Please," the wounded father said, "don't take my son. Today's his birthday." Tears were spilling down the child's face.

"Rod Man," Tyrone said, "it's time to go."

Harwell stood, then walked around the car. Her Glock remained in her hand but was pointed towards the ground. "You're not getting into that plane, Tyrone."

Tyrone then forced the barrel into the boy's mouth. Harwell stopped. He said, "Oh, yes I am. Junior here is my flight insurance. He's going on his first plane ride after all. As long as I feel safe, Junior lives. Then, after we land, he and Charlie are free to fly back here and this story has a happy ending."

"Then take me instead."

It was Danny. He laid his gun on the hood of the cruiser, and walked toward Tyrone, hands out to his side. "C'mon, Tyrone. All you need is a hostage. I volunteer. Let the boy go home with his father."

Tyrone smiled, aimed his gun at Danny and pulled the trigger. Danny immediately fell to the ground. The child screamed, terrified by the noise, and began to struggle frantically to free himself from Tyrone's grip.

Harwell rushed over to Danny. She knelt beside him. "Danny!" she cried. He wasn't moving. She got up and began walking to Tyrone.

He aimed his gun at Harwell. "Stay where you are, Detective. Do not come any closer."

"You won't kill me," she said, "Remember? You don't kill cops."

"I don't see a badge," he said, then put his gun against the child's forehead. "but if you take another step, bye-bye Junior." Harwell hesitated, just a couple of feet away. She could almost touch him.

She laid her Glock on the tarmac. "Let him go, Tyrone," she said, "and take me instead."

"Take *you* now? Have we got any other volunteers?" Tyrone yelled at DJ and Jessup.

Harwell kept talking. "This isn't your style. I'll be your hostage, your insurance policy. Let the child go."

While she had everyone's attention, DJ slowly dropped to the ground. He quickly scanned his limited targets, extended both arms underneath McCaskey's cruiser and carefully aimed his weapon.

"Look at his father, Tyrone. Put yourself in his place. What if someone had a gun against Kristin's head? How would you feel?"

Harwell had hit a nerve. Tyrone hesitated. Suddenly, a shot rang out and one of the tires on the airplane exploded. Instantly, more shots rang out and Rod Man went down, hit in both legs. As he laid on the asphalt, Rod Man tried to return fire, but he was no match for DJ's skill and training. DJ fired first, and put a bullet into the gangster's chest. Rod Man was done.

Distracted, Tyrone moved his eyes away from Harwell. It was all she needed. She pulled the boy from Tyrone's grip and threw him tumbling toward his father. Despite his injury, his father gathered him up, then took him inside the hanger. Enraged, Tyrone swung his weapon around, wanting to pummel Harwell's face. But she was ready.

Her time had come.

She jumped, and with a powerful kick, knocked Tyrone's gun from his hand. As he watched it go skidding across the tarmac, she reached up, grabbed Tyrone's head with both hands and, with every ounce of her strength, slammed his face into her knee, caving teeth and cartilage. He staggered on the edge of consciousness, but before he could recover she threw a vicious right cross into his bloodied mouth. All the frustration she had borne for years went into that punch. Images of Timecia and Kristin spiked a sky high adrenaline level, and her strength surged accordingly. Tyrone's head swung violently to his right, and his body followed. He went down, but somehow remained conscious.

"That was for Timecia," Harwell said.

Danny, now standing next to Harwell, said, "That was pretty bad ass, Detective. Maybe *you* should be Mr. T."

Tyrone looked at him, squinting until he was finally able to focus, then shook his head in disbelief. "*Shit*! How many lives do you *have*, Danny?"

Danny pulled his shirt up, revealing the bullet-proof vest he was wearing. "Little present from our new friends in Arkansas."

Tyrone shook his head. "Should've aimed higher."

Harwell looked at McCaskey. "Jessup, radio Matz and tell him to move in."

"Way ahead of you, Detective."

"Good. Then come cuff this pussy."

Her words stung. Tyrone was on his hands and knees. There was blood dripping from his nose and mouth. He attempted to stand upright.

"What's the matter, Tyrone?" Harwell sneered. "Dizzy?"

He looked at her. "You'll regret this, Detective," he said, pulling a handkerchief from his pocket and getting shakily to his feet. "My lawyers will eat you alive."

She laughed. "You *still* think you're all that, Tyrone? Like you're still *somebody?* You're *nothing* Tyrone. There's no more

Family. You have no one left."

"I don't *need* anyone," Tyrone hissed, then looked at Danny, "and *you* won't be able to hide from me. You can't walk away, Danny Boy. I won't *allow* you to walk away. Once Family, *Always* Family, remember? You think I'm beaten? I'm not beaten. Not by a long shot. I am *Ty-rone Reed!*" he said, beating his chest with each syllable of his name. "I am head of the goddamn *Family!* You can't hold *me!*" he screamed, "Not for long! I am *invincible!*"

Harwell shook her head. "You still don't get it, do you?" She walked over to McCaskey. "Let me see your cuffs." He handed them to her, and she walked behind Tyrone and cuffed him. "The bottom line," she whispered in his ear, "is this: My family just kicked your family's ass!"

He laughed. "Just a whole lot of tough talk," he said, "Strange comin' from a girl whose momma blew her own brains out after boy-toy shoved his dick down your throat."

His words hit Harwell like a slap in the face. "What did you just say?"

"Tell me something, detective," Tyrone hissed, looking over his shoulder, "did Grandpa take over where boy-toy left off?"

Without a word, Harwell walked over and picked up Tyrone's gun, then started back toward him.

"Detective," said Danny, "what are you doing?"

Harwell ignored him. She stood in front of Tyrone and aimed the gun at his forehead. "Tyrone," she said, "it just now occurred to me. It's time for you to go."

"Alright. You win," he said. "Take me in. But I promise you this. I'll beat you in court."

"You're never going to see the inside of a courtroom, Tyrone. I'm passing sentence right now."

"Angela," McCaskey said, walking toward her, "you don't want to do this."

DJ held an arm out, stopping McCaskey. "Let it play out, sir. She knows what she's doing."

Tyrone's face registered confusion at first. Then he understood.

"You're going to *shoot* me?"

"That's just *exactly* what I'm going to do."

"No!" he said, "This isn't right. This isn't your decision." He stumbled backwards and fell, but his eyes never left the gun.

"Oh, yes it is," she said, standing over him, the barrel of the weapon never wavering from his head. The wail of police sirens filled the air, but Harwell didn't flinch. "How does it feel, asshole, *knowing* you're going to die?"

He was suddenly back on the streets in Nutbush, standing over Harrington and reliving what he'd said just before his first kill died. It was nearly his very words. Now he knew exactly how his victim felt. He was alone. He felt helpless. He felt something he'd never known before. He was completely petrified.

"Five seconds, Tyrone."

"Detective, please," he said, "I'm sorry. I shouldn't have said that about your grandfather."

"Four seconds."

"I'll do anything."

"Three seconds."

"No. Please don't."

"Two seconds."

"I'm begging you. Please don't kill me."

"Time's up, Tyrone."

Tyrone closed his eyes.

"This for my grandfather, you son of a bitch!"

Her finger tightened on the trigger.

No, Angel! a voice whispered in her head. It echoed over and over. A vision of her grandfather went through her mind.

She pulled the trigger. The gun fired. The bullet screamed toward its target.

Tyrone's world went suddenly black.

****

As scores of Memphis Police began to arrive on the scene,

Danny walked over, looked down at Tyrone, then looked at Harwell. "Sweet Jesus, Detective. Why the hell did you do that?"

"He deserved it." She handed Tyrone's gun to McCaskey.

Danny looked at his body laying on the ground, utterly still. He looked beside Tyrone, at the hole the bullet left in the asphalt. "You know, just a couple of inches to the left and he'd be dead for real.
You cut that awful close."

"I had every intention of blowing his head off."

Danny looked at her, puzzled. "You mean you missed?"

"I never miss."

"Then what changed your mind?"

She was thoughtful. "A guardian angel," she finally said. "My whole life, all I ever wanted was for my grandpa to be proud of me. Still do, and I almost blew it. He may be gone, Danny," she continued, then tapped her chest over her heart, "but he'll always be here. Tyrone could never take that away. It's the only reason he's still alive."

Danny knelt down and slapped at Tyrone's face. "Poor bastard's fainted. Probably just as well, 'cause when he looks in the mirror and sees what's left of his face? Damn! I busted up a few folks when I was fighting, but not like this. Remind me to *never* piss you off."

"Danny," she said softly, "that was one of the bravest things I've ever seen. How did you know he'd aim at your chest?"

"I didn't," he said, smiling, "but I was sure hoping."

Harwell walked over and stood in front of DJ. "Great shooting, DJ. The way you took out Rod Man? Damn."

DJ shrugged. "You needed a diversion, I gave you one."

"Yeah, but the tire? Brilliant."

"There was no way they were getting on that plane."

Just then two MPD cruisers pulled up and stopped next to the hanger. An ambulance pulled in directly behind them. One Paramedic went to attend to the wounded father and another looked over Rod Man. He was still alive, but barely.

Two of Memphis' finest headed straight to Tyrone.

Lt. Matz got out of the lead car. He walked over to Harwell, and said, "Well done, Detective. Because of you, we got all the top Family members locked up, screaming for lawyers or wanting to cut a deal."

"I had help, sir."

He walked over to McCaskey and offered his hand. "We want to thank you and your men from our neighbor across the river. Just an outstanding effort. If there's anything we can ever do for the state of Arkansas, please feel free to call."

"I appreciate that Lieutenant," McCaskey said.

He then went to DJ and shook his hand. "I can't begin to express my gratitude to you and the United States Navy."

"We didn't do anything, sir. We were just conducting an exercise."

Matz nodded. "I understand."

He stepped in front of Danny and looked him over. "You know, son," he said, "our gang unit could use a man like you. You ever thought about being a cop?"

Danny smiled. "You know, I believe I'd like that. And I need a job. Company I used to work for just went out of business."

Matz nodded. "Come and see me."

He then pulled out a badge from his jacket pocket and tossed it to Harwell. "I believe this belongs to you." She caught it, looked at it, smiled, then put it on her waist.

"Welcome back, Detective."

"It's good to be back, sir."

He looked at Tyrone as he was being led to a squad car. "What happened to his *face*?"

Harwell smiled. "He... fell, sir."

Matz laughed. "Hell of a fall."

****

A few hours later, Harwell walked into Timecia's room at the Med and found her there with her mom and Kristin. She said, "We got him, Timi, and he'll never hurt you, or anyone else, ever again."

Timecia's eyes brimmed with tears. "Oh my God, really?"

Harwell nodded. "Really."

Timecia drew her hand to her mouth, and her eyes showed disbelief. Then, removing her hand, she said, "My daddy told me that there was an angel watching over me. He meant you, detective."

"Your daddy?" Harwell said. She knew he'd died a long time ago. "You mean when you were a little girl?"

Timecia shook her head. "No," she said, "It was after all this happened. God sent him to me, the same way God sent you to us."

Harwell felt something stir deep inside her. She said, "Thank you, Timecia."

"Thank *you*, Angel," she whispered, "for everything."

And then tears fell as the weight of the world lifted, just like that, off her shoulders. She'd lived in fear for years, and now suddenly didn't have to be afraid anymore. Her mother stood, and wrapped her arms around Harwell. "Detective, I don't know what to say."

"Don't say anything. Just take care of my girls."

Harwell drove home. She went straight to her bed and tumbled into it, exhausted. She whispered, "Thank you, Grandpa."

She then fell into a deep sleep.

****

Jasmine turned onto her street and noticed her garage door was open. She saw Danny sitting on the porch steps, waiting for her.

She stopped short of the garage, unbuckled her sons from the car seats and let them out first. Bonnie and Clyde bounded after the twins, beating them to Danny. He knelt down and played with them briefly, grateful for what they'd done for him. The boys were screaming, "Daddy! Daddy!" and rushed to his arms. Danny picked them up, and savored the moment.

Jasmine watched as her sons hugged their dad. Danny whispered something to the boys, set them down and they dashed into the house. The dogs followed. Danny and Jasmine stood where they were for a minute, then rushed into each other's arms. They held each other, almost afraid to let go.

Jasmine whispered into his ear, "You're sure about Tyrone? Is he really gone?"

"Well, let's just say that I'm unemployed right now."

Jasmine kissed him. "We'll manage, honey. We'll be fine."

"Actually," Danny said, "I may have a job. Lieutenant Matz wants me on MPD's gang unit."

Jasmine looked at him in disbelief. "You're going to be a *cop*?"

He shrugged. "Don't know for sure. Maybe." He patted her stomach. "How's Isabella doing?"

She covered his hand with hers. "She's just fine, Danny. She missed her Daddy."

"And I missed her momma."

They walked into their home, arms around each other.

The garage door closed behind them.

****

DJ opened the apartment door, and stepped inside. His mother and sister were seated on the couch, watching the news. His sister stood, then rushed to her brother.

"Oh, DJ! Are you alright?"

He nodded. "I'm fine."

"We were so worried." She leaned back from him, nodded toward the TV, then said, "Did you do all that?"

"Not by myself," he said, "I had a lot of help."

DJ sat beside his mother on couch. Her eyes remained glued to the broadcast. "Are those the boys who killed your daddy?"

DJ put an arm around her, and said, "Yes, ma'am."

She nodded, set her jaw, and said somberly, "Good. I hope they burn in hell."

$$**********$$

McCaskey drove his cruiser back to his office in West Memphis. His team was waiting on him. They began applauding and hooting as he got out of the car. He smiled and took it in. The men settled down.

"Boys," he said, "today we made history. Y'all gonna be all over the TV and the Internet. You did a hell of a job. I ain't never been prouder. Not bad for a bunch of rednecks." The men all laughed. McCaskey continued, "We sent the whole world a message this morning."

"Don't fuck with Arkansas?" one of the men asked.

"You goddamn right!" McCaskey said.

The cheers and laughter were long and loud.

$$**********$$

Rico watched the story as it unfolded on his computer. He shook his head, then sighed deeply. "I tried to tell you," he said to Tyrone's picture. "Remember? But you just wouldn't listen."

He closed out the window then sat back in his chair. He mused, "I don't know. Maybe I'm working for the wrong guys. Maybe the good guys need someone like me. Smaller budget, maybe, but way better job security."

He decided to seriously think about it.

Epilogue

"Timecia Harrison."

As members of her family erupted in joy, Timecia walked across the stage and accepted her diploma. Annie was perhaps the loudest of them all.

"You go, girl!" she screamed. "I told you you was smart. I *told* you!"

Harwell sat with Timi's family, clapping loudly and beaming with pride as if she was her own sister.

And in a way, she was. Kristin sat on Harwell's lap, her tiny hands mimicking all the others who clapped for Timecia. Her mother sat beside Harwell, and she took her arm in both her hands and laid her head on Harwell's shoulder.

"This is a day," she confided to Harwell, "that I was afraid to dream would ever happen. My little girl, once lost in a sea of drugs, walking across that stage and getting her diploma. Thank you, Detective. Thank you! You have made such a difference in her life!"

Harwell smiled. "That's all I've ever wanted," she said.

Mrs. Harrison raised her eyes towards the heavens. "Your grandfather," she said, "is as proud of you today as I am of Timecia." She turned and made eye contact with Harwell. "Know that. Know that for a fact!"

****

The tardy bell rang in the hallway of Edwin Markham Middle School, and the few students still loitering hurried to their classrooms. The school was in Watts, a neighborhood of Los Angeles notorious for riots, gangs and poverty. Kids here were largely Latino and African-American and raised in single parent homes.

The students in Mr. Chandler's history class immediately

noticed the stranger seated next to their teacher's desk. Behind him on the board was written: *Mr. Manning.* As soon as they were all seated, Mr. Chandler stood and got them quiet.

"Class," he said, "this is Mr. Manning. He is a guest of ours this morning. I want you all to pay very close attention to what he has to say." He then left the classroom, closing the door behind him.

Mr. Manning rose, and said, "I asked Mr. Chandler to leave because I want all of you to feel free to say absolutely anything that comes to your minds. I'll start with this question." He raised his own hand above his head. "How many here belong to a gang? Or want to be in a gang?"

There was hesitation, then one student raised his hand. Then several hands went up.

Mr. Manning chose the one who looked the toughest and said, "Do you know how big a fool that makes you?"

He got exactly the response he wanted. "What the fuck you know about being in a gang?"

Mr. Manning smiled, then put his dreadlocks behind his back. "I'm so glad you asked." He unbuttoned his shirt, then opened it, revealing The Family tattoo.

Joe turned slowly, giving everyone in the classroom visual evidence of his past.

"Now that you have my credentials," he said, "I'd like to tell you a story."

He had their undivided attention.

****

Captain Jessup McCaskey and Detective Angela Harwell walked together, arm in arm, thru a tunnel and onto the field at Redbirds Stadium. It was a beautiful late fall afternoon, and a brisk breeze kept the flags around the stadium whipping and snapping smartly against a cobalt blue sky.

They were both in full dress uniform, as were the hundreds of officers who lined the walls, two and three deep in places, around the entire stadium. They were in the parade rest position, feet apart and hands behind their backs, and had traveled from near and far to show respect for their fallen comrade. And while Harwell knew they'd be here, she wasn't prepared for the impact it had on her. It took her breath away and she unconsciously gripped McCaskey's arm a little tighter.

"You okay?" he asked.

She looked at him. "Seriously?"

He smiled, and patted her hand. "You'll be fine."

She took an urn from her shoulder bag, and they made their way around the field. Each officer snapped to attention as they approached, and held a salute until they passed. Every badge on the field had a black band across it and the American flag in center field flew at half-mast. Harwell was glad McCaskey was with her. She wasn't sure she'd have made it otherwise.

It took nearly half an hour to make it back to home plate, and when they were finally at the end of the long line Harwell began to cry. There stood DJ, in full dress Navy uniform, and Danny, proudly wearing his new MPD uniform, saluting their friend.

She smiled through her tears. "Oh, DJ, thank you for being here."

"Wouldn't have missed it, Detective."

She looked at Danny, approvingly. "You look good in that uniform, Danny."

"I look good in everything, Detective."

Harwell laughed. "Same old Danny."

As she walked by them, DJ muttered under his breath, "Same old bullshit is what it is."

"You lucky we ain't in no ring, Navy boy."

"Anytime, big man. I got nothin' to do after this."

Harwell turned and smiled at them, letting them know she'd heard the exchange. McCaskey led her to a microphone, tapped it to make sure it was on, and then stood to the side.

Harwell, clutching the urn with both arms against her chest, began to speak.

"My grandfather," she said, her voice echoing around the park, "was a man of few words. I plan to follow his example. What he would say to you all, if he could, would be, 'Go home. Why are y'all here? Season doesn't start for another four months.'" Laughter spread through the ranks. She continued. "He was a simple man who liked simple things. Things like baseball, family and being a police officer. Your being here today, honoring my grandfather, means the world to me. For a time, I thought I had no more family. I was wrong. I look around this field and realize I am surrounded by family. Thank you, all of you, for making this day so very, very special."

She stepped away, and McCaskey turned the mic off. There was a drum roll, and then a lone bugler began to play taps. Harwell walked over to third base and was glad the wind was blowing from behind her, towards the outfield. She removed the top of the urn, poured some of the ashes into her hand and held them for a while. "I'm sorry it took me so long, Grandpa," she whispered, "but I just wasn't ready to let you go." She threw the ashes straight up, and watched them fly into left field. She then emptied the urn into the wind, and as the last ash settled into the grass, the final note from the horn faded.

Rodney Rocorro was laid to rest.

Later, after everyone had gone, Harwell sat alone in the third base stands, just behind the dugout, in the very seat she occupied at their last game together. She reached in her bag and drew the two bottles of beer that her grandfather had placed in the footlocker. She opened one, then put the bottle in one of the cup holders. She opened the second bottle, took a long swig, then smiled.

"We should have a pretty good team next year, Grandpa," she said. "Good hitting. Pitching looks solid as well."

They talked for some fifteen minutes while they enjoyed their last beer together. She told him of her plans; she shared her hopes and dreams with him. She shed a tear here and there, but mostly she smiled. They talked until her beer was finished.

Finally, standing, she gazed into left field and said, "Good-bye Grandpa. I love you." She walked quickly up the steps and left the stadium.

Her grandfather's beer remained, untouched, her empty bottle beside it.

****

Tyrone Reed knelt at the altar of the prison church, early on a Monday morning. He began every morning here, and he was nearly always alone. He was just about done saying his daily prayers. He had found Jesus, as so many of the inmates did. There's not much else to believe in, and with so much time to think about your sins you become frightened of what may be awaiting you after you die. He thought about death often these days. He'd never worried about his own mortality, until that morning at the airfield when he was sure Harwell was going to shoot him with his own gun.

He and his lawyers had meekly agreed to a lifesaving plea. Tyrone received a 199 year sentence. If, somehow, he ever did get out, with good behavior perhaps, he figured he would be well over 150. And even after only just over a year here in the West Tennessee State Penitentiary he'd felt his health decline. He realized it was unlikely he would ever see 50, much less 150.

It was a life sentence, and he knew it.

He finished his prayers, and made the sign of the cross over his torso. When he was a little boy his grandmother had taken him to a Catholic church, and this is what he'd chosen here. No reason except he was vaguely familiar with it and some of the customs. He was surprised with what he remembered at his first mass there. Like riding a bicycle.

Unlike most of the other inmates, Tyrone never had visitors. Also, for his own safety, he was kept isolated in Protective Custody, away from general population. It was like she'd said at the airfield. He was utterly alone. The Family that once meant everything was now nothing more than a tattoo on his chest. With all of his top lieutenants in jail as well, the entire organization had crumbled. It was his own fault. He'd been stupid, consumed with greed. He'd lost everything on that horrible day, the day he was so sure he'd have riches beyond his wildest dreams, but instead ended up broken and defeated. The depression was overwhelming. He wasn't sure how much more he could take.

He stood, and made his way to the end of the pew where he kneeled and crossed himself one last time. When he got up to leave Tyrone found himself face to face with a large Hispanic prisoner he'd never seen before. Tyrone attempted to walk around him.

"Excuse me, please," he said timidly. His power was gone. The position of authority and muscle that he'd once enjoyed as head of The Family was barely a memory now, and that had been a difficult adjustment.

The Hispanic man gripped Tyrone's arm. "Are you sure you have said all of your prayers, amigo? I can wait a little longer should you need more time."

"No, no," Tyrone assured the man, "I'm finished. The sanctuary is all yours."

The man's other arm swung around, and plunged a razor-sharp six-inch shank deep into Tyrone, just under his rib cage. He left it there a moment, then sliced diagonally across his abdomen before removing the blade. Tyrone felt his head being pulled back, then sharp pain as the homemade knife cut deeply across his throat. The man released Tyrone, and let him collapse to the floor.

As Tyrone bled out, the man said, "Ricardo sends his regards, and he says to tell you that your debt is now paid in full."

Tyrone remembered that morning in Ricardo's jet. He had said, "They are always surprised when I find them with my judge and jury. They are found guilty, and then they die."

Tyrone, fading quickly, actually smiled. He was glad Ricardo had found him.

He looked at the altar. He saw Jesus on the cross.

His life flashed before his eyes.

Someone asked, "Who are you?"

"I am Tyrone Reed," he heard himself say. "Head of The Family."

The same voice said, "We've been waiting for you."

As a curtain of darkness enveloped him, he began to hear cries of anguish in the distance. They were low at first; wailing, screaming. But then the tormented voices grew louder and louder until he found himself awash in a horrifying cacophony of suffering and despair.

Tyrone Reed began falling...

Falling...

Falling...

The End

Author's Note

Thank you for reading my book, *Driven.* I hope you enjoyed it.

I would love to hear from you. Feel free to email me at rick45@aol.com.

Rick Jacobs

About the author:

Rick Jacobs lives with his wife, Susie, in Bartlett, TN, where he serves court papers for Shelby County. He is the author of two self-published works of non-fiction, *Let Life Begin* and *Life Has Begun.* He writes an occasional column for his hometown newspaper, *The Bartlett Express.*

Driven is his first novel.

Perhaps, though, not his last.